CRITICAL ACCLAIM FOR *DEADLY ALIBI*

'Curves I never saw coming' – *For the Love of Books*

'You are not going to want to put it down' – **Jo Robertson, My Chestnut Reading Tree**

'Of all the Steel books so far, this will be one that stays with me for a long time' – *So Many Books, So Little Time*

CRITICAL ACCLAIM FOR *MURDER RING*

'A great murder mystery in its own right and highly recommended' – *Fiction Is Stranger Than Fact*

'Smoothly professional fare from the always-consistent Russell' – *Crime Time*

CRITICAL ACCLAIM FOR *BLOOD AXE*

'A great story with some interesting and unexpected twists and turns. It ends with some scenes of high drama and a clever and surprising outcome' – *Fiction Is Stranger Than Fact*

CRITICAL ACCLAIM FOR *KILLER PLAN*

'Her previous six novels featuring DI Geraldine Steel marked her out as a rare talent, and this seventh underlines it' – **Daily Mail**

'I will be looking out for more from this author' – *Nudge*

'A fast-paced police procedural and a compelling read' – **Mystery People**

'Fans of the series will enjoy reacquainting themselves with Leigh Russell's work' – *Crime Fiction Lover*

'The plot was excellent with plenty of twists and red herrings' – *newbooks*

CRITICAL ACCLAIM FOR *RACE TO DEATH*

'Unmissable' – **Lee Child**

'Leigh Russell has become one of the most impressively dependable purveyors of the English police procedural' – **Marcel Berlins, Times**

CRITICAL ACCLAIM FOR *STOP DEAD*

'All the things a mystery should be, intriguing, enthralling, tense and utterly absorbing' – ***Best Crime Books***

'*Stop Dead* is taut and compelling, stylishly written with a deeply human voice' – **Peter James**

'A definite must read for crime thriller fans everywhere – 5*' – ***Newbooks Magazine***

'For lovers of crime fiction this is a brilliant, not to be missed, novel' – ***Fiction Is Stranger Than Fact***

'Geraldine Steel sticks out as a believable copper and *Stop Dead* flows easily' – ***Electric Lullaby***

'A well-written, a well-researched, and a well-constructed whodunnit. Highly recommended' – ***Mystery People***

'A whodunnit of the highest order. The tightly written plot kept me guessing all the way' – ***Crimesquad***

CRITICAL ACCLAIM FOR *DEATH BED*

'Earlier books have marked her out as one of the most able practitioners in the current field' – **Barry Forshaw, *Crime Time***

'*Death Bed* is a marvellous entry in this highly acclaimed series' – ***Promoting Crime Fiction***

'An innovative and refreshing take on the psychological thriller' – ***Books Plus Food***

'Russell's strength as a writer is her ability to portray believable characters' – ***Crimesquad***

'A well-written, well-plotted crime novel with fantastic pace and lots of intrigue' – ***Bookersatz***

'Truly a great crime thriller' – ***Nayu's Reading Corner***

'*Death Bed* is her most exciting and well-written to date. And, as the others are superb, that is really saying something! 5*' – ***Euro Crime***

'The story itself was as usual a good one, and the descriptive gruesomeness of some scenes was brilliant' – ***Best Crime Books***

CRITICAL ACCLAIM FOR *CUT SHORT*

'*Cut Short* is a stylish, top-of-the-line crime tale, a seamless blending of psychological sophistication and gritty police procedure. And you're just plain going to love DI Geraldine Steel' – **Jeffery Deaver**

'Russell paints a careful and intriguing portrait of a small British community while developing a compassionate and complex heroine who's sure to win fans' – *Publishers Weekly*

'An excellent debut' – *Crime Time*

'It's an easy read with the strength of the story at its core... If you want to be swept along with the story above all else, *Cut Short* is certainly a novel for you' – **Crimeficreader**

'Simply awesome! This debut novel by Leigh Russell will take your breath away' – *Euro Crime*

'An excellent book...Truly a great start for new mystery author Leigh Russell' – *New York Journal of Books*

Cut Short is a book I had to read in one sitting... excellent new series' – *Murder by Type*

'A sure-fire hit – a taut, slick, easy-to-read thriller' – *Watford Observer*

'Fine police procedural, with a convincing if disconcerting feel of contemporary Britain' – *The Compulsive Reader*

'*Cut Short* featured in one of Euro Crime's reviewers' Top Reads for 2009' – *Euro Crime*

'*Cut Short* is not a comfortable read, but it is a compelling and important one. Highly recommended' – *Mystery Women*

'Gritty and totally addictive debut novel' – *New York Journal of Books*

Titles by Leigh Russell

Geraldine Steel Mysteries
Cut Short
Road Closed
Dead End
Death Bed
Stop Dead
Fatal Act
Killer Plan
Murder Ring
Deadly Alibi

Ian Peterson Murder Investigations
Cold Sacrifice
Race to Death
Blood Axe

Lucy Hall Mystery
Journey to Death
Girl in Danger
The Wrong Suspect

LEIGH RUSSELL

MURDER RING

A DI GERALDINE STEEL MYSTERY

NO EXIT PRESS

First published in 2016 by No Exit Press,
an imprint of Oldcastle Books Ltd,
PO Box 394, Harpenden,
Herts, AL5 1XJ, UK

noexit.co.uk
@noexitpress

A CIP catalogue record for this book is available from the British Library.

ISBN
978-1-84344-677-4 (Print)
978-1-84344-678-1 (Epub)
978-1-84344-679-8 (Kindle)
978-1-84344-680-4 (Pdf)

2 4 6 8 10 9 7 5 3

Typeset in 11.25pt Times New Roman
by Avocet Typeset, Somerton, Somerset TA11 6RT
Printed in Denmark by Nørhaven, Viborg

To Michael, Joanna, Phillipa and Phil

Acknowledgements

I would like to thank Dr Leonard Russell for his expert medical advice, and all my contacts in the Metropolitan Police for their invaluable assistance.

I would also like to thank the inimitable Annette Crossland for her loyal support.

Producing a book is a team effort. I am fortunate to have the guidance of a brilliant editor, Keshini Naidoo, and I am very grateful to Ion Mills and Claire Watts, along with all the dedicated team at No Exit Press, who transform my words into books.

My final thanks go to Michael, who is always with me.

Glossary of acronyms

DCI   – Detective Chief Inspector (senior officer on case)
DI   – Detective Inspector
DS   – Detective Sergeant
SOCO – scene of crime officer (collects forensic evidence at scene)
PM   – Post Mortem or Autopsy (examination of dead body to establish cause of death)
CCTV – Closed Circuit Television (security cameras)
VIIDO – Visual Images Identifications and Detections Office

Prologue

STAGGERING OUT OF the restaurant, David was up for another drink before catching the train home. One by one his staff made their excuses until he was left alone on the pavement.

'Well, sod you,' he mumbled, 'lightweights the lot of you.'

Still fumbling with the buttons on his new leather jacket, he stopped outside a bar. 'Here it is then. One for the road.'

A young woman with pink hair came over to serve him. Coloured glass glittered on her fingers as she put his pint down on the bar.

'Get one for yourself,' he told her, handing over a tenner. He glanced down at her fingers. 'You like jewellery?'

'Sure.'

In a convivial mood, he was ready for a chat.'I had my wife's engagement ring reset. Just got it back today.' He leaned against the bar and raised his voice, eager to impress her. 'It wasn't cheap. Must take you a year to carn what her ring cost me.'

'Really? Your wife's lucky.'

'She deserves it,' he said solemnly. 'She has a lot to put up with – me!'

He burst out laughing. Sometimes he forgot how witty he was. The girl behind the bar laughed too, displaying perfect teeth. Her smile gave him a warm feeling.

'This is a nice place,' he said. 'And you're a very nice girl. I can see that. Would you like to see my wife's ring? I've got it right here.' He patted his trouser pocket. 'It cost me over twelve grand.'

'You shouldn't shout about it in public.'

David was about to speak to her again, but she moved away to serve another customer. Finding a seat at a corner table, he hung his jacket carefully over the back of his chair before sitting down. At the bar the pink-haired girl was talking to someone else. Finishing his pint, he stood up. He felt a little woozy. With a last glance over his shoulder at the girl behind the bar, he staggered out. The night air sobered him slightly, making him shiver. All he wanted was to go home and lie down. The pavement along Oxford Street was crowded. Turning on to a side street he walked more quickly, heading in what he thought was the right direction.

Hearing footsteps pounding along the street behind him he looked over his shoulder, fleetingly worried, then laughed because the street was deserted. All the same, he felt uneasy. Everything looked different in the dark. He was bursting for a slash, so he turned off Wells Street into a narrow unlit lane. There was no one around to see him stagger over to the wall. Before he could unzip his trousers he heard footsteps approaching, and a hoarse voice called out. Turning his head, he made out a figure hovering in the shadows.

'Gimme the ring.'

'What?' Sober enough to understand what was going on, he was drunk enough to be angry. 'If you think I'm going to hand over my wife's ring –'

As the shadowy figure raised one arm, the barrel of a gun glinted in the moonlight.

1

GERALDINE WENT TO bed early but she couldn't sleep. For years she had dedicated herself to her career as a police detective. While her personal life was unfulfilling, her track record on murder investigations was excellent. Nothing had ever interfered with her focus on her work. Until now. With the murder of a close colleague, she had discovered that years spent observing the bereaved had not prepared her to deal with grief of her own. She wondered if she would ever feel ready to investigate another murder, or if every corpse from now on would take her back to that one unbearable death. Rigid with misery, she sat at her kitchen table considering whether she ought to resign. At last she went back to bed.

She must have fallen into a deep sleep because when her phone rang, she reached out to switch off her alarm. A few seconds later, it rang again and she realised it was her phone. Cursing, she reached out to answer the call. It was ten to nine. Hearing the curt voice on the line, she was instantly awake, automatically registering the details and dressing hurriedly. Passing through the hall she grabbed a waterproof jacket. She had no idea what the weather was like. Her phone rang again as she opened her front door, car keys in hand.

'I'm on my way.'

A body had been found in Central London, in a narrow cul-de-sac north of Oxford Street, halfway between Oxford Street station and Tottenham Court Road station. Geraldine drove straight to the location. It was not far in terms of distance, but the morning London traffic was heavy. As she drove, she listened to the report that had been sent. It gave only the basics. In a way she was relieved because that made it easier to process the information while she was driving. By the time she arrived at Wells Street she knew that a middle-aged man had been shot, once, in the chest. He had no wallet on him, suggesting he had been mugged. So far they were assuming the victim's name was David Lester, the owner of the Oyster card found in his pocket, although his identity had yet to be confirmed.

The doctor had left by the time Geraldine arrived. The cul-de-sac where the dead man had been found was cordoned off. Several uniformed officers were standing at the end of the close, stopping any pedestrians from viewing the site. A scene of crime officer filled Geraldine in on the details. The body had been discovered by someone using the back entrance to one of the office blocks. The man who had reported the body had given a brief statement. Geraldine glanced through it before turning her attention to the victim.

'What can you tell me?'

The scene of crime officer could add little to what Geraldine already knew.

'The doctor placed time of death an hour or two before midnight last night. She couldn't be more precise than that because he's been lying here all night. She estimated he's in his early to mid-fifties.'

Geraldine nodded. That tied in with the date of birth on the Oyster card, according to which the victim was fifty-two. Although the body was partly sheltered by an external fire escape, it had been exposed to rain which confused the evidence. Geraldine turned her attention to the victim, lying on his back, brilliantly illuminated inside the forensic tent. Apart from the dark patch on his chest, his blankly staring eyes and ghastly pallor proclaimed him dead. White-clad scene of crime officers were busily examining every inch of the scene, scraping and collecting traces of evidence. She drew closer and crouched down beside the body.

Behind her a familiar voice said, 'Great start to the day.'

Geraldine turned to greet her sergeant. Sam grinned. Her short, spiky blonde hair gave her an elfin look despite her stocky build.

'The body was moved post mortem,' a scene of crime officer said.

'In order to rob him?'

The other woman shrugged. 'That's for you to work out. It's not my job to draw conclusions from the evidence, just to gather it.'

'Yeah, yeah,' Sam chimed in. 'We know that. But what do you think?'

The white-clad officer blinked at Sam in surprise, then laughed. 'I think he was moved so he could be robbed, because he has no money and no plastic on him, just a set of keys and an Oyster card. Most likely he had a wallet or at least loose cash on him, although we don't know that. But he's well dressed. Why would he be here, in Central London, with no money on him at all? I think he was moved shortly after he was killed, by whoever it was mugged him.'

Sam nodded. 'Makes sense.'

'That doesn't mean it's necessarily true,' Geraldine said quietly. 'Now, he was killed an hour or two before midnight. There must have been people around at that time on a Monday night. Someone might have heard the shot.'

'In Central London? With all this traffic?' Sam said. 'You are joking.' The scene of crime officer agreed with Sam. 'And in any case, how are you going to trace all the people who were in the vicinity? I'm sorry,' she added, seeing Geraldine's expression, 'that's not my job. What do I know about it?'

She turned away as one of her colleagues called out.

'We've got another one.'

'What have you found?' Geraldine asked her.

The officer turned back. 'So far we've got three bullets, apart from the one that hit the victim.'

'Were they all fired from the same gun?'

'They'll need to be examined properly to confirm that.'

'But what's the chance there were two guns fired?'

'Almost zero, I'd say. I may be sticking my neck out here, but the bullets have all got an irregularity on one side, visible with the naked eye, so it looks very much as though they were all fired from the same handgun.'

'What do you mean an irregularity?'

'A tiny ridge, or dent down the side, more like a scratch, where the barrel's damaged.'

'And all the bullets were aimed at the victim?'

'That's difficult to say really.'

'Depends on how good his aim was,' another scene of crime officer added, overhearing Geraldine's question. 'He might have missed, he could have been firing around to scare the victim, or more likely he was so out of it he didn't know who or what he was trying to hit.'

All they could tell for certain was that more than one bullet had been fired, probably from the same gun.

'So we know he was fifty-two.' Geraldine paused, staring down at the body. 'What was he doing here at night?'

'Going home from work, perhaps?' Sam suggested.

'Towards midnight?'

'The guy finishes work at eight, eight thirty, goes for something to eat, a few drinks, then he's on his way home at ten thirty, eleven, to catch the last train – perhaps there was a drinks do if someone was leaving from his office – or maybe he had a romantic tryst after work – there's any number of reasons why he might have been on his way home at that time.'

'Sam, you're not being helpful.'

'All I'm saying is there's nothing out of the ordinary about him being here in the evening.'

'You're right. In any case it's far too early to start speculating like this. Let's get back to the station and see what else we can find out about David Lester.'

'We don't know that's who he is,' Sam muttered. 'Now who's speculating?'

2

WHEN THEY HAD finished talking to the scene of crime officers it was nearly time for the morning briefing, so they went to the police station. There was nothing more to learn from the crime scene. Geraldine was keen to be on time for her first meeting with her new detective chief inspector, her previous senior investigating officer having taken early retirement. The traffic lights were with her and she reached the police station with time to stop off at the canteen for a quick breakfast.

'Mind if I join you?' Sam asked as she plonked a tray down on Geraldine's table.

It was a rhetorical question.

Geraldine looked at Sam's plate. 'Are you sure you've got enough there? I'd hate to see you go hungry.'

'Best to stock up while we can. You never know when we might have an opportunity to eat again.'

'Bloody hell, Sam. You must use that excuse at least three times a day. We're not explorers crossing the Arctic!'

Sam grinned as she tucked in to a plate piled with fried eggs, toast, sausages and beans.

'How can you survive on that anaemic muck?' she asked, with a nod at Geraldine's bowl.

'Porridge is very healthy.'

'Boring!'

Neither of them had met the new detective chief inspector before. As she ate, Sam related the gossip she had heard about him. Adam Eastwood had been working as a detective inspector in South London before his recent promotion.

'And,' she went on, spooning beans on to her toast and cutting a dripping square, 'he recently got divorced, which might explain all the fuss some of the other girls are making, because apparently he's drop dead gorgeous. If you like that sort of thing.'

'By that sort of thing you mean men?'

Sam wrinkled her nose, her mouth full.

'What else have you heard?'

Sam shook her head. With a last gulp of coffee, Geraldine stood up. Sam remonstrated, gesturing at her plate.

'I'll see you there then,' Geraldine said. 'Don't be late.'

Geraldine had to concede that Sam's praise was justified. Detective Chief Inspector Adam Eastwood was certainly an attractive man. Tall and slender, everything about him gave an impression of neatness, from his cropped, dark hair to his navy fitted jacket and polished shoes. He was clean shaven and his features were well proportioned. Although his voice was soft, his diction was so precise it was possible to distinguish every word as he ran through what they knew of the victim.

'You know what to do, so let's get going,' he concluded, gazing round the team before they split up to carry out their allotted tasks. 'You might want to double-check with the duty sergeant before you start. We're not going to have any cock-ups.'

Scowling at a couple of female constables who muttered crudely about fancying a cock-up from their detective chief inspector, Geraldine hurried away. Her first task was to question Andy Hilton, the man who had reported the body to the police. Concerned that he had probably already forgotten most of what he had seen, she was keen to speak to him as soon as possible. Sam was put in charge of organising a team of constables to watch film from CCTV cameras in the streets surrounding Wells Mews. There were cameras along Oxford Street, but none in the little cul-de-sac itself. It was a huge job involving many hours of work, but vitally important.

Andy lived in a converted Victorian terraced house along the Caledonian Road. In his twenties, he had sandy-coloured hair and a very long nose that dominated his pinched face.

'Are you the police? They said you'd be coming.'

'Yes, I spoke to you on the phone.'

He barely glanced at her warrant card.

'Well, come in.'

Sitting opposite her in his small kitchen, he launched into an account of how he had discovered the body, adding little to what she already knew. He had been out drinking with his work colleagues on Monday evening, celebrating someone's birthday.

'I'm not a great drinker,' he added apologetically, as though it was a shameful admission. 'But I was a bit pissed, because we'd been drinking, you know? Anyway,' he gave an embarrassed laugh, 'I went along Wells Mews –'

'Why did you go there?'

His cheeks flushed as he shrugged without answering.

'This is a murder investigation,' Geraldine said firmly. 'It would be criminal as well as foolish to conceal anything.'

'It's a quiet dead end. I was desperate for a pee. We'd been drinking.'

'So, you needed to urinate and went into Wells Mews.'

'Yes. That's not illegal is it?'

'I'm conducting a murder investigation. Let's focus on that, shall we?'

'Yes, yes. Of course. Well, I went to the end of the mews and was taking a piss, when I saw this bloke lying there. Actually, I kicked him, by mistake. He didn't budge. I can't remember much else but I must have called the police and next thing I knew there were police everywhere and I was being asked all these questions and that's all there is to it, really. I told them what had happened, that I'd seen this body lying there.'

'How did you know he was dead?'

'I didn't know if he was dead or out cold, not at first. Then I saw his eyes were open and he was just staring, not blinking. When I saw the blood on his clothes, that's when I put two and two together and called the police.'

'Well?' Sam asked when Geraldine returned to the police station and went to check on her progress with the CCTV.

'Well what?'

'What do you think of our new DCI?'

'What do *you* think?'

'He looks like Ken.'

'Who's Ken?'

Sam rolled her eyes. 'Didn't you have Barbie dolls? No, I guess they were after your time.'

'No, they weren't after my time. And in any case, I do have a niece.'

'Please tell me you haven't bought her a Barbie doll.'

'Of course. She's got all sorts of frilly pink outfits, and high-heeled shoes, and –'

'Oh shut up. Anyway, what's your impression of him?'

Geraldine considered. 'I think he speaks very clearly.'

'Let's hope he thinks clearly.'

3

LENNY WOKE WITH a pounding headache. At first he thought he was still in the nick. He turned and bashed his head on the seat in front of him. Hearing a noise, he looked up. A line of people was filing past his face. The stench made him feel sick. Coming to, he realised he was lying across the seat of a bus. The rough fabric felt damp against his cheek. He hoped it was just wet with his dribble. Someone shook his arm.

'Fuck off!'

'Oy, wake up!'

Travelling on the night bus had been unpleasant. For hours he'd sat hunched in a seat, face to the window, trying to shut out the raucous bursts of laughter from kids who were intoxicated, high, and volatile; a pathetic collection of riotous clubbers and despondent, neglected youngsters who had spent a few hours together sheltering from the night.

Daylight was just beginning to break as he made his way home, approaching from the opposite direction to Central London and the quiet corner where he had stumbled across a bit of luck. No one had seen him in the mews. He had been clever enough to distance himself from the stiff and, to cap it all, he was a hundred quid better off. Gina would never know he had blown his official dosh. It was all working out just fine, which was fair enough. A bloke couldn't be dogged by bad luck all the time. Sooner or later he had to have a break, although to be fair he'd made his own luck by having the wit to nick the stiff's wallet when he had the chance. That cash would save him getting it in the neck from Gina, at least for a while. He couldn't have coped with one of her flare ups just then. On top of a foul hangover, he had slept fitfully and had woken with a sharp pain in his neck from lying with his head twisted round in an awkward position. All he wanted to do was get home to his own bed.

He hoped she'd be out when he got there, but no such luck. Her grating voice cut through him as soon as he opened the door.

'Where the hell have you been?'

Some homecoming. He didn't even bother to answer. She knew perfectly well where he'd been for the past eighteen months. He slipped past her into the hall muttering that he just wanted to go to sleep, and a cup of tea wouldn't go amiss. She spun round, slamming the front door. Her mousy hair was a mess. In a face pitted with acne scars, her eyes shone blue and beautiful.

'Lenny, I'm talking to you.'

'I can hear you.'

'I asked where you been?'

'You know bloody well where I been.'

'Why would I be asking where you been, if I knew where you been?'

'I been in the nick. You can't have forgotten.'

'Course I know you was in the nick. I seen you there. And I know you was out Monday. And I want to know where you been since then.'

'What, since Monday you mean?'

'Yeah, since Monday. I been waiting here for you to come home.'

It was only Tuesday. He had been out less than twenty-four hours, meeting up with some mates. At first he couldn't be bothered to answer but she kept on and on at him until he lost his temper. It was always the same with her. She could never leave it alone.

'I suppose you been at your mum's, and she took all your pay off you what should've come to me.'

'I haven't spoke to my mum.'

He reached into his pocket for the wallet. In the daylight he could see it must have cost a fair bit, real leather by the looks of it. He drew out a handful of notes. That shut her up. Eyes fixed on the dosh, she took a step forward and snatched at it. He let her have it. Poor cow, it must've been a struggle for her while he'd been inside.

'How you been managing, babe?' he asked.

He watched her count the money. Sixty quid. That meant he still had over forty for himself. He grinned as she stuffed the notes in her pocket.

'You can feed yourself up a bit,' he said. 'You look skinnier than ever. You don't eat properly.'

'Where's the rest of it?' she demanded, hands on hips.

'That's all they give me.'

'Liar.'

Just then he remembered the small blue box he had nicked off the stiff along with his wallet. He felt in his pocket for it.

'Look, I got you this!'

'What is it?'

'It's a present. I got it for you.'

She took the little box, scowling. When she opened it her chin dropped and her eyes grew round with wonder. Poor cow didn't get many presents.

'Where the hell did you get this?'

He hesitated an instant too long and cursed himself for failing to prepare his story. 'Never mind that. It's for you. Do you like it?'

'I bloody love it!'

He was taken aback by her enthusiasm. She picked the ring out of the box and slipped it straight on the third finger on her left hand. Without taking her eyes off the jewel, she waved her hand in the air.

'It's beautiful.'

Just as he began to relax, she spoke again. Her voice was soft but her words shocked him.

'I thought you never wanted to get hitched. And now look at us. We're engaged! Where did you get it, honest?'

'I been saving up,' he faltered. 'I been working –'

'Working? What you talking about? You been in the nick –'

It was worse than being interrogated by the police. At least she was distracted by the ring. He carried on, doing his best to convince her he had scrimped and starved just for her, even sacrificing the chance of a packet of fags so he could save a few extra quid.

'Over eighteen months, it all adds up, you know.'

'What does?'

'They give you jobs in there, you know. I saved every scrap so I could get you something. I wanted to make it up to you.'

Her eyes narrowed. 'How much did it cost then?'

He glanced at her hand. It was quite a rock. He licked his lips and hesitated. He hadn't realised what a nice bit of ice was in that box. If it was real, it would be worth a fortune.

'How much?'

'Enough.'

'Where the hell did you get hold of something like this?'

'Jesus, Gina, a bloke can't get nothing past you. All right, for fuck's sake, this is how I come by it. There was this stiff in an alley way –'

'A stiff?'

'Yeah. He'd been shot.'

'Did you do it?'

'Fuck off. I only just come out the nick. You wanna hear this or not?'

She nodded.

'So I checked his pockets – it would've been stupid not to – and that's what I found. So I waited all night to get a bloke I know to check it out. That's why I never come home until now.'

He smiled, admiring his own deftness in getting out of trouble.

'And? What did he say?'

'He told me it's worth a lot. A good few thousand, he reckoned. So I thought to myself, when am I ever gonna get anything like that for my girl? You know I always been good to you.'

'But –'

'It's special,' he pressed on. 'Only the best is good enough for my girl, that's what I thought. It's a real rock. It's what you deserve.'

'It didn't cost you a penny.'

'I could've sold it and kept the dosh, but I wanted to give it to you. You're worth more than any amount of dosh to me.'

She looked dubious, then she fluttered her hand in front of his face. The diamond sparkled. Different colours seemed to shine from it, mesmerising. It might be really valuable, worth far more than he could ever afford.

'I thought you'd be pleased. Of course, if you don't want it –'

'Don't be daft. Of course I want it. Anyway, it's mine now, ain't it?'

He considered, while she waved her hand in front of his face. The diamond glowed at him with a seductive inner fire. She was right. Bloody hell. It could be worth thousands. He had to get it back. Seeing the ring sit loosely on her finger, he had a brain wave.

'It don't look right. It's too big. It might fit on your index finger.'

She fell for it at once. 'No way. It goes on this finger. It's an engagement ring, isn't it?'

'I'll have to get it fixed then, so it fits proper, like it was made for you. You don't want it falling off because it don't fit.'

'You want me to give it back to you?'

'Just till I get it made so it fits proper.'

'But we'd still be engaged?'

'If you want. Yes, yes, of course,' he changed his answer quickly, seeing her expression darken. 'That don't make no difference. Come on, give it here so I can get it fixed proper. You wouldn't know where to take it. You can't trust a stranger with a rock like that. Rip you off as soon as look at you. Any old jeweller's going to replace a real diamond with a shit bit of glass, and you won't even know.'

'This is a real diamond, ain't it, Lenny?'

'Only the best for my girl, that's what I said. Look, I'll take it to a geezer I know and he'll sort it just like that, no questions asked. You'll have it back in no time.'

'How do I know I can trust you not to nick it off me?'

'What you talking about, you daft cow? I gave it you in the first place. It's worth a fucking fortune and that's what you're worth to me.'

She couldn't argue with that. Reverently she slipped it off her finger and replaced it in the box. Pocketing it, he suppressed a grin. He had plans of his own for her new trinket. He was going to clean up, and she would never know.

4

ENTERING HER OFFICE, Geraldine was surprised to see someone occupying the desk that had belonged to her former colleague, Nick. No one living knew that she had been involved in a brief affair with him before he had been murdered. She braced herself to be civil to the man now sitting in Nick's place, on his chair, at his desk, fingers moving swiftly over the keyboard that had felt Nick's touch.

'Good morning.'

Her new colleague spun round then sprang to his feet, one hand extended in greeting. Fighting to control her distress, she was aware of laughter creases around blue eyes that smiled a welcome. He was young and fair haired. With candid eyes, straight nose, slightly sunken cheeks and a neat pointed chin, he was charismatic rather than good looking. He gave an impression of energy, a physical dynamism that she couldn't help finding attractive.

'Neil Roberts,' he said as he shook her hand firmly. 'You must be Geraldine.'

They sat down and chatted briefly. Neil was also a detective inspector, and recently promoted to the Met from Surrey.

'I'm really excited to be in London,' he added with boyish enthusiasm.

Geraldine couldn't help smiling.

'You're on this new case, aren't you? The mugging.'

'Yes.'

'I'm on standby right now, so if there's anything I can do –'

Geraldine turned away, momentarily overcome. Nick had made the same offer once.

'Thank you,' she mumbled. 'And now, I need to crack on. I've got to go and tell the wife.'

David Lester had lived with his wife near West Acton station, straight through on the underground from Central London. Laura was considerably younger than him, and they had only been married for two years. They had no children. Aware that the traffic could be slow moving, Geraldine decided to take the underground. If there were delays, at least she would be able to work on the train. Arriving in West Acton, she walked along a street of small black and white houses. With a wide, leafy central reservation running along the centre of the road, it was an attractive estate. She turned off into a side street and found the house she was looking for, a small end of terrace cottage. A plump blonde woman came to the door. She looked about thirty. For a moment Geraldine wondered if she was David Lester's daughter.

'Are you related to David Lester?'

'He's my husband.'

'May I come in?'

On learning who Geraldine was, the young woman fired a series of questions at her.

'What do you want? What's this about? Has something happened to David? He didn't come home last night. Where is he? What's happened? Is he in trouble? He's in trouble, isn't he? Where is he?'

Geraldine urged Laura to invite her in. 'It would be better if you sat down.'

The other woman's face grew pale, as though she understood what was coming, but she persisted with her aggressive questions. 'Why? What's happened?'

At last they went inside. Laura sat down on a pink leather sofa. Geraldine perched on a matching armchair and glanced around the room. On a mantelpiece above a boxed-in fireplace she saw what she was looking for: a photograph of the dead man with one arm around the woman who sat facing her.

'Mrs Lester,' she began softly. 'I'm really sorry to bring you some bad news.'

She remembered hearing about the death of her own adoptive mother, and the initial feeling of disbelief that had protected her. In those first moments, being the bearer of terrible news was worse than receiving it. Only later would reality hit, once the shock had subsided.

'I'm afraid we have reason to believe your husband, David, has been the victim of a fatal mugging.'

'What? I don't understand. He didn't come home last night – or at least, he wasn't home when I went to bed, but they were going out for a meal because someone was leaving, so I knew he'd be late. That's all. He must have come home in the early hours of the morning, and gone out again before I woke up. It's nothing more than that. I'm sorry for your trouble but you've got this all wrong. You've made a big mistake. I never even reported him missing.' She gave a high-pitched laugh. 'You ask David, he'll tell you, I'm the worrier. If there's anything wrong, I'm always the first to suspect it, but he's fine, I know he is. He knows how to take care of himself. He always takes care of me. I'm the one –'

She stopped talking abruptly and burst into tears. Geraldine gave her a moment before asking if there was anyone who could come round.

Laura shook her head. 'I want David, I want David.'

As gently as she could, Geraldine told the distraught woman what had happened. Laura cried and shook her head. All at once she raised a tear-stained face.

'Mugged?' she repeated. 'You said he was mugged?'

'It appears that way. We need you to identify the body to be sure it is your husband.'

The newly bereaved widow nodded her head.

'Laura, I know this is difficult, but there are certain questions I need to ask you. Can you think of anyone who might have wanted your husband dead?'

'You said he was mugged.'

'That's what we think, but we have to consider every possibility.'

Ignoring Geraldine's question, Laura wanted to know what had been stolen.

'We don't know. We assume his wallet was stolen as he had no money or phone on his person, only a set of keys and an Oyster card.'

'What about my ring? Did he have my ring? You need to check his pockets. It'll be in a box.'

Geraldine sat forward. 'What ring?'

'He was taking my engagement ring to London to get it resized, I told him not to take it all the way up there. He could have lost it, or... he said he was going to try and get to the jewellers yesterday to take it in, but he rang when he finished work and said he hadn't had time to get there but he said he'd take it in today. That's why he was mugged, wasn't it? My ring, my ring. It was my engagement ring.'

Laura broke down in tears, ostensibly more distraught at the loss of her engagement ring than the death of her husband. Geraldine waited a moment for her to regain control of herself. The theft of the ring could be significant.

'Laura, listen to me. I need you to tell me about your ring.'

'It was my engagement ring.'

'Do you know how much it was worth?'

Laura looked up, nodding. 'It was one point seven carat, a nearly perfect brilliant cut white solitaire set in white gold.'

Geraldine shook her head. 'What would that be worth? Do you know?'

'I can get the insurance certificate.'

The ring had been insured for fourteen thousand pounds. Even if it could be sold for half its replacement value, it came to a tidy sum.

'Did the ring have any distinguishing features?'

'What do you mean? It was a ring, an engagement ring.'

'It wasn't engraved or scratched?'

'Oh, I see what you mean. No, nothing like that.'

'Did anyone else know your husband had your ring on him?'

'He said he wasn't going to tell anyone at work. He wasn't an idiot. Not that he didn't trust his colleagues. He'd been there for years. But still, you can't be too careful.'

Laura covered her face in her hands and began to sob again. Watching her heaving shoulders, Geraldine was shaken with helpless fury. Death was always dreadful, an unnatural death harder to accept than the result of illness or even accident; casual murder in the course of a mugging must be almost unbearable.

'I'm so sorry,' she muttered, embarrassed by the inadequacy of her words.

'I don't suppose I'll ever get it back,' Laura sobbed.

Geraldine attributed Laura's preoccupation with her stolen jewellery to displacement. It was disturbing to believe she could be more upset about the loss of her ring than her husband. Yet Geraldine knew she couldn't rule out the possibility that the weeping widow in front of her might be responsible for her husband's death.

5

LEAVING THE VICTIM'S family home, Geraldine drove to the mortuary. When Sam offered to meet her there, Geraldine said the sergeant would be more usefully employed supervising the team checking CCTV near the crime scene. It was an unspoken secret between them that Sam was queasy around cadavers.The pathologist, Miles Fellowes, was waiting for her when she walked in. Hazel eyes crinkled in a smile, he held up his bloody gloved hands in a welcoming gesture. After they exchanged greetings, she turned her attention to the body. Nearly bald and developing a paunch, David must once have been a good-looking man. Clean shaven, with a large straight nose and thin lips, Geraldine had seen in photographs that his closed eyes were dark and attractive. The original chiselled outline of his lower jaw was easy to see above his double chin. Below rounded shoulders his arms looked muscular, and his legs were toned. He had the appearance of a middle-aged man who ate well and worked out regularly or played a lot of recreational sport.

'He looked after himself,' Miles said, confirming Geraldine's initial impression of the dead man. 'He looks flabby, but he has impressive muscle tone, and he was in good condition, physically. There's not a lot wrong with him, in fact – apart from being dead,' he added with a grin.

'I wonder if he knew what was happening?'

'There are no defence wounds. It looks as though he collapsed at once. He was pretty drunk.'

In some ways it wasn't a bad way to go. A quick death, in his prime.

'You said he was drunk?'

'Yes. He'd eaten a good meal about an hour before he died. Steak, chips, some sort of gooey trifle, all washed down with at least one bottle of red wine, and a generous shot of brandy.'

The bullet had been removed. A bloodless hole showed clearly in the centre of the dead man's chest. Miles laughed when Geraldine said the entry wound looked too small to have been the cause of so much trauma.

'The bullet slipped neatly between his ribs just at the right spot and pierced his heart, and pouf!'

'Was it just the one shot?'

'He was hit once, right in the chest, with a Smith and Wesson. I'm no ballistics expert. You probably know more about the gun than I do. But I can show you exactly where one of the bullets ended up.'

Geraldine nodded. 'Other bullets were found at the scene, fired from the same gun. Do you think this could have been a lucky hit in a random round of shots?'

'Not very lucky for him,' Miles replied, with a lopsided grin. 'We've stripped him of a lambswool jumper and a shirt which have gone off to the forensic lab.'

'And I seem to remember he was wearing dark trousers?'

'You've got a good memory for details.'

'That's my job, to notice things.'

Miles nodded. 'Smart navy trousers. Anyway, as I was saying, the bullet reached his heart and he was dead, almost instantaneously.'

'I thought it took four minutes for a person to die.'

'Technically, yes. But this wound was going to be fatal, four minutes or no four minutes. My guess is our fellow here lost consciousness almost immediately, from the shock, and then, you're right, it took four minutes for all vital signs to cease.'

'Could he have been resuscitated? I mean, if he'd been given medical attention straight away? What if his attacker had tried to stop the bleeding and called for an ambulance?'

'Even if a paramedic team had reached him straight away, I don't think he could have been saved. His heart was too badly damaged. The bullet went through the left ventricle and severed the root of the aorta.'

'Was there anything to suggest his attacker tried to stop the bleeding?'

'Any bruising around the wound, you mean? No. Nothing at all. But like I said, he was as good as dead once the bullet entered his heart. Even if he had received medical attention straight away, there was too much damage to his heart for him to recover.'

'But his attacker wouldn't have known that. Whoever attacked him ran off leaving him to bleed to death, without even trying to save his life.' She paused, staring at the dead man. 'It's possible this was a premeditated murder, planned to look like a mugging that went wrong.'

Miles shrugged. 'It's beyond my remit to indulge in that kind of speculation.'

'But it's possible?'

'Not my job, Geraldine. All I can tell you is that he was shot in the chest and the bullet reached his heart –'

'What're the chances of that?'

Miles gazed at her, his hazel eyes momentarily troubled. 'I wish I could answer that. I wish I could answer all your questions – but then of course you'd be out of a job.'

He grinned again and she smiled back, although he couldn't see her mouth behind her mask.

By the time Geraldine finished writing up her report and left her office it was quite late, so she stopped for a takeaway on her way home. Sitting at her kitchen table, she paused, remembering how she had sat in the same place the previous night. In the urgency of the opening stages of a new investigation she had forgotten about her personal loss. A warm comforting aroma of chips and vinegar rose from the greasy paper on her plate, but she no longer felt hungry. Grief for her dead colleague overcame her and she wept for him, and for all the victims whose killers she had pursued. She had investigated so many murders. She remembered them all.

6

AT HALF PAST nine the following morning, Laura came to the mortuary to formally identify the body. It wasn't necessary for Geraldine to be there in person, but she wanted to observe the young widow's reaction to the sight of her dead husband. Geraldine met Laura in the visitors' room. Her fluffy black coat looked brand new, as did her patent leather shoes. Geraldine wondered if she had bought them after learning about her husband's death. There hadn't been much time.

'Are you ready?' Geraldine asked.

The widow dabbed at her heavily made-up eyes with a tissue, and nodded without speaking.

'Would you like another minute?'

'No.' Laura's voice was barely louder than a whisper.

She stood up, her face pale, her lips trembling. With a pang, Geraldine remembered she was not yet thirty, very young to be facing this personal tragedy.

'Is there someone who could pick you up afterwards? You might not want to be on your own...?'

Everything Geraldine said to this young woman felt crass. Since Nick's death, she was realising for the first time how inadequate all her words of intended comfort were. Whoever took Laura home, the house would still be empty. Nothing could bring her husband back.

'No, I'll be fine,' Laura whispered.

'Are you ready?'

'Yes.'

Geraldine led her into the small chapel where David was laid out. His face was unmarked. Apart from his extreme pallor, he looked much the same as he must have looked in life.

'Poor lamb,' Laura whispered tearfully.

Geraldine was surprised to hear the young woman use a maternal term of endearment about a man legally old enough to be her father. It questioned the assumptions Geraldine had made about the marital relationship. Geraldine had imagined David had been a father figure to Laura. Perhaps the opposite had been the case, and Laura had been the adult in the relationship. Geraldine knew Laura was his personal assistant. She would have taken care of his arrangements, and looked after his interests at work. One word had challenged Geraldine's impression of their relationship.

She observed Laura approach the body, waiting for her to break down, but the widow remained silent. Tears streaming down her cheeks, she turned to Geraldine and nodded.

'You can confirm this is your husband?'

'Oh yes. It's David.' Her voice broke but she didn't sob.

Geraldine took her back to the visitors' room and offered her a cup of tea. She shook her head and asked for a glass of water. Although she was shaking, she still didn't break down.

'No sign of my ring then?'

'No, I'm sorry.'

'You must think I'm a gold digger, and that I care more about my jewellery than my husband, but it's the sentimental value. It was my engagement ring. He'd just had the stone reset.' She sighed and turned in her seat to look directly at Geraldine. 'I know David was older than me, a lot older, but we were happy. We loved each other.'

'We checked his trouser pockets.'

'What about his jacket?'

'He wasn't wearing one.'

'Really?' Laura looked irritated. 'He must have left it at the office. It wasn't a nice night. It was raining and the damp gets to his chest. He should have been wearing his jacket. I don't understand why he didn't have it on. We only bought it last week. I wonder if my ring's in his jacket pocket?'

'Once the forensic team have finished with his clothes, they'll be returned to you,' Geraldine said gently. 'I'll make sure we return everything to you. But not his shirt or jumper, I'm afraid.'

Laura nodded. 'I understand. They must be...'

'Would you like some more water?'

'I'm OK, really. I'd like to go home now, if we're done here.'

'We're finished. I'm sorry again for your loss.'

Having completed the necessary documents concerning the identification of the body, Geraldine went to David's office to collect his jacket. A harassed-looking woman greeted her and introduced herself as the office manager.

'We're all devastated about it,' she said when Geraldine introduced herself. 'What a thing to happen. He was such a nice man. A real gentleman. Oh, I know he left his wife and married Laura. It caused a lot of gossip at the time, the way she behaved.'

'The way she behaved?'

'Throwing herself at him like that. But he went through with it. He married her. So she must have had something. I mean, we all thought she was nice enough when she was working here, but look what happened.'

Geraldine listened to her gossip for a while before asking if the office manager knew of anyone who might have wished to harm David.

'Harm him?'

'Did he have any enemies?'

'Apart from his ex you mean? I don't suppose she was too pleased with him.'

'Anyone else?'

The woman's eyes widened in surprise as she understood the reason for the question. 'We were told he was mugged. The young constable who came here to ask about David told us it was a mugging that went wrong. We all thought David must have fought back. We'd been out together for a meal on Monday night because one of the staff's leaving. We're a small team here so we like to do that. David had drunk rather a lot, I think. Do you think it was something else then, not a mugging that went too far? Is that what you came here to tell us?'

Geraldine reassured her that she was just asking routine questions while she was there. She had come to collect David's leather jacket.

'His jacket? I haven't seen it.'

They looked on his chair and under his desk in case his jacket had fallen down. There was no sign of it. The office manager was sure he had been wearing it when they went out on Monday evening.

'I can't think why he wouldn't have been wearing it. It was a miserable night, quite chilly as I remember, and he had this lovely jacket, really soft leather, you know. It must have been expensive. You can tell.'

Geraldine couldn't overlook the possibility that someone in the office had stolen the jacket, possibly with a view to pocketing the expensive ring David was carrying. There was only one way to be sure David had removed his jacket from the office himself.

The manager of the restaurant where the staff had gone for dinner on Monday recalled the party of six but couldn't remember whether David had been wearing a leather jacket or not. He offered to show Geraldine footage from the security camera at the entrance. After some fiddling around, he found the right section of the film. Geraldine stood behind him, watching over his shoulder, as he ran it on his computer screen. At seven thirty, David's office party arrived. He was wearing his jacket. The manager grew defensive, insisting no one had left a jacket in the restaurant that evening. Geraldine wondered whether he was protesting too forcefully. There was no reason for him to grow so agitated, unless he had found the jacket and pocketed the ring himself.

'Can we find the frames where he's leaving?'

'Wait, I'm looking.'

Geraldine waited as the film sped by. At last the manager stopped it. Together they watched David leave the restaurant. It was ten thirty on Monday evening. He was wearing his jacket.

Geraldine's next visit was to David's ex-wife. He had been married to his childhood sweetheart, Elaine, for twenty-seven years, before he abandoned her to marry his twenty-nine-year-old personal assistant. His two children were not very much younger than his second wife. Elaine and her children still lived in their family house in Edgware. Geraldine drove there after checking in at her office for any new developments. Having logged her report, registering the suspected theft of a valuable diamond ring and a leather jacket, she set off. Elaine lived in a large house, set back from the road. A statuesque woman, she was visibly shocked to hear about her ex-husband's death. White-faced, she stared at Geraldine, shaking her head in disbelief. Geraldine had to repeat the information three times before the other woman seemed to take it in.

'He's dead then?'

'I'm afraid so.'

'I can't believe it. You said he might have been murdered? How can I tell my children?'

As though she knew Elaine was thinking about her, a young woman burst into the room. She looked about the same age as Laura, not yet thirty. Geraldine was correct in assuming she was the dead man's daughter. Seeing her mother in tears, she demanded to know what was going on. When Geraldine told her that her father had been shot during the course of a mugging, the young woman burst out crying.

'How could anyone do that?' she spluttered through her tears. 'How could it happen? How?'

By contrast to her hysterical daughter, Elaine was tearful but controlled. She thanked Geraldine, who left her attempting to console her daughter.

7

HE HAD TOLD Gina he knew a guy who could give him an honest valuation of the ring. That wasn't true. Most of his loot went to an old bloke called Joe who ran an antique shop in Portobello Road. He took what he could, no questions asked. That was all Lenny needed, a regular fence who didn't give him any grief. The trouble was, this ring was out of Joe's league. There was a chance it could be worth a lot of money. Lenny had the ring in his pocket, and he needed to turn it into cash. On Gina's finger, it was of no use to him at all. A chance like this didn't come along every day. He needed someone to buy the ice off him directly, without a middle man, for a good price, and replace it with a nice bit of glass.

He asked around and tracked down a contact he thought would be able to help him.

'So you're going to sell the rock, and replace it so she don't see no difference, and you get to pocket the dosh?' Berny nodded his head. 'Nice. If you don't mind ripping off your old lady.'

Lenny shrugged. 'Don't make no difference to her. She'll never know.'

'So what are we talking about?'

Lenny took a swig of his pint and narrowed his eyes, weighing up how much he should tell his former cell mate. They had become close, sharing so much time together. Prison could do that. But he didn't trust the weaselly man facing him across the table.

'It's just a piece of jewellery,' he said. 'I'd show you but I haven't got it on me right now.'

'Of course you haven't.'

Neither of them spoke for a moment. No doubt Berny was speculating about why Lenny wasn't taking this piece to his usual fence.

'So? Do you know anyone?' Lenny asked.

'Not directly. But I know who would know.'

The longer this went on, the more people were going to hear about Lenny's find. He needed to get rid of it quickly, and get his hands on some dosh. But he had to have a ring to return to Gina. He couldn't afford to piss her off too much. She had too much on him, enough to put him inside many times over. He wouldn't put it past her either. She could be a vindictive cow when the mood took her. He leaned forward.

'Look whoever takes it on gets his hands on a nice rock at a knock-down price. I ain't gonna ask much for it, a lot less than it's worth that's for sure. Only it's got to be replaced right or she'll know I done her.'

Berny made a crude joke about Gina being screwed and Lenny pretended to laugh.

'Look, can you help me or not? Only I ain't got all day.'

'Tell you what, I know exactly the right bloke for the job.'

'And he won't talk?'

'What he knows could put a whole bunch of us away for years. Silent as the grave he is. I'd trust him more than me own grandmother, who's rotting in hell.'

Lenny nodded. This sounded promising.

'It'll cost you, mind.'

Berny narrowed his eyes, considering how much Lenny might cough up in exchange for the contact. 'He's worth his weight in gold to you.'

'How much?'

They haggled for a while. They both knew they'd reach a

figure sooner or later. However hard Lenny tried to hide his desperation, Berny had him over a barrel, and he knew it.

'I could take it elsewhere,' Lenny blustered. 'There's this bloke I know…'

'No worries,' Berny nodded. He finished his pint and stood up. 'See you around then.'

'No, wait.'

Berny sat down again, a faintly puzzled expression on his wrinkled face.

'What you after now?'

'You know bloody well what I want. What we've been talking about all this time.'

'Oh,' Berny pretended to be surprised. 'And there was me thinking you'd decided to go elsewhere. Well, you know my price.'

Lenny scowled. It was steep, but it was that or nothing. Gina wasn't the only one getting screwed. With a sigh he nodded.

8

ALTHOUGH THE CANTEEN food wasn't bad, Geraldine would have preferred to get away from the premises altogether. Ready for a break, she regretted having agreed to meet her sergeant for a late lunch.

'Something smells good,' Sam said with a smile as she joined Geraldine in the queue.

'I thought you'd never notice my sexy aftershave,' a constable replied, putting his head on one side with a silly grin.

They sat down, Geraldine with a salad, Sam with a plate piled high with sausages and a heap of chips.

Sam broke the silence. 'You seem a bit glum.'

Geraldine shrugged.

'What happened about your mother?'

Geraldine put her fork down with a sigh. Adopted at birth, recently she had decided to contact her birth mother. Her request for a meeting had been refused. Geraldine knew it was irrational to take the rejection personally. All the same it was depressing to know that the woman who had given birth to her didn't even want to meet her.

'Nothing,' she admitted. 'She didn't want to see me.'

'I'm sorry.'

'Let's talk about something else. There's plenty to discuss.'

The disappearance of the victim's leather jacket puzzled Geraldine. Somewhere between leaving the restaurant and being shot, it had vanished.

'What it is this obsession with leather?' Sam replied. 'I

never had you down as a secret fetishist. You think you know people...'

If another sergeant had addressed her like that, Geraldine might have been tempted to reprimand her for cheek. As it was, she smiled.

'Look,' Sam went on in a more serious tone, 'don't you reckon the killer must have taken the jacket off him before he shot him? Otherwise it would have been bloodstained and no use to anyone. There was no point in ruining an expensive jacket when he could walk away with it himself. It was nearly new, wasn't it?'

'Yes. Laura said he'd only had it a week or so.'

'There you go then.'

Geraldine nodded. 'So what you're saying is, find the jacket and we find the killer.'

'That wasn't exactly what I was thinking. I mean, all we'd have to do is find someone wearing a leather jacket in London. Can't be more than a million or so of those walking around.'

Geraldine agreed the imagined scenario made sense. They hadn't been able to see the jacket clearly on CCTV film, but Laura and the manager at David's office had both remarked on how smart it was. Laura had told Geraldine it was expensive. It might have caught the mugger's fancy, when he had been about to ask David to hand over his money. In the time it took for David to remove the jacket – perhaps fumbling with the buttons in his panic – he would have had a good look at the mugger's face. It might have been that, or something David said, that caused the mugger to turn killer. Realising what he had done, or perhaps simply satisfied with his haul, the gunman had run off.

'So something – or nothing – provoked him to shoot and he ran off before anyone came along to see what the noise was about. My guess is he scared himself off. I agree it sounds stupid, but I daresay the killer isn't Brain of Britain. Probably high as a kite and didn't know what the hell he was doing.'

'And we sit back and let someone like that run around with a gun.'

'We can't stop it.'

Geraldine sighed. 'We could try.'

Looking for one particular gun in London had become as difficult as looking for a specific leather jacket.

'How?' Sam challenged her. 'If we ask nicely, everyone in possession of an illegal firearm will meekly hand it over, is that the idea? Oh, except those people who actually want to keep it. And why would that be? Because they might want to use it one day? It's a no brainer. Only the good guys will play ball, law-abiding citizens who probably aren't comfortable owning a gun anyway. It's naive to the point of idiocy to think otherwise. Society's riddled with illegal weapons and the sooner we arm ourselves the better.'

'The day the police walk the streets with guns will be the start of a bloodbath.'

'Why? Don't you trust your colleagues not to go around shooting at people?'

'That's not the point. Do you have any idea how many people are shot every day in America? About three hundred. That's every day. And the police there are armed. They say one in three people in America know someone who's been shot. It's like the witch burnings here in the Dark Ages. People are being killed, Sam. Arming the police doesn't solve anything.'

'That's because everyone in the US has a gun. It's nothing to do with the police being armed.'

'Look, we'll have to agree to disagree for now, because we need to get back to work.'

'You mean you know I'm right.'

'Bollocks. It's self-evident that an armed police force solves nothing. But now we do need to get back to work. So, ballistics have confirmed that the bullets were all fired from the same gun, an old Smith and Wesson double action. There are a lot of them around, mostly illegal, so that's not much help. Let's focus on the jacket for now.'

There was a chance the jacket could give them a lead. Geraldine instructed Sam to set up surveillance of film from security cameras along Wells Street. With a team searching for a figure leaving Wells Mews in a jacket like the one they had seen on the victim, they might be able to see the direction the killer had taken after he had shot David. The chances of recognising the victim's jacket were slim, but it was possible. Geraldine left the canteen and made her way along the corridor to the detective chief inspector's office. Not having worked with him before, she thought it best to explain her decision to him face to face. She was asking for a team of officers to search through hours of CCTV footage for a glimpse of a jacket they were unlikely to recognise.

Before she reached his door, there were sounds of a disturbance behind her and Adam burst from his room.

'I know,' he told Geraldine. 'I'm on my way to the incident room now.'

Baffled, Geraldine turned and followed him back along the corridor. Clearly some new information had been received, but before she had a chance to ask what had happened, he disappeared into the incident room. Entering behind him, Geraldine saw Sam and hurried over to her.

'What is it? What's happened?'

'You mean you haven't heard?'

'I was away from my desk for a moment. Honestly, you only have to blink in this place. What is it? What's happened?'

'They've got the killer's DNA!'

Geraldine gaped as the detective chief inspector began to speak.

'You must all know by now that forensics have found the

killer's DNA. It seems he was stupid enough to spit at his victim. At any rate, saliva has been found on the victim's face, and it isn't his own.'

A cheer went round the room. A grinning Adam held up his hand for silence.

'It gets better.'

'Please tell us we have a match,' Geraldine muttered.

'We have a match,' Adam went on, and this time the cheering officers were not so readily quietened. 'His name is Leonard Parker, known as Lenny. He was released from the nick on Monday and went on a bender – his saliva was mostly alcohol. Let's go and pick him up.'

9

ROSA PUSHED HER straggly hair from her face with the back of a hand without taking her eyes off the kid. His thin arms and legs jerked with frog-like spasms as he kicked a football at the wall. As far as she could tell, he was trying to hit the exact same spot each time. Mostly he missed. His flat face was screwed up with concentration, and he mumbled to himself each time the ball hit the wall.

In response to the regular thudding of the ball, there was a sudden knocking from the other side of the wall. The next-door neighbour began shouting at the kid to stop his bleeding racket.

'Shut the fuck up! Some of us are trying to sleep!'

'It's two o'clock in the bloody afternoon!' Rosa yelled back, as loudly as she could.

Her thin voice didn't carry far. She hoped the miserable old geezer next door could hear her. If he didn't leave it out she'd set Jack on him, see how he liked that.

'Wait till my Jack gets home!' she added.

'Shut the fuck up or I'll have that fucking crazy kid locked up! Stop banging on the bloody wall!'

Theo stopped his kicking. He wasn't really a kid any more. His widely spaced black eyes stared at her from his pale face. 'Wait till my Jack gets home!' he screeched suddenly, the words tumbling out in high-pitched mimicry of his mother.

Rosa gave a nod of approval although she wasn't sure he understood a word he was repeating. Inside his twenty-two-year-old head he had the mind of a small child. It was time he learned to stand up for himself; if you didn't fight back, they crushed you. People on the estate scented fear like sharks smelling blood. She had seen it happen. Jack's father had been so scared of gang members on the estate he'd left without even saying goodbye. He had told her right from the very first night together that he wasn't planning on staying around for long. For more than a year she listened to him babbling about finding a better life, away from London.

'Where will you go?'

'Anywhere away from this hellhole.'

She had been a fool to believe he would take her with him. He had hung around for a few months after Jack was born, until she dared hope he would stay forever. Then he had gone, leaving her with a three-year-old problem child and a baby. She rarely thought about him now.

'We don't need no old man round here,' Jack had told her, and he was right. 'I ain't never had no father and I ain't starting now. If he ever walks back in our lives, he won't walk nowhere again.'

Her younger son's vicious words frightened her, but she needed him. If it wasn't for the wages Jack brought home she and the kid would struggle to cope. She watched Theo kick his ball repetitively against the wall. He was never going to get a job, not like Jack. Fat chance when there were no jobs any more. It was a miracle Jack had managed to keep hold of his for so long. He was off his face more often than not. She lived in dread of him coming home one day to tell her he'd been laid off. Jack laughed at her fears with the confidence of youth. Theo was completely different. Even the school hadn't wanted him. They had given her a load of bullshit about home visits which had never happened, and tests and assessments, but it was clear they hadn't known what to do with him. All they had ever wanted to do was take him away from her.

'They come for him, I'll kill them,' Jack said.

For once she had agreed with him.

'You carry on,' she told the kid, nodding at his ball.

The football was nearly flat anyway and only made a dull thudding noise when it hit the wall. She wasn't going to be bullied by some stupid git next door. Where the hell was Theo supposed to kick his ball? There was no way she could let him go outside. The kids on the estate would beat the crap out of him.

'He's not right in the head, that son of yours,' the neighbour yelled.

'He's more right than what you are, you arsehole!'

Theo needed somewhere to let off steam. She hoped the exercise would develop some muscle in him, making him stronger and better able to defend himself. Right now he looked like he could be snapped in two, like a dead twig. Someone banged so violently on the front door of the flat that the flimsy wooden frame shivered. She knew who it was. There was no way she was going to open the door to him. Apart from the fact that she didn't want to see her neighbour's ugly mug glaring at her, whenever she unlocked the front door Theo tried to run off and it wasn't safe for him to go out alone.

'Oy!' her neighbour shouted through the door. 'I told you to shut it! I'm trying to get some kip here. That crazy kid of yours needs to be locked away in a padded cell.'

'Fuck off, you old git!' she yelled back. 'You got no right telling us what to do in our own home. He can play all he wants.' She turned to Theo. 'Don't stop.'

'Don't stop,' he repeated in his high monotone.

'I'm trying to sleep!'

'I hope you have nightmares!' she called out. 'Have nightmares and die in your sleep!'

'Fuck you!'

'Fuck you!'

'Fuck you!' Theo piped up, still kicking his ball.

She turned away from the door and smiled at him. For all his spindly frame he wasn't such a pushover any more. He was a sweet boy, but when his temper was roused he could bite and kick and scratch like a wild cat. She had been worried about him when he was younger, he had always been so puny, but he was shaping up well. Playing with his football helped.

'Don't you stop kicking that ball,' she told him. 'I'll make us some tea. Jack brought cakes home yesterday. Do you want some cake?'

Theo didn't answer. He carried on kicking the ball. As she walked past she heard him singing softly under his breath. She tried to make out the words but it sounded like a foreign language.

She had just reached the kitchen when there was a sudden crash as the front door was kicked open.

10

SAM DROVE THEM to the block of flats in Haringey where Lenny lived with his girlfriend. The exterior brickwork of the building was crumbling in places, the window frames were old fashioned and looked draughty, the paintwork was cracked, and the short path leading to the front door was pitted with broken stone.

'Watch where you put your feet,' Sam called out as she avoided stepping on a dog turd. 'Nice.'

She rang the bell to number seven and shuffled sideways to position herself right in the doorway. While they waited, a gust of wind whipped past them, making Geraldine shiver in her thin jacket. She thrust her hands deeper into her pockets.

'Come on,' Sam muttered, jigging impatiently from foot to foot.

Geraldine watched her colleague out of the corner of her eye. Sam appeared to have fully recovered from a recent ankle injury that had prevented her from working for a couple of months. Now she looked even more robust than Geraldine remembered her. Solidly built and good tempered, impatient to crack on with the job, she didn't seem to mind the cold. There was something earthy and grounded about her that was very reassuring.

'I missed you –' Geraldine's words were carried away by another gust of wind.

Before she could speak again, the door opened a crack. A

woman peered out and demanded to know their business.

'Who the hell are you? What you selling?'

As she spoke, the door was already closing. Sam darted forward, put her foot over the threshold, and pushed the door open with her shoulder. The scrawny woman inside had no chance against the force of Sam's muscle. Barely thirty, Gina could have been fifty. She glared at them with heavy-lidded eyes.

'We're looking for Leonard Parker.'

'I don't know what you're talking about. Who the hell's that?'

'We know who you are, Gina, so there's no point in trying to fob us off with lies. We know who you are, and what's more, we know Lenny lives here with you.'

'Yes, well, I know who you are and all,' the woman replied sullenly. A large wart on her chin seemed to tremble with the motion of her jaw as her speech grew increasingly agitated. 'And all I got to say to you is that you had my Lenny locked up for eighteen bleedin' months and all for nothing because he done nothing, and you can bloody well leave him alone now. Go on, get lost, the pair of you. Hey, get out of it. What you think you're doing?' Her voice rose in anger as Sam stepped into the hall. 'Sling your hook, or I'll –'

'You'll what?' Sam spoke calmly but Geraldine could tell she was enjoying being back on the job. 'Are you going to call the police?'

'This is harassment. This ain't legal. You got no right –'

'We just want to talk to Lenny.'

'Well, he ain't here.'

'You don't mind us coming in and taking a look around?'

'I bloody well do mind. What a fucking cheek! This is my home. You got a search warrant or what?'

Ignoring her increasingly shrill objections, Geraldine followed Sam into the flat. Gina had been honest about one thing at least. They didn't find Lenny.

'I told you, he ain't here. Don't believe me, will you? And before you ask, I don't know where he is. And if I did know –'

'Yes, OK, we've heard it all before,' Geraldine interrupted her wearily, 'if you did know where he is, you wouldn't tell us.'

Gina grunted. 'But I don't know, and that's God's truth.'

'Can we sit down?'

'What for?'

'I need to talk seriously to you.'

'You can say whatever it is you got to say right here right now, and then you can piss off.'

Geraldine weighed up the risks of telling the truth. On the point of warning Gina that they believed Lenny to be armed and dangerous she hesitated. Gina didn't strike her as easy to scare, besides which she was loyal to Lenny and no friend to the police. Plenty of people were willing to aid a villain to escape the law, just in order to spite the police. Gina was probably one of them. Geraldine didn't believe Gina was in any danger. Lenny wouldn't harm her. But she might well alert him to the fact that the police were after him, if Geraldine revealed the reason they were looking for him.

'Gina, we only want to talk to Lenny. He's not in any trouble,' she lied. 'We think he might be able to help us with an enquiry. That's all. But it's very important we speak to him as soon as possible. Will you ask him to call us the minute he gets home?'

'Pull the other one. Think I was born yesterday? Think I'm going to fall for any of your gobshite? You fitted him up once. You ain't going to get away with it a second time. Not if I got anything to do with it. I got friends will sort you lot out if you try and touch him again. Friends that know the law better than anyone. Better than any lawyer.'

'Gina, this is important. You need to contact us as soon as he comes home. Will you do that?'

'Oh fuck off out of it. I know your game, putting innocent

people away. Listen to me, you smart-talking cow. You leave my Lenny alone, you hear me? He's done his time. Leave him alone.'

There wasn't much point in staying. They tried to persuade Gina to tell them where Lenny might be, but she insisted she had no idea.

'I told you, I ain't seen him, not since before he was nicked. God knows where he is. Out the country by now, if he's got any sense, with you lot after him the way you are. Bloody hell, can't you leave him alone? What's he ever done to you? And before you ask any more, I ain't saying another word. Not one more word.'

Back in the car, Geraldine requested twenty-four-hour surveillance of the flat, and instructed a sergeant to set up a watch for Lenny at stations and airports. With luck he would be completely unaware they were looking for him and would return to the flat where he would be picked up straight away. But they had to be prepared in case he had somehow got wind of the evidence they had found. After a short wait they saw an unmarked vehicle draw up, and they left for the police station.

'It won't be long till we find him,' Sam said. 'He won't get far.'

Geraldine didn't answer. The idea that they had allowed a killer to slip through their fingers was too depressing to contemplate.

11

SAM WAS WHISTLING as she drove Geraldine back to the police station. Every red light seemed to be against them yet she didn't complain. Even a minor traffic jam at some road works didn't bother her.

'How can you be in such a good mood, when the suspect wasn't there?' Geraldine burst out in exasperation. 'And stop bloody whistling. It's getting on my nerves.'

'Ooh, someone's touchy,' Sam grinned, but she stopped whistling.

'You do realise this could turn into a major manhunt all over London?'

'He'll probably roll up at his flat drunk this evening, and we'll have him behind bars before bedtime.'

'Do you think so?' Geraldine waited, but Sam didn't respond. 'What do you think the DCI's going to say?'

'Ah, so that's what this hissy fit is about. You're not really worried about whether we get the bastard behind bars now or later on today, you're just upset that the good-looking, new DCI won't heap praises on you for a job well done.'

'That's not true. And you needn't adopt that familiar tone with me when we're working.'

'This is just like old times. It's great to be back. I love my job!'

Geraldine was silent, wondering if Sam was right. There was no doubt Adam was good looking. But that was beside the point. If Adam had been a middle-aged woman, Geraldine would have been equally keen to make a good impression on her new detective chief inspector. It was a matter of professional pride, as well as ambition, to want to impress her superior officers.

'Just shut up and drive,' she told Sam.

Until now Adam had seemed aloof, although courteous and pleasant. Even as his eyes focused sharply on Geraldine, she sensed that he remained detached, his fury a calculated performance.

'What do you mean, he wasn't there?' His pale face flushed with anger. 'How can you have lost him? He's only been out of prison for two days, for Christ's sake.'

He stood up. Geraldine wasn't short, but he seemed to tower over her from behind his desk.

'This is crass ineptitude! We identified David's killer, and you let him get away.'

Geraldine frowned, her dismay at having failed to apprehend Lenny momentarily subsumed by the need to defend herself. If she had worked with Adam before, she might not have been so defensive. As it was, Adam knew nothing about her. Keen to make a good impression on him, she seemed to have messed up royally in her first week.

'You let him vanish from under our noses! We had him. Jesus, he's only been out for two days. How can he have disappeared? He came out, shot someone, and went to ground before we even knew it was him. It's unbelievably inept. What the hell have you been doing?'

His accusation was so unreasonable that Geraldine suspected he was judging her on her response to his ranting, rather than on her performance so far. The facts bore out that she had done nothing wrong. At the same time, her detective chief inspector must realise that she was watching him as he assessed her reaction. Unsure what to make of this goading, she kept her face impassive and spoke as calmly as she could.

'There's no reason why he would have disappeared. He doesn't know we're on to him.'

'He just shot a man. How can he possibly think we're not looking for him?'

'But he has no idea we know it was him. Why would he? And we don't know he's done a runner. He just wasn't at home when we went round there.'

'So now you've managed to barge in and warn his girlfriend that we're on to him.'

'I stressed that he's not in any trouble. I said I just want him to help us with an enquiry –'

'And you think she's not going to see through that? She was probably on the phone to him as soon as you walked out, warning him to keep out of sight. We may never find him now. He'll move on, and it'll be down to some other force to pick him up, because we let him slip through our fingers. We'll be a laughing stock.'

He wasn't testing her reaction to his verbal attack after all. He was genuinely put out at her failure, because it reflected badly on him. Adam was feeling under pressure himself, and was passing it on in the hope that she would somehow achieve a result. With a flash of empathy, she hurried to reassure him.

'We're doing everything possible to find him. We've got officers watching the flat twenty-four hours a day. If Gina goes out, we'll follow her in case she leads us to him, and we'll still have someone watching the flat all the time. We'll keep it up until we find him. And we *will* find him. We've sent a notification to security at all the airports and stations in the UK, in case he got wind we suspect him. He won't get away.'

'He *has* got away. We can't keep up this twenty-four-hour surveillance indefinitely. Where the hell is he?'

'We'll find him.'

She met his gaze levelly and his expression altered. His shoulders sagged as he sat down.

'I'm sorry, Geraldine. I was out of order just then. I thought we had him, you know. It would have been a coup, arresting a killer so quickly.' He gave an embarrassed laugh. 'This is my first case as DCI.'

She nodded, reassured and at the same time dismayed. She wanted a superior officer devoid of emotion, a kind of modern Sherlock Holmes with a firm grasp of facts and a piercing intellect. Adam had those qualities, but his cool manner, which she had mistaken for professional detachment, was a façade. Underneath it he was insecure. With a few more investigations under his belt, he might develop into a brilliant team leader. In the meantime, he was worryingly vulnerable. All the same, Geraldine warmed to him more now than she had before, when he had seemed so cold.

'We'll find him,' she repeated. 'He can't stay off the radar indefinitely.'

'Well, I'm going home. It's late and I'm knackered. Why don't you call it a day as well? There's nothing more we can do tonight.'

She nodded. 'With any luck he'll be safely locked up by tomorrow morning.'

'Let's hope so, for all our sakes.'

12

ROSA'S HEART POUNDED. Trembling, she snatched up her phone. In a panic she grabbed the bread knife with her other hand. She had to be prepared. Her neighbour might turn violent. Later she would worry about how to convince the police she had acted in self defence. For now all that mattered was Theo. She would stop at nothing to protect him. Quickly she pressed Jack's number, praying that he would answer. She had no one else to turn to, but even if she got through to him straight away it might take him an hour to get home. In the living room a phone began to ring and she heard a familiar voice.

'Ma? It's me. Where are you?'

Almost crying with relief, she ran out of the kitchen. Jack was standing in the doorway. Theo raced out of his room, wildly happy to see his brother.

Jack stepped forward, kicking the door closed behind him. 'Wait till you see what I got for you, bro.'

Theo reached him in one bound, arms flapping in excitement. Rosa watched the brothers embrace with a faint pang of envy. Theo wouldn't allow her to hug him, and Jack would never tolerate any show of affection, except from his crazy brother.

'You nearly give me a heart attack, coming in like that, crashing and banging,' she complained. 'Why'd you have to make such a racket?'

Jack took a step away from Theo and turned to look at her. 'What you mean? Why you crying, woman? What you scared of?'

She realised her mistake straight away. 'It's nothing, nothing at all,' she said quickly, wiping her eyes on the back of her hand. 'I ain't scared of nothing. I just thought you was at work, that's all.'

He caught sight of the bread knife she was still clutching. 'You going to shank me?'

'I was thinking of making toast,' she muttered.

'Don't stop! Don't stop! Wait till my Jack gets home!' Theo screeched suddenly.

Jack frowned. 'Who's been upsetting you, ma?'

'No one.'

Jack turned to his brother. 'What's going on, kid?'

'Wait till my Jack gets home,' Theo repeated, over and over. 'Wait till my Jack gets home!'

'Oh yes,' Jack said, 'I nearly forgot, I got something for you.'

Theo stopped talking. He giggled as Jack reached into his bag and pulled out a giant Toblerone.

'Well? You want it? Huh?'

He raised the chocolate bar as high as he could above his head but Theo grabbed it and scuttled to his room. They could hear him chortling and chattering to himself. Rosa laughed. Theo loved to squirrel things away.

'It's a wonder he ever finds anything in there,' she said. 'Have you looked in his room lately?'

'Leave it out. He's got little enough. I'm not surprised he wants to keep whatever he can get his hands on. You leave him alone.'

'I don't take nothing off him. And I never go in that room no more. He screams if I even touch his door.'

Jack muttered about a person being entitled to some privacy.

'I can't even get in there to clean. It stinks in there.'

Theo came back in the living room and stood in front of Jack. 'Wait till my Jack gets home!'

Jack nodded. 'I hadn't forgotten, bro. What happened? Who's been upsetting ma?'

Theo flapped his arms, laughing.

Jack turned to Rosa. 'You got to tell me, ma. Something happened. Was it that punk next door?'

Shaking her head, Rosa insisted nothing was amiss. Theo was just talking shit. She could see Jack didn't believe her for a minute.

'It was that old git next door, wasn't it?'

Theo picked up his deflated football and began kicking it at the wall making a regular thumping sound. As though he had been waiting for a signal, the bloke next door banged on the wall, and began shouting at Theo to shut the fuck up. Theo giggled.

'I bloody knew it.'

Jack spun on his heel and strode out of the room with Rosa trotting to catch up with him. At the front door she reached out and seized his arm.

'What you doing, Jack? Don't make no trouble. It's us got to live here.'

'Shut it, ma. That old fucker ain't nothing but trouble. I'm going to shut him up, once and for all. That's all. Don't fuss. I aint' gonna hurt him, not unless I have to.'

'Leave it, Jack. He ain't worth the trouble.'

'No, but you are. No one gets away with pissing you off, not if I can help it.'

'He ain't pissed me off, he –'

'Well, he's pissed me off.'

He shook himself free of her grasp and went out. He wasn't gone for long. When he returned he seemed energised. There was a lightness in his stride and a brightness in his eyes.

'Oh Jack, what you gone and done?'

'It needed sorting and someone had to do it.'

'What's that on your hand?'

Jack glanced at a wide streak of blood on the back of his hand. Theo stared at it too, his eyes wide with admiration.

'That?' Jack said with a dismissive shrug. 'Ain't nothing. It ain't as if it's mine.'

He laughed loudly. Watching him, Theo clapped his hands together and giggled. 'Wait till my Jack gets home!' he crooned, over and over.

'Oh shut up for fuck's sake,' Rosa grumbled. 'He's been saying that all afternoon.'

'Come on,' Jack urged his brother. 'Show us how to kick a ball.'

He handed the flat football to Theo and sat down, watching as his brother kicked the ball repeatedly against the wall.

'That's great, Theo. You keep it up.'

'He can do that for hours,' Rosa said proudly. 'The doctor said exercise is good for him.'

'I ought to get him a new football,' Jack mused. 'That one's shit. Of course a new ball's going to be full of air, and really hard. It'll make a lot more noise as it hits the wall.'

He looked at Rosa and grinned.

13

THERE WASN'T MUCH else Geraldine could usefully do that night. Realising how tired she was, she followed Adam's advice and went home. Once there, she regretted having left her desk. Although she had no appetite she fixed herself some supper, and switched the television on. There was nothing worth watching so she picked up a book and tried to read. But whatever she did, it was impossible not to think about the case. The general mood at the station had been upbeat, most officers seeming to agree with Sam. Even if they hadn't yet managed to put David's killer behind bars, at least they now had a suspect. The trouble was, Geraldine wasn't convinced they were after the right man. She had a number of reservations going round and round in her mind. It was maddening. Eventually she gave up trying to read and jotted down her questions. The next morning she would go into work early and raise them with Adam. With that decision made, she went to bed and fell asleep almost straight away. It had been an exhausting day.

The following morning she requested an early meeting with Adam. He greeted her even more coldly than usual. At pains to present a calm and measured outward appearance at work, she suspected he was mortified by his outburst the previous day. She wanted to assure him that she wouldn't tell anyone about it, but she wasn't sure how to approach the subject. In the end she decided not to mention it at all. He would learn for himself that she was discreet. Instead of referring to his conduct, she read him her list of concerns.

'First of all, Leonard Parker had only just left prison. Where would he have got hold of a gun?'

'He could have got it anywhere, once he left. Remember he'd been out for over twelve hours when David was shot. It doesn't take long to source a gun if you know where to look. And criminals talk. They may be scum, but they network, same as everyone else. Probably better than most.'

'Secondly, what happened to David's jacket?'

'Ask Lenny. I thought we agreed the killer could have taken it.'

Geraldine frowned. 'So the mugger asked him to take off his jacket before shooting him? Really?'

Adam shrugged. 'Makes sense to me. It's perfectly feasible. It was an expensive jacket, according to the wife.'

'Well, finally – and this is really the most important – I've looked into Lenny's background. He's never been involved in any gun crimes. He robs houses, not people on the street. He's never mugged anyone.'

'Not that we know of. Look, Geraldine, we're not the judge and we're not the jury. No one's asking you to convict this man of murder. But we do need to find him, and we need to bring him in, because right now he's the only suspect we've got. So get out there and track him down. We need him brought in yesterday.'

'I just don't believe he's a killer, Adam.'

'No one is until the first murder.'

Leonard Parker's mother lived in a poky one-bedroomed flat in Acton. Geraldine and Sam drove there, accompanied by a couple of constables. They set off before the rush hour hoping to avoid the traffic. The earlier they turned up, the more likely they were to surprise their suspect. The armed response team was already in place by the time they arrived.

Lenny's mother came to the door in a grubby dressing gown, blinking as though she had just woken up. She had short, straight, dyed blonde hair, and very broad shoulders that made her look even more dumpy than her stout figure warranted. Beneath a thick double chin, she appeared to have no neck at all.

'What do you think you're doing, calling on people at this ungodly hour of the morning? Ain't you people got homes to go to? Here, what you doing? You can't come in here. You got a search warrant?'

Geraldine assured her that a warrant had been issued, and the old woman stood aside, grumbling, as an armed team went in to check if Lenny was there. Once she had been assured there was no sign of him, Geraldine went and sat with Cynthia in a front room that seemed to be crammed with all sorts of junk.

'We want to speak to your son,' she began.

'Which one?'

'How many do you have? Three, isn't it?'

'If you know, why ask? Two in Australia and one here with me.'

'Your oldest son, Leonard. He's –'

'Oh no,' Cynthia interrupted firmly. 'He's done his time. You can't touch him no more.'

'Just what I was about to say.'

'What you want with him then? Can't you leave the poor kid alone? He's learned his lesson.'

Geraldine doubted that very much.

'We think he might be able to help us with an investigation.'

'And you think he's going to tell you? Huh! You can bloody well take yourself off out of here, and don't bother to come back. If my boy does know anything, he ain't going to tell you, not after what your lot done to him.'

Geraldine glanced around the room while they were talking. On several low tables an assortment of random objects was displayed: a large box inlaid with mother-of-pearl that probably contained jewellery of some description, pens, glass ornaments, at least half a dozen expensive watches, carriage clocks, and numerous knick-knacks. On the floor a cardboard box was piled high with iPads, iPods and other small electronic devices. She wondered why Cynthia had brought her into a room full of what were obviously stolen goods. She could only assume there were similar items in the other rooms in the flat.

'What you looking at?'

'You've got quite a lot of stuff here.'

'So? Is that any business of yours? We do the markets, if you must know, me and my Lenny. We sell gear and we buy gear. A lot of it gets stored here in between markets and boot sales. I know what you're thinking, but it's all legit. We do a hell of a lot. It's bloody hard work, I can tell you, and it's all a load of crap as you can see.'

'Mrs Parker, we need to know where Lenny is. If we don't find him very soon, he could end up in serious trouble –'

'Bollocks. You got nothing on him. Now bugger off, the lot of you, before I make a complaint.'

'We need to know where he is,' Geraldine repeated quietly, without shifting in her chair.

'I ain't got the foggiest. But when you find him, you can tell him from me that I'd like to know where he's been an' all. He's been out four days, and he ain't so much as picked up the phone, let alone come to see his mother, after I pined for him day and night for eighteen months. What sort of son does that to his mother?'

'One more question, Mrs Parker. Have you ever seen Lenny with a gun?'

'A gun? Bloody hell, what sort of family do you think we are? Now bugger off out of it and leave us alone. He's done his time.'

14

CYNTHIA WAS LIVID. First off Lenny had been stupid enough to get himself nicked which put the whole family under the spotlight as far as the law was concerned. It was never a good idea to attract attention like that, but Lenny had always been a moron. He was bound to get caught sooner or later. She had thought he'd be in the clear once he was out, only now she'd had a visit from some bloody inspector, and everyone knew what that meant. Any contact with the police was too much as far as Cynthia was concerned. She'd seen the way that inspector's eyes had roamed all over the room, taking in the watches and other stuff. Of course, she kept the obviously dodgy gear well out of sight. She wasn't stupid, unlike her idiot of a son. But there was enough gear lying around to arouse suspicion in a block of wood, and that inspector was no fool. When Lenny surfaced, Cynthia was going to give him a piece of her mind. If he wasn't a grown man, she'd tan his hide, just like she used to do when he was a kid.

There was no point in hiding the gear in her bedroom now. The police inspector had already seen it all. The valuable bits and pieces were out of sight, in the top cupboard in the kitchen. Cynthia hoped they were safe up there. That idiot Lenny had a lot to answer for. As soon as the front door closed behind the inspector and her lackeys, Cynthia rushed to the kitchen and put a few more tins in front of the bags of jewellery stashed there. Most of it was Lenny's stuff. He was always on at her. 'Hide this for me, mum,' and, 'put this somewhere till I come for it.' She understood he didn't want his girlfriend, Gina, getting her hands on his loot. She'd rip him off as soon as look at him, that one.

Grumbling to herself, she put the kettle on and made herself a cup of tea. Really, she could do without all this stress at her age. Her son ought to be looking after her, not giving her endless grief. Just as she sat down with a cup of tea and a slab of cake, she was disturbed by a knock at the front door.

'Oh fuck it all, what now?'

She was tempted to ignore it. She'd just sat down and got the weight off her feet. The knocking came again, more loudly this time.

'All right, all right, I'm coming. Give me time. I'm not a bleeding athlete.'

Expecting the police, she steeled herself to tell them to get lost. They had no business coming back and pestering her again. She hadn't broken any laws. She was just a poor old woman doing her best to make ends meet. She opened the door a crack and saw Lenny's skinny little bitch, scowling and biting her lip.

'Gina! What the hell you doing here?'

'Looking for Lenny, that's what.'

'Not you as well. Seems like the whole world's looking for Lenny.'

'Why? Who else is after him?'

Cynthia hesitated before inviting Gina in. 'Oh well, you'd better come in out the cold seeing as you've come all this way. I suppose you had your tea?'

'Don't put yourself out on my account.'

The words were kind enough, but Gina contrived to sound hostile. Cynthia regretted inviting her in as soon as the front door closed behind them.'I won't,' she muttered, leading Gina to the front room.

They sat in silence while Cynthia finished her tea. She

did her best to ignore her visitor, but she couldn't enjoy her cake, not with Gina perched awkwardly on the edge of a chair watching her every mouthful.

'That was delicious,' Cynthia said with fake enthusiasm, wiping crumbs from her mouth with the back of a hand. 'You don't know what you're missing.'

As soon as Cynthia put her cup down, Gina started on her. 'Where is he then?'

'How the hell would I know? I ain't seen him since he got out, and that was Monday.'

Aggrieved, Cynthia launched into a litany of complaint.

'Yeah, yeah, I know.' Gina interrupted her. 'You was pining for him every day. You told me.' She leaned so far forward in her chair, Cynthia thought her boney arse might slip right off it. 'What I want to know is where is he? He's got something of mine and I want it back.'

She sounded so earnest, Cynthia was curious.

'What is it? What you got that's so bloody important?'

'Mind your own bleeding business.'

'Whatever it is, anything you got is thanks to him and you'd do well to remember that. Anyhow, you can sit there till you're blue in the face, it won't do you no good because I already told you I don't know where he is. But I do know you're not the only one who wants to find him.'

'And what the hell's that supposed to mean? You going to tell me or what?'

'The rozzers was here, asking for him.'

'Never! They were round at mine last night looking for him but he'd gone out for the evening and he never come back.'

'Have you seen him since he got out?'

'Yeah, I told you. He came home Monday night – no, Tuesday morning – and he went out again yesterday and I ain't seen him since. But the pigs was round at the flat last night looking for him. Oh Christ, Cynthia, something's not right.'

Tears started in her eyes and she hung her head. She was trembling. She looked so forlorn that Cynthia couldn't help taking pity on her.

'Don't take on so. Lenny knows what he's doing. He's got wind of it, and he's laying low for a while. He'll be in touch when he's ready, don't you worry.'

'What if they're waiting for him? We got to warn him.'

'And how the hell can we do that if we don't know where he is?'

The two women stared at one another, their petty rivalry swept aside in mutual anxiety.

'He'll be all right, won't he?' Gina asked.

'Don't you worry yourself, pet,' Cynthia repeated, although she could see no reason to be confident. It was pretty clear Lenny had gone and done something stupid, or the law wouldn't be so interested in him. 'Whatever it is, those interfering bastards will find something else to busy themselves with soon enough. Now, I'll go and put the kettle on. And I got some nice Dundee cake that's not even stale. You could do with a bit of fattening up. You look like a bleeding skeleton.'

15

LENNY HAD DONE a runner, but they were confident they would find him. He couldn't hide from them forever. His home and his mother's home were under surveillance. Sooner or later he would surface and the police would be there, waiting for him.

Adam seemed upbeat about losing him. 'The instant he returns to his flat, he'll be picked up,' he said. 'We're keeping a watch at airports and stations, although I don't think he'll get far so there's no need to go overboard there. It's not like we're hunting for Brain of Britain. He's not even been particularly successful as a petty house burglar. He didn't manage to get away with that. And right now, he's only just come out of prison. With no passport, and no money, how's he going to take himself off anywhere? I'm sure he's just lying low, and he'll show up soon enough. He'll have to turn up at his home, or go to see his mother, because apart from anything else, he'll need to get hold of some cash. Don't forget, he's broke. And when he turns up, that's when we'll get him.'

'He may be broke, but he mugged David Lester at gun point. What's to stop him doing that again if he's desperate for money?' a constable asked.

'And he can get hold of a fake passport, if he's been out mugging people for cash,' someone else pointed out.

'All patrols are on the alert to look out for him. If he's roaming the streets, anywhere in the country, he won't stay out there for long. And if he's gone into hiding, well, he can't hide away forever with no money. Let's not overestimate him. This is no more than a temporary hold up. He's not clever enough to stay on the run for long. We'll try Gina again tomorrow, see if we can pressure her into telling us who his associates are, because chances are he's enlisted help. In the meantime, we need to check up on any of his contacts who might be sympathetic to him, plus anyone he was inside with who's now out, and the wives and girlfriends and families of anyone still inside. Whoever's sheltering him probably has no idea they risk becoming an accessory to murder. We'll put an alert out on Crimewatch, and we need to stress that he's killed once, and he may be armed and is certainly dangerous. Members of the public need to warned off approaching him, and if anyone is hiding him, hopefully they'll think twice about putting their own arse on the line. Right, that's it for now.'

They could do nothing but wait for Lenny to be picked up. Geraldine and Sam went for a drink after work. Instead of going to the pub nearest the police station where most of their colleagues often dropped by for a pint, they went to a pub they knew along the Edgware Road that served good food.

'We could just go for a drink,' Geraldine suggested.

'I'm not going anywhere that doesn't serve decent food.'

Geraldine laughed. 'OK, The Heritage Arms it is. And it's on you.'

'Hang on, I'm not expected to pay for the pleasure of your company, am I? I see you every day at work as it is.'

Geraldine was pleased to have a chance to catch up with Sam. Since her colleague had returned to work, they had been too busy to go out together. As if by an unwritten agreement, neither of them mentioned work that evening. Geraldine began by asking Sam about her relationship status. The last she knew, Sam had been seeing a woman called Emily. Sam grinned.

'Oh yes, we're still together. We just get on well, you know? She's really easy to be with. She stayed away when mum was around and I really missed seeing her.'

Geraldine was surprised. 'But your mother must know about you?'

'Oh yes, she knows I'm a lesbian. She's cool with it. I think she's always known, even before I told her. But she's ambivalent. I mean, she's used to it, but deep down I think she still hopes I'll change. She imagines I'll wake up straight one morning, or meet Mr Right who will change my mind. Change me.' She laughed. 'It's not going to happen. We both know that. The trouble is, my cousin's just had a baby and mum's desperate for me to follow suit. She gets kind of broody, you know, and she talks about my cousin all the time. She never used to mention her.'

'That must be hard for you?'

'Not really, but it's bloody boring.'

Geraldine gave a sympathetic smile. 'My sister's pregnant.'

'So congratulations are in order? You're going to be an aunt all over again. They all seem to be at it these days.'

'Everyone except us.'

'Yes. But would you really want to? Find a bloke, I mean, have a family, and all that. Somehow I don't see you as a domestic goddess.'

'No.' Geraldine stifled a sigh. 'I've not met anyone anyway, so it's immaterial.'

'But if you did, meet someone I mean, would you want children?'

Geraldine shrugged. 'It's not something I've ever really thought about,' she lied.

Driving home, she tried not to think about Sam's question. Apart from a long-term relationship in her twenties, the only man she had seriously fallen for had been a colleague, murdered shortly after their affair began. After losing him, she couldn't imagine ever daring to fall in love again. She seemed destined to investigate the dead without ever engaging with the living. Blinking, she was surprised to discover that she was crying.

16

GINA SAT DOWN on an empty bench, the slats hard and cold against her thighs. She shifted her weight forward. A dreary wait on a draughty platform was all she needed. Travelling all the way to Acton to see Cynthia had taken up most of the day, and had achieved nothing. Cynthia had grunted when Gina refused her offer of tea. 'My cake not good enough for the likes of you?' She hadn't offered again.

Gina had hoped to find Lenny there. It turned out Cynthia didn't know where he was either, or if she did know she wasn't letting on. The trip had been a waste of time. If it wasn't for her engagement ring, Gina would be tempted to question whether Lenny was worth all the stress. He was a stingy sod most of the time. When he was home she lived in fear of him, when he was banged up she lived in fear of the other men on the estate. But her life was about to change. No one had ever given her anything beautiful before. It made her feel really special.

She was nearing the end of her journey when the rush hour began. The crush of commuters was terrifying. At least she had a seat. She tucked her feet in and kept her head down, impatient to get off the crowded train and close her front door against strangers. Finally, she reached her stop. It was growing dark. She hurried out of the station and turned off the main road into the side street where she lived. There was still a long walk ahead of her, along a deserted pavement.

When an occasional car shot past she trembled in case it stopped. They took her back to the time when she used to get in cars with men. She had lived in constant terror of being hurt, but she had gone with strangers anyway. That was before Lenny had brought her to London with him. She clenched her left fist, rubbing the back of her ring finger with her thumb. She was engaged. Lenny was going to make an honest woman of her. That made her smile, in spite of her aching feet. Once they were married, everything would be different. Lenny would stay at home with her and keep her safe.

Finally, she shut her front door. Slipping off her shoes, she went into her small living room. Only one light bulb was working. The room looked shadowy. She shivered. She didn't like being at home on her own. All the time Lenny had been inside she had been nervous. Now he had been released and she was still sitting in the flat by herself. He liked to boast how easy it was to get into a house, as long as you knew what you were doing. There was nowhere he couldn't break into. He went on about it until she had insisted he put a chain on the door. But the windows were large enough for a man to climb through. When she asked Lenny if they could install a burglar alarm he had nearly pissed himself laughing at the idea.

Without Lenny to protect her, every night she went to bed terrified of being attacked while she was sleeping. Lenny's violence was nothing compared to being raped and battered to death by a stranger. There were constant reports of muggings and burglaries on the estate. The police didn't care. No one took any notice.

Lying in the dark, she heard a door open somewhere nearby. Terrified, she listened, knowing there was nothing she could do to protect herself from an intruder. She heard footsteps outside the bedroom door. Holding her breath, she kept perfectly still, praying he wouldn't find her. One of her legs was dangling out of the side of the bed but she lay rigid, not daring to pull it under the covers. The edge of the duvet tickled her bare leg, but she didn't move a muscle. Pressing her teeth together she listened, ears searching the darkness. Apart from the familiar drone of snoring from the flat downstairs, and the distant hum of traffic, all was quiet. Whatever had disturbed her must have been a dream. She started to relax but then it came again, the sound of shuffling footsteps. If she'd been asleep, she might not have noticed them. Once heard, they were impossible to ignore.

She tensed, listening. A few seconds passed before she heard the noise again. This time there was no doubt. Someone was in the flat. Creeping stealthily was not Lenny's style. He was never worried about waking her up when he came in late but would barge in, high on adrenaline, loudly demanding booze and food and sex, eager to show off his spoils. With an effort she stopped herself crawling under the duvet. There was nowhere to hide, and no escape. The bedroom door was ajar. The slightest sound might be heard by the intruder. Best to lie still and hope he didn't come into the bedroom.

Without any warning the door flew open. A stream of dim light poured in from the living room window. Through half-closed eyes she watched in terror as a dark figure burst into the room. She closed her eyes and held her breath, praying that he wouldn't notice her. It was ironic. Lenny earned his dosh robbing houses, and now here she was, the victim of a burglar while Lenny had buggered off God only knew where. A soft whimper escaped her. She couldn't help it. She screwed her eyes tightly shut. The worst thing she could do was be caught watching. If he thought she had seen his face, he would make sure she could never identify him. Her last thought was that it served Lenny right. He should have been there to protect her.

17

THEY ARRANGED TO meet outside Camden Town station when Sophia finished work. Jack had the night off and they were going out. She wasn't there when he arrived. He wandered a few paces away from the throng of kids hanging about on the pavement. Keeping a close eye on people surging out of the station, his gaze flitted past the girls, sizing up the blokes as they passed him. The threat of violence hovered everywhere on the streets, and he had to stay alert. No one had taken him down yet, but they tried from time to time. He had no intention of being caught out, not now he was doing so well.

His business venture was starting to thrive. Word was, Axel was watching him. That sort of attention wasn't dished out to just any small-time drug dealer. New on the scene, Jack had become a serious player very quickly. So far so good. He wasn't just ambitious, he was clever. He hung on to his job at the bar. He no longer needed their stingy wages, but it gave him a legitimate cover for his earnings. Not that his money went far, even now he was doing so well. Some of it went to his mother. She was smart enough to keep her trap shut when he said he had earned it doing an honest week's work. He knew she spent most of it on his brother, Theo, but that was all right. Theo was simple. He couldn't take care of anything for himself. Other than that, Jack spent some of his earnings on himself. He liked to dress sharply, and he had to keep himself in drugs, fags and booze. The rest of it went on his girl. He spent a fortune to keep her happy, and she still kept him hanging about waiting at the station. He swore under his breath. He was not a happy man.

His anger vanished the minute he saw Sophia's huge eyes searching the crowd streaming out of the exit. He stood still for a moment, watching her, hardly able to believe that she was there just for him. There were other guys all around her. He started forward, calling her name. When she caught sight of him waving, her face lit up with a smile that spread a warm glow right through him. He pushed his way through the crowd and seized her arm. It drove him nuts the way other blokes looked at her. It seemed every man in sight was at it, young blokes, old blokes, all running their eyes up and down her body, checking out her long brown thighs, lingering on her tits, shifting to her arse as she passed by.

Not that he blamed them. Her glossy hair, the curves of her body, the rhythmic sway of her hips, everything about her made him ache to possess her. It wasn't only lust, although even the mere thought of her body aroused him. He could have conquered that. She touched him in a manner that was more potent than any physical desire. Every time he saw her was like a wild explosion in his head, maddening and wonderful. He had never experienced anything like it before. There had been plenty of girls before her. With his athleticism and good looks, he had no trouble attracting tarts. But since meeting Sophia he had lost interest in other women. The change in him had been instantaneous. He simply didn't want anyone else.

'I been thinking about you,' he muttered as she put her cheek up for him to kiss.

He didn't add that he thought of little else. Wherever he was, she was present inside his head. Images of her smile, her laughter, her beautiful eyes, her sinuous body, flashed across his mind in a tantalising kaleidoscope. She visited him in his dreams. If she refused to see him it was torment. She was like a drug. He worried constantly that she would leave him for someone else. He tried to explain his feelings, but she laughed. When he persisted, she grew sullen. He was reduced to feeling grateful that she saw him at all.

There was no reason for her to look elsewhere. He took her out all the time and bought her expensive gifts. Often it was stuff he nicked, but sometimes he let her choose and watched her eyes as he handed over the notes. He kept her in booze and fags, and bought her nice clothes. One time she asked him for perfume. The stink was overpowering, but she was pleased with it. He couldn't understand why anyone would want to walk around smelling like that. It was all part of her mystique. He would never know what was going on inside her head, although he thought about her all the time.

'What do you really want from me?' he asked her once.

'Apart from your cock you mean?' she laughed.

He wasn't sure if she was insulting him or not. Somehow he never knew with her. Was that all he was to her? A bloke with a cock? If that was true, then she could go with anyone. No bloke in his right mind could resist her. If some bloke with more money than him were to hit on her, would she turn him down?

It sounded stupid, but he had to ask. 'You do like me, don't you?'

It didn't make him feel any better when she just nodded, as though it wasn't important. If anything, he felt even more frustrated.

'If I ever catch you playing jiggy with another guy, I'll kill you,' he said. For answer she tossed her head, like a horse flicking away an annoying gnat.

'You better believe it,' he muttered, 'because I ain't joking.'

18

'GINA? GINA? YOU awake?'

She opened her eyes, crying out in relief.

'Jesus, Lenny, what the fuck?' She heaved herself up on to one elbow. 'What the hell you doing, creeping around like that in the middle of the night like you was going to murder me in my bed?'

He flicked the light on. 'What you talking about, you dumb bitch?'

'You're pissed.'

'What's it to you?'

'I been worried about you.'

'You're a daft cow.'

'Where you been all this time?'

'None of your fucking business. I can come and go as I please, go where I like. I'm not in prison now.'

That reminded her. She frowned. 'They been looking for you.'

He sat down with a bump on the edge of the bed. Slipping off his shoes, he chucked them at the radiator.

'Don't do that. Jesus, Lenny. Anyway, you can't stay here.'

'Who says I can't? It's my home, innit? What you on about, you daft cow?'

He pulled off his socks and threw them after his shoes as she was talking.

'I'm telling you, Lenny, they come here looking for you. They'll be back. And they was at your mum's flat, asking her where you were and all. They're after you. That's why you can't stay here. You got to get away. Go somewhere they won't find you. Lenny, I'm scared. What do they want with you?'

She began to cry. He twisted round to look at her.

'What is it, Gina, baby?' he asked kindly. 'What you on about? There's nothing to get upset about. I'm here now. We're going to be all right. Go on, budge up, there's a good girl.' He stood up and took his trousers off. 'Come on, lie down.' He lifted the duvet and fell on the bed.

She shook her head, still sitting up, and crying so hard she could barely speak.

'I'm telling you, it's not safe for you here. Jesus, why won't you listen to me? The pigs was here, looking for you, and they was round at your mum's too, asking where you was. They're after you, Lenny. You got to get away. It's not safe for you here.'

He sat up and leaned on one elbow. 'Gina, baby, what the fuck are you talking about?'

Carefully, she explained. At last he understood what she was telling him. He swore aloud and thrashed the bed in his anger.

'Why the fuck can't they leave me alone? I done my time. Those bastards. Once they got you, they think they can pin anything and everything on you. Some prick's gone and robbed a house and now they want me to go down for it, so they can meet their bleeding target. No matter it wasn't me. Someone got robbed. Let's do Lenny for this one. He's just out. We can send him back and hit a target. Bastards. Well, I ain't going down for nothing, just so's they can talk shit about how they done a good job and got one more piece of scum off the streets. No way. They ain't going to pin this on me. I'll fight it, Gina. I won't go down without a fight.'

Watching him work himself up in to a temper, she waited for him to calm down enough to listen to her.

'Don't be a mug, Lenny. What you going to do? Call the whole police force a liar? If they say you done it, who's going to believe you?'

'Bastards!'

He knew she was right. Now he had form, he was a sitting duck. They could accuse him of burglary and any judge or jury would convict him without even listening to a word in his defence. He was a marked man.

'You ain't done nothing since you come out, have you?' she asked.

'Only robbed that stiff. Oh shit. You know what? The bastards are going to want to pin that on me, aren't they? Call me a bloody murderer. Well, they got to find me first.'

'That's what I been saying. We got to get away. It's not safe here.'

'If I gotta run, I ain't taking you. Where the fuck am I supposed to go? I ain't got no money. How much you got, baby?'

Without a word she climbed out of bed and fetched her purse. There was just over thirty quid in it.

'Give it here.'

'What? All of it? What am I supposed to live on for the rest of the week?'

'You'll get more. Come on, give it here.'

Reluctantly she handed over the cash. 'It's all I got. We'll find somewhere, won't we?'

'We? What you on about, you daft cow. I told you, I gotta go alone. You'll slow me down.'

'But you'll send for me, won't you? When you got somewhere to live?'

'Send for you? What you talking about? You got any idea how stupid you sound? How am I supposed to find somewhere to live? I ain't got no money. I got no job.'

She climbed back into bed. 'You got friends?'

There was no point pretending he would be able to find somewhere for them to live, not without fear of the law catching up with them. He would be on the run.

'Maybe you should just stay here. Tell them it weren't you. Whenever it happened, I'll say you were with me.'

'Like those bastards are going to listen. No, I got to get away. It won't be forever,' he promised her, putting one arm round her and pulling her close. 'One last night together, before I'm off.'

'You will send for me won't you?'

'Yeah, yeah.'

'And before you go, I want my ring back.'

'Oh shit. I forgot about that.'

'Where is it, Lenny? You promised.'

He explained that he had taken the ring to be resized, as they had discussed.

'Where? Where did you take it?'

'Just leave it out will you? I'll sort it when this is all over.'

'No, I want it, Lenny. I want it back now.'

She didn't tell him that she had a plan. She would sell the ring for whatever she could get for it, and they could use the money to move away. They could go up North, maybe to Scotland. That was as good as another country. No one there would be after him. They could find somewhere to live and start out again, without his bloody mother breathing down their necks every five minutes. It might even turn out for the best in the long run.

'Where is it, Lenny? Where did you take it?'

'Shut up will you? I said I'd sort it. Now lie down for fuck's sake. I ain't got all night.'

In the early hours he climbed out of bed. Forlornly, she followed him into the kitchen and watched him stuff what little food she had into his rucksack, before he slipped out of the flat, leaving her sobbing in the narrow hallway. It was worse than him being in the nick. At least then she had known where he was, and he hadn't been able to drift in and take all her money, leaving her with nothing to eat and an empty purse.

19

GETTING AWAY WAS always the hardest part. Tonight was particularly tricky because if what Gina told him was true, the police would be outside, keeping an eye on the flat. It was lucky he had not simply marched up to the front door where he could easily have been seen. It was almost like he had a sixth sense, and knew they were looking for him. Still, slipping in and out of properties unseen was his special talent. It made a change effecting an escape from his own home. At least he knew the territory better than anyone else. The most obvious escape route was out the back but he noticed that was under surveillance from a second-floor window overlooking the yard. Lenny was expecting that. He spotted the watcher first. Keeping close to the fence, he edged his way to the end of the yard an inch at a time, his progress masked by the tangled bushes that no one ever pruned. Reaching the back fence he pressed himself against the wooden slats, and waited patiently. At last the opportunity came. The watcher in the window turned as a second figure appeared, probably his replacement. As they faced one another, Lenny made his move. It was the work of a second to slip through the gate and press himself up against the far fence, out of the watcher's line of vision. Unable to see up to the window where they had set up their surveillance, he waited. There was no sound of pursuit.

The passageway that ran between the blocks of flats was unlit. Ignoring sharp stones that pierced the skin on the palms of his hands, he slithered along the ground in the darkness. It wasn't far to the end of the path, but he seemed to be crawling for hours. At last he reached the road. Straightening up, he brushed the dirt from his jeans and jacket and set off towards anonymity and freedom. He had to restrain himself from running. He couldn't afford to draw attention to himself. Reaching the main road, he paused. Finsbury Park station wasn't far away. It was tempting to head straight there, nip down the stairs and jump on a train. On the other hand he wasn't wearing a hood, and the underground network was riddled with CCTV cameras. On balance he decided it wasn't worth the risk of being picked up on a security camera. Reluctantly, he walked past the station and carried on, collar up, head down, eyes fixed on his scuffed shoes, listening for any sound of pursuit.

As he strode along, he formulated a plan. Any one of his contacts could be an informer. Even if they didn't grass regularly, they might buckle under police threats or inducements. He couldn't think of a single person he could rely on to face police hostility rather than betray him. Not even his own mother was trustworthy. He worked himself up into a fury as he marched along, ducking his head whenever a car went by. Gina would give him up for cash. She was always out for what she could get. He would screw what money he could out of her and then disappear. Admittedly she had stuck by him all the time he was inside, but she was becoming a drag, harping on and on about getting married. As if he didn't have enough problems. It was time he moved on.

Before it grew light he needed to be out of sight. The only place he could think of to hide at such short notice was in one of the lock-up garages at Alfie's place. Most of them were used for storage so there wasn't much risk of being spotted. Alfie was usually out visiting scrapyards on Fridays so, with luck, he wouldn't be around much. By Saturday Lenny would be gone. He just needed to get some cash in his pocket first. As he drew near Alfie's motor repair yard, he pulled out his phone.

'What you doing, calling me on the mobile? Didn't you listen to what I said? The police was here. They can track you –'

'Shut the fuck up, Gina. All you got to do is listen. And don't worry, I'm using a mate's phone.' It was one he'd nicked just after he got out of prison. Not that it was any of her business. 'I need to get my hands on some readies. What you got?'

'You know I ain't got nothing. You took it all last night.' She began to cry. 'Where are you, Lenny? Where you hiding?'

'I'm at Alfie's, round the back, in one of the lock-ups. Only I can't stay long. Alfie don't know I'm here. No one knows. Only you. So you get some cash together and bring it round, like a good girl. Anyone asks, you're going to the shops. Go and see a few other people first, and some more after, as many as you can, so it looks like you're trying everywhere, in case they're following you.'

'What you mean, following me? Who's following me?'

'I mean in case the pigs is following you.'

'Why would they do that? I ain't done nothing.'

'Course you ain't but they're looking for me, ain't they? Jesus, Gina, don't be so bloody thick.'

'Oh fuck off.'

'Don't let anyone suspect I'm here. You got to be clever about it, Gina. Use your head for Christ's sake. But you bring me some dosh soon. Maybe you can get some off me mum. I'll be banged up again if I don't get out of here soon. And don't call me back. I'm going to chuck the phone somewhere no one's going to find it so you won't get me on it. Now get going, will you?'

'Where the hell am I supposed to get any money?' she whined.

He rang off. There was no point trying his mother. She never answered his calls. There was no one else. He glanced around before slipping the phone down a drain. He hoped Gina would come good for him.

20

GERALDINE AND SAM set off early to visit Gina. They were almost certain Lenny wouldn't be there. He would have had to steal past two officers sitting in a patrol car a few doors away, watching the property.

'He's a house burglar,' Sam had pointed out that morning. 'He knows how to creep in and out of houses without being spotted.'

'Not under our noses,' Adam had replied. 'We've got officers watching the house, front and back.'

Although she tended to agree with the detective chief inspector, Geraldine had to admit it was possible Lenny had slipped home undetected. He had been caught only after successfully entering hundreds of properties undetected. Men like him knew how to move around unseen. She shared her views with Sam who grinned with excitement at the suggestion that they might find Lenny at home.

'Just imagine if he's there!' she crowed. 'All these alerts and messages flying around, all the surveillance teams, and even an announcement on Crimewatch. Jesus, everyone in the whole of the Met, the entire force, the whole country, must know about the fatal mugging and the killer who got away. He vanished into thin air, and now we're going to march into his house and arrest him, just like that. It's awesome! Think how good it's going to look on our CVs. I can just picture it. There might be promotion in it. And as for my mum, always banging on about how I should give up the job, and how I'm risking my life for nothing, this'll shut her up, won't it? You and me, simply walking in and arresting a dangerous killer. He could be armed. Shit, I love this job!'

'He probably won't be there,' Geraldine said, but Sam refused to be deflated.

As they drove, Geraldine thought about what Sam had said. There had certainly been a fuss about David Lester's death in the media, especially since Laura had been persuaded to grant an interview to one of the news channels. Young, blonde and tearful, she had been a reporter's dream accompaniment to a dramatic account of a violent death on the streets of London. It was only one of several accounts criticising the police for failing to catch the perpetrator immediately.

'The victim did not belong to a gang, or associate with criminals. He was simply a law-abiding member of society who was shot dead in Central London for the contents of his wallet. What,' the reporter had concluded, 'are the police actually doing to protect our citizens from such violence on our streets?'

To begin with, Gina tried to refuse to allow them in the house.

'Don't do this, Gina. You know we're here with a search warrant and a full team. If you resist, we'll only end up having to break the door down. Let us in. We just want to take a look around. Then we can call the search teams off and leave you alone.'

'Why the hell would you want to search my flat? What you looking for anyway?'

'We need to find Lenny.'

Finally, with much grumbling, Gina opened the door to let them in. If anything, she looked even more gaunt than the first time Geraldine had seen her. She was visibly agitated. Her legs trembled as she leaned against the wall in the narrow hallway for support.

'You won't find him,' she muttered. 'There ain't no one here. I ain't seen him since he was in the nick.'

Geraldine spoke gently to the terrified woman, as though she was speaking to a nervous child.

'Gina, I need to talk to you about Lenny. Let's go and sit down, shall we?'

Taking Gina's elbow, she steered her into the cramped living room where they had spoken before. While an armed team searched the flat, Geraldine kept an eye on Gina to make sure she couldn't warn Lenny they were there. Gina perched on the edge of a worn upright chair, biting her lip and squinting askance at her uninvited guest. Geraldine glanced around the room. Small and sparsely furnished, it was ugly and uncomfortable. Apart from the two matching chairs she and Gina were seated on, there was an armchair of worn tan leather that looked as though it belonged in a different room. A low table was covered in stained tea cups. Around a dozen gin bottles, mostly empty, were lined up against the wall. Above a grotty gas fire fixed to the wall, empty beer bottles stood in a row on a narrow shelf. There was nothing else in the room, apart from worn grey carpet and threadbare orange curtains.

'You can look all you like, you won't find him,' Gina snarled. 'You think I don't see your game? Well, you won't find nothing. And they better not nick my purse neither. I know what's in it.'

Geraldine chose her words carefully. 'Gina, you may see this on the television, so I'm going to tell you now to your face. You need to listen to me. Lenny's in trouble.'

'Oh fuck off. He ain't done nothing. You'll never make this stick, whatever it is you're trying to fit him up with. It's all a set up. I weren't born yesterday.'

'We think he killed someone.'

'Who did?'

'Lenny.'

Gina threw her head back. Her scrawny neck juddered as she gave a bark of laughter.

'Well I don't believe you, not for one minute, and you won't get no jury to convict him because you won't have no proof. You can't just bang a man up any time you feel like it, even if you are the police.'

Her bravado was pathetically transparent. She was terrified.

'We have reason to suspect he mugged a man on the street and shot him dead.'

'Shot him?'

'Yes, with a pistol –'

'Oh bugger off. Now I know it's all a pack of lies. Lenny never had no time for guns.'

'He's armed, and he's dangerous. If you know where he is, or if he comes to see you, you need to call us straight away. We can protect you –'

'I don't need protecting. Only from you. You're a fucking liar, and you know it. Lenny ain't done nothing. You better leave him alone.'

Geraldine stared at her. 'Gina, if it turns out you know where he is, there's every chance you'll go down as an accessory to murder. At the very least you'll be done for withholding information from the police and obstructing our enquiry. These are serious offences, Gina. We're conducting a murder investigation.'

'Fuck off out of it. I told you, he ain't here.'

'I put the wind up her,' Geraldine told Sam as they walked back to the car together. 'She was nervous all right. But she stuck to her story.'

The search team had found nothing incriminating in the flat.

'You wouldn't know he lives with her,' one of them said. 'There were no men's clothes in the wardrobe, hardly any clothes at all in there, just a huge pile of soiled women's clothing in the bathroom, not even in a laundry basket, just lying on the floor.' He screwed up his nose. 'And there wasn't a single photo of him to be seen anywhere.'

'She might have pictures of him, just not out on display.'

'It must have been concealed beneath other things then. Who keeps photographs hidden away?'

Geraldine thought about the one precious photograph she had of her birth mother. It was an old picture, probably taken before Geraldine was born. Her mother looked about twelve in it, but she had only been sixteen when Geraldine was born, and probably not very different to the thin, wide-eyed child in the photograph Geraldine kept hidden away in the drawer beside her bed. Until now, it had never struck her as strange that her mother had asked the social worker to give the picture to the daughter she had abandoned at birth and now refused to see. For the first time she wondered if that was significant.

'Geraldine? Are you listening?' Sam asked. 'They couldn't find anything.'

Geraldine shook her head. What they were looking for wasn't going to be hidden away in a drawer or a tin in the kitchen.

'Where is he?' she muttered.

'We'll find him,' Sam replied. 'He can't have gone far. Sooner or later he'll stick his nose up out of whatever sewer he's hiding in, and then we'll have him.'

21

GINA COULD HAVE laughed when the police turned up to search the flat, because there really was nothing there. Not even a loaf of bread. Luckily the inspector believed her when she said she didn't know where Lenny was. If they had suspected she was lying, they might have treated her differently. Everyone knew the police put themselves above the law. If they'd bothered to check her phone, they would have seen she had received a call only about an hour earlier. Not that it would have helped them, because he was using a stolen phone. Still, they might have been able to trace where he was when he made the call. You couldn't be too careful with the police. They were up to all sorts of crafty tricks, always trying to catch people out. No wonder everyone hated them. That was what Lenny said, anyway.

'It's like living in a police state. You can't hardly take a piss without some fucking copper coming up and nicking you.'

And the police weren't the only ones hassling her. While they were pestering her for information, Lenny was on at her for money. When she had asked him where the hell he expected her to get hold of any cash, he had hung up. But he was just being careful. She had to remember he was going to marry her, and in the meantime he was relying on her to save him. There was only one way she could save Lenny and herself too. If she got her ring back she could pawn it and share out the cash between herself and Lenny. Once she had saved enough, she would retrieve her ring. She would have it resized and never take it off again. Grabbing her mac, she ran out of the flat and went haring up the road. Lenny needed her and she wouldn't let him down. She would get him through this, and then they could get married.

She went straight to the antiques shop where he took most of his gear.

Although it was late by the time she arrived, the shop was still open. Averting her eyes from a mangy stuffed fox that seemed to be staring right at her, she approached the white-haired bloke behind the counter. He smiled at her over his rimless spectacles.

'Lenny's girl?'

She nodded, pleased he had recognised her. That would make her task easier. She had been afraid he wouldn't believe her when she said Lenny had sent her to fetch her ring. She did her best to sound confident, but her voice shook.

'Oh yes, the diamond.' The old man nodded. 'I remember it, but I ain't got it. He needed a jeweller to swap the stone for a piece of glass, so no one would be able to tell the difference. He wasn't one to pass up an opportunity.'

After all they had been through together Gina couldn't believe that Lenny could be so mean. All the time he had been locked up she had stood by him, asking nothing in return, and he had given her nothing but grief. The engagement ring had made up for everything he had put her through. He knew how much that ring meant to her. It held a promise that he wanted to take care of her for the rest of her life. That was the point of being engaged. Only now he had taken even that away from her. He was more interested in converting her diamond into cash than in making her happy. If he had suggested they sell the ring and split the readies, she would have agreed. She would have accepted a different ring, if there was money in it for her. But he had lied to her, planning to pocket the cash himself and fob her off with a piece of glass.

When she reached the car repair yard, there was no one in sight. From inside one of the lock-ups came the noise of machinery whirring and droning.

She walked swiftly past to the end door and tapped on it.

'Oy, Lenny, you in there?'

There was a sound of scrabbling and the door lifted, just enough for her to stoop and go in. The door clanged shut softly behind her.

'I got you some cash but I ain't handing it over till you tell me where my ring is.'

'Give it here and I'll let you have your ring.'

She handed over a twenty quid note she had kept back for emergencies. If her plan worked, there would be no more emergencies, not for her anyway.

'Did you bring me anything to eat?'

'Like what? I can't afford nothing, not after you took all my dosh. I just give you all I had left. Now I got nothing.' She glared at him, her hands on her hips. 'Where's my ring?'

'It ain't your ring. And keep your voice down.'

'What? You give it me, that means it's mine.'

'Yeah, well, you give it back, didn't you, so now it's mine. I wanted to give it you, only now I need it back.'

She took a step forward. 'Where is it, Lenny?'

She would never wear it as an engagement ring now. That dream was busted. But she sure as hell would sell it and be better off than she was now.

Lenny was no different to any other man she had ever met, a cheating, lying, selfish swindler.

'Give it here. It's mine.'

'Even if I had it here I wouldn't give it to you. Now, what you still doing here?' He walked over to the door. 'Go on. Get out of here unless you want to get caught with me, and then they'll bang you up too.'

Gina panicked. 'Where you going? You can't leave, not just

like that, not without telling me where you're going.'

'Keep your voice down, you stupid cow.' He reached for the door control. 'I'm going to open that door and soon as I do, you get out of here. Don't let anyone see you or we'll both be nicked.'

The door rolled upwards. 'Go on,' he urged her. 'Be quick for fuck's sake, before someone sees, or we'll both be for it.'

Gina ducked down and scrambled out of the lock-up. The door slid shut behind her.

Safely out of the yard she legged it up the road, relieved to have got away from there without any more bother. She was fuming. One way or another she was going to get her ring back from that thieving bastard or he'd be sorry. He had given the ring to her. It was her property. As she walked away, she knew what she was going to do. Lenny had underestimated her for the last time.

22

THERE WAS ONLY one person Jack wanted to impress but her phone went straight to voicemail. At first he wasn't too bothered, and left her a cheery message.

'Hi babe, it's me. Give us a call.'

Not wanting to spoil the surprise, he didn't say any more. Instead he went for a drive in his new car. It was a bright day. Reaching the motorway he put his foot down, enjoying the sensitive response of his wheels. This was how life ought to be, and he deserved every scrap of it. Playing hard and fast he had earned the right to sit behind the wheel of a Mazda MX5 sports car, as smart a motor as any he'd seen, and as smooth a ride as anyone could wish for. With its glossy metallic paintwork, soft top and leather seats, it could have been brand spanking new. It was a dream car and no mistake, a car reeking of success and oozing sex appeal.

Leaving the main road half an hour later, he left a second message. 'Hi, it's me. I got a surprise. Call me.'

He was impatient to show her, but another hour went by and still she didn't call.

He called again and left another message. 'Where the hell are you? I got something to show you.'

Realising the bitch must have left her phone at home, he waited and called again when he thought she would be home but she still didn't pick up. Annoyed that she was ignoring him, he texted her 'WTF' and called again. There was no reply. Swearing at her, he went for another drive but the novelty was wearing off. Driving up and down all by himself lost its appeal after a while. He wanted Sophia at his side, squealing with terror as he overtook some jerk, or gasping with excitement as he accelerated along an open stretch of road, her long thighs spread across the leather seat beside him.

There was no light under the door of her room when he knocked. She didn't answer. Supposing she must be asleep, he knocked more loudly.

'Oy, shut it,' one of her neighbours called out. The woman opened her door a fraction and glared at him. 'What you making such a bleeding racket for? I don't see no fire. Bugger off or –'

Jack lunged forward, fist raised, and she slammed her door shut. He didn't hear any more out of her. He gazed disconsolately along the drab corridor before he turned and knocked on Sophia's door again, calling her name repeatedly. Even when he yelled at her, there was no answer.

He tried her phone again. 'Sophia, answer the fucking phone, will you? I been calling you all day. Where the fuck are you?'

It wasn't the first time this had happened. Several times he had gone to see her recently, only to discover she was out. When he complained, she told him that she had gone out with her girlfriends.

'What's your problem anyway? I can go out with my girlfriends any time I want. I ain't just sitting at home in case you come by.'

'You must have a lot of girlfriends. You're never bloody in.'

'We like going out. That's what girls do.'

'You ought to be going out with me. Why didn't you tell me you was going out?'

'You'll be wanting me to tell you when I breathe next.'

She complained if he turned up at her flat unannounced, but what the hell was he supposed to do when she didn't answer her phone? She was his girl. He should be able to see her whenever he wanted. He kicked the door in frustration until it juddered in the door frame before he loped back downstairs, thinking all the while about her pale pink duvet cover and matching pillows. Her bed was pretty and feminine, just like she was. Although he had bought her bed linen, she had chosen it. Just as well. He would never have gone for girly pink flowers.

'Either it's a gift or it ain't,' she had scolded him when he wanted her to choose a different design. 'If it's a gift, I can choose whatever I want.'

Picturing her in bed, fast asleep, he wondered if she was lying naked between the sheets, and imagined slipping in beside her. It was agonising thinking about her, but he couldn't stop himself. The bitch had refused to give him a key but he would get one cut anyway. He wouldn't be shut out like that by his own woman.

'Fucking bitch,' he grumbled as he reached his car. 'Fucking whore.'

He ought to go out and find himself a willing bitch, one who would appreciate him and his money. Sophia didn't deserve him. The trouble was he didn't want anyone else, not like he wanted Sophia. With all his other bitches it was just sex. He decided to wait in his car for a while. If she was out with her mates she would be back before the last train. She didn't like getting the night bus. He lay back in his seat and closed his eyes. It was getting late. He hadn't heard from her all day. He didn't even know where she was. She could be sick or injured. With a curse, he called her again.

'Where the fuck are you?'

His voice seemed to echo down the silence on the line. After that he must have dozed off because he woke with a start as a car drew up in front of him. He sat up. The driver got out, slamming his door behind him. At the same time, a familiar figure climbed out of the passenger seat. As the couple turned up the drive he caught a glimpse of the girl's face. She was laughing.

For a moment Jack was too angry to react, although he wasn't surprised at seeing another guy taking Sophia home. He argued with himself as he watched the two figures walk side by side up the path. The driver could be the brother of one of Sophia's girlfriends, as she had claimed in the past when Jack had caught her in the company of another man. There was still time for the guy to step back, wave goodbye and return to his car. Instead he waited while Sophia unlocked the front door to the block before following her inside. Jack waited, drumming his fingers impatiently on the steering wheel. No one came back out. After ten minutes, he leapt out of his Mazda and ran to the other car. It was just an old banger. He keyed it viciously all along one side, then all the way back along the other. About to slash the tyres, he paused. Thrusting his knife back in his belt, he hurried back to his own car to wait.

This wasn't over yet.

23

'FANCY GOING FOR a drink?' Neil asked.

Geraldine had just slung her bag over her shoulder and was about to leave for the evening. She paused and turned to look at him.

'It's Saturday night and it's been a long week,' he said.

She was standing close enough to see the delicate skin around his eyes crease in a smile. At the end of his first week at Hendon, Geraldine was flattered that Neil wanted to mull over things in her company. He had started working on a different investigation and probably wanted to compare notes.

Doing her best to look as though she regretted her refusal, she shook her head. She felt slightly guilty. Recently arrived in London, Neil didn't know many of their fellow officers. Probably he was hoping she would show him where they all usually went for a drink after work. She knew what it was like, trying to settle in to a new post. It wasn't long since she had relocated to London herself.

Her new colleague's suggestion gave her a painful sense of déjà vu. The detective inspector who had shared her office before Neil's arrival had nagged her for months to go out with him, just for a drink. They had finally ended up in bed together, a few nights before he was killed on a job. Of course all that had nothing to do with Neil who knew nothing about her relationship history, but his invitation reminded her of someone she was trying to shut out of her mind. She hoped her smile didn't look forced as she apologised for having to turn him down.

'Another time I'd love to, but I've already made plans for tonight.'

'Sure. No worries. Another time then. Have a good evening.'

He was very personable. Before long he would doubtless make connections with other colleagues, and be off drinking with them after work. It was best that way. Leaving their shared office, she went to look for Sam. They had agreed to go to Central London and get something to eat. Sam was keen to try a new Chinese restaurant that had just opened in China Town, near Leicester Square.

'How do you know about all these places?' Geraldine asked. 'You always know where to go to eat. It's like you've got a secret radar system where food's involved. Do you belong to some kind of secret food critics' network?'

'Someone told me about it,' Sam replied vaguely. 'You don't mind if Emily comes with us? I said we'd call for her on the way.'

Geraldine had been looking forward to spending the evening with Sam, but she could hardly object.

'It'll be nice to get to know her,' she said, hoping she wouldn't end up feeling like a gooseberry.

'You'll really like her. She's such fun. And she'll stop us talking shop. To be honest, I'm beginning to go stir crazy. It's so frustrating knowing who did it, and not being able to find him. We don't seem to be getting anywhere looking for him.'

'It's only three days since we established his identity,' Geraldine replied. 'The TV announcement went out yesterday, and that might end up getting us a genuine lead. And who knows, Laura's performance might even help. We just have to hold our nerve and be patient. We'll get there. I'm going to talk to Adam about a reconstruction. Someone might have seen David shortly before he was shot. Laura's already picked out a jacket that looks similar to the one that's gone missing.'

Geraldine thought ruefully how much more coverage Laura's

tearful interview had been given by the media than the serious statement Adam had read out on the news, urging anyone who had been in the area of Wells Mews on Friday evening to come forward. The detective chief inspector had trotted out the usual formulae. 'Any information, however apparently trivial, might help us to catch this killer.' Unfortunately, they all knew that such announcements prompted a host of unrelated and crazy calls, all of which had to be checked and followed up.

'You're right,' she added, smiling at Sam. 'It would be good to get away for a few hours.'

They had just set off when Geraldine's work phone rang.

Scowling, Sam told her to ignore it. 'It's Saturday night, for Christ's sake. We're entitled to some time off. And anyway, we've got to eat. I'm starving. Aren't you?'

Geraldine didn't bother to reply but took the call, as they both knew she would. As soon as she heard who it was, she put her hand over the phone and mouthed 'Gina', in a stage whisper. Sam raised her eyebrows and braked. By now Geraldine had finished with the call and was on the phone again, arranging back up with an armed response unit.

'I hope we don't get there too late.'

With an exaggerated sigh, Sam pulled over and called Emily to cancel their arrangement for that evening.

'I don't know what time I'll be back,' she was saying as Geraldine hung up. 'Look, I've got to go. I'll see you later. Love you too.' She turned to Geraldine. 'Where are we going?'

Geraldine considered for a second before giving her the address, adding that they might as well go straight there.

'What else were you thinking of doing? We've hardly got time to eat now.'

'It's not far so we might be first on the scene, but we'll have to wait until the armed unit arrives. They won't be long. We can't do anything before that.'

Sam nodded. She was a martial arts expert and a match for

most men, but she wouldn't be foolhardy enough to tackle an armed man. All the same, she put her foot down. When Geraldine reminded her that they couldn't do anything on their own, Sam grinned.

'Whatever happens, we're going to get this bastard. He can't be allowed to walk the streets, shooting innocent passersby.'

'This isn't the Wild West,' Geraldine laughed, slightly unnerved by Sam's exhilaration.

'I just want to get us there as soon as we can. They're about to nail an armed killer and I don't want to miss it. Come on, Geraldine, you've got to admit this is exciting.'

'There's nothing exciting about guns.'

'I'm sure even your cold blood's pumping faster knowing there's going to be a shoot-out.'

'Sam, there isn't going to be a shoot-out. We're going to witness the arrest of an erratic gunslinger –'

'Gunslinger? Gunslinger?' Sam burst out laughing. 'Now who's indulging in fantasies about the Wild West? So come on then, admit that it's going to be exciting!'

'We'll have to agree to differ on that because I doubt very much it's going to be exciting. Quite the opposite. If you ask me, it'll probably turn into a long, drawn-out siege, where nothing happens for hours on end and we all just stand around waiting.'

'Well, that's exciting too. We've got no idea what's going to happen.'

Geraldine didn't answer. In a way Sam was right. They couldn't be sure what might happen when they reached the car repair yard. All they knew for certain was that Lenny had been there earlier that day. He might still be hiding there. And they knew he was armed and dangerous.

24

THERE WAS STILL about an hour of daylight when they approached the car repair yard where Gina had reported that Lenny was hiding. It was located just off the A504 near Seven Sisters tube station, at the back of a church. With the approach roads blocked by patrol cars and police vans, there was no way Lenny would be able to leave unseen, if he was still on the premises. As Geraldine and Sam jumped out of the car a helicopter roared by overhead, its bright light sweeping the area. Geraldine hurried over to a sergeant manning the cordon.

'We're just waiting,' he said.

Nothing was happening, but the atmosphere was tense. All at once a loud voice rang out. A stocky bald man had approached a uniformed constable and was shouting at him.

'I demand to know what's going on. Who the hell's in charge here?'

Geraldine walked over to him. 'Mr Berry?'

'Yes, Alfred Berry. That's my name. And this is my car repair outfit, and it's all perfectly legit so I've no idea what the hell you think you're doing here. All I can say is, whatever you suspect is going on here, you're making a serious mistake'

After introducing herself, Geraldine asked if he had given anyone a key to one of his lock-ups. He was adamant he had not, nor had he noticed anything unusual.

'I was out at the scrapyards all day, I visit them most weekends. I came by to lock up. Now, are you going to tell me what the hell's going on?'

'Armed response unit's one minute away,' a sergeant called out.

'What the fuck –?' Alfred spluttered, rubbing the top of his bald head nervously as he glanced up at the helicopter circling overhead.

'We've had a report that an armed fugitive is hiding in one of your lock-ups,' she answered. 'If you know anything about it, you'd best tell me right now.'

Alfred shook his head in helpless dismay. Geraldine hesitated to send him home. There must have been a reason why Lenny chose this particular site for his hide out. She thought Alfred was telling her the truth, but she could be wrong. If she sent him away, he might be on the phone to Lenny straight away to warn him. At the same time, she couldn't allow Alfred to stay where he was. The whole area had to be kept clear. As the armed response unit moved swiftly into place, she told a constable to take Alfred to the police station where he would be safe.

'Hang on,' he protested, 'why don't I just go home? That's far enough away from here to be safe.'

'I don't have time to discuss this now, Mr Berry. Just accompany the constable, please. As soon as the suspect's secured, you can be on your way.'

'What if he's not secured? What if he's not here at all?'

Grumbling loudly, he was led away. Geraldine looked around. Everything was ready. She nodded at the negotiator who picked up his tannoy.

'Lenny! We have this entire site surrounded. You can't possibly get away from here.' He paused. 'Lenny, we want you to come out now with your hands above your head. Be sensible, and no one's going to get hurt.'

There was no answer from the lock-ups. The negotiator let his arm fall to his side before he turned to Geraldine.

'It's going to be a long night. Do you want to go home and get some sleep?'

'I'm not tired.'

'We could go and get something to eat?' Sam suggested hopefully.

The negotiator nodded, misunderstanding. He raised his loudspeaker again.

'Lenny! Are you hungry? We can get you something to eat. What would you like?'

He turned back to Geraldine. 'What would appeal to him?'

'Anything but prison food,' Sam muttered.

'Shall we bring his girlfriend here?' Geraldine asked. 'He won't know she told us where he was.'

The negotiator nodded and Geraldine made the call. It was getting dark by the time a car arrived with Gina. One of the female constables who had brought her explained to Geraldine that Lenny's girlfriend had been reluctant to accompany them.

'If you hadn't told us to mention that she might get her ring back, she'd never have agreed to come with us. I've no idea what that was about, but it worked a treat.'

Geraldine nodded and walked over to Gina. Carefully, she explained that they wanted her to stand with the negotiator while he tried to make contact with Lenny. They were hopeful he was still there. She didn't add that it would prove an expensive mistake if he had already moved on. The helicopter alone was a costly piece of equipment, not to mention the armed response team. Gina was trembling.

'I did see him here,' she stammered. 'He was in the end lock-up and he wanted cash off me. I give him my last twenty quid but he wouldn't tell me what he done with my ring. He's a bastard and he deserves to be banged up again. I hate him so much!' She burst into tears.

'Gina, you can help us. This is Jonathon. He's a skilled negotiator. He's going to try and make contact with Lenny, and he might want to ask you some questions.'

'What sort of questions?'

Jonathon's smile was tense. 'First off, Gina, can you tell me what he likes to eat?'

'To eat?'

'Yes. We want to make him comfortable. That way we can gain his trust. If he's hungry, he's more likely to fly off the handle and end up shooting someone.'

Gina looked surprised. 'Lenny ain't got no gun. He ain't going to shoot no one.'

Geraldine and Jonathon exchanged a glance. 'Very well,' he replied, his voice almost devoid of emotion, 'but will you help us get him out of there?'

'Well, he can't stay in there forever,' Gina said.

'Will you help us, Gina?' the negotiator asked again.

She shrugged. 'Don't look like I got much choice. But I don't get why you don't just go in there and get him out. If you ask me, all this is a whole lot of fuss over nothing. Ain't you lot got nothing better to do on a Saturday night? It's only Lenny in there, ain't it?'

There was a sudden hush. Something was happening. A voice was yelling from inside the lock-up where Gina had reported seeing Lenny.

'I ain't done nothing,' he was shouting. 'I was with my mum when that bloke got shot. I know who told you I was here but don't you believe a word that lying bitch tells you. Look what she done to me. Fucking bitch. I know it was her.'

The negotiator's calm voice boomed through the PA system, drowning out the sound of Gina's shrill retort.

'Open the door, Lennie,' the negotiator urged. 'Come on out so you can talk to the police and tell them what happened. They're waiting to hear what you have to say.'

'Like fuck they are.'

Slowly the door opened.

'Come out with your hands above your head!'

'Whatever he's done with the gun, it's not in his hand,' someone said, and it sounded as though everyone watching exhaled in unison.

25

ADAM LISTENED IN quiet disapproval while Geraldine outlined her reasons for organising such a large-scale back-up team to arrest Lenny.

'Granted he's now in custody, we're still talking about apprehending one man who was hiding in a shed,' he said. 'When I gave you a free hand to do what was necessary, I never expected you to take so many officers with you. And I can't see why you wanted a helicopter. It's not as if you were conducting a search of the area, because you'd been told exactly where the suspect was hiding, and the yard was surrounded. He couldn't get away.'

Geraldine reiterated that they had reason to believe the suspect was armed at the time they received a tip off about his whereabouts.

Adam nodded. 'But there's still no sign of the weapon?'

A team had been searching the area all night without success. The gun could be anywhere.

'It wasn't found at his flat, or at his mother's place,' Geraldine confirmed, 'so it seemed reasonable to assume he might have it on him, if he actually shot David.'

'Well, let's hope he's prepared to cooperate fully now we've got him.'

Geraldine hoped Lenny wouldn't realise that without establishing his prints were on the weapon, they would only be able to prove he had been with David, not that he had killed him. Lenny was the only person who could tell them where he had disposed of the gun, perhaps together with the ring that

Gina wanted back. Geraldine was slightly intrigued by her obsession with it.

'Lenny give it to me,' was all she would say.

Given that Gina had informed the police where to find Lenny, the ring could hardly have sentimental value for her. Presumably Gina believed it was worth a lot of money.

'The only way he could get hold of an expensive ring would be if he nicked it,' Sam said, as they sat over an early breakfast in the canteen. 'He's only just come out of prison. And he didn't stay out for long,' she added cheerfully.

'Of course!' Geraldine slapped herself on the head. 'It's so obvious! Lenny stole the ring from David. It's the one Laura was so upset about losing.'

'If it is Laura's engagement ring, it must be worth a few thousand quid.'

'No wonder Gina wants it back. We need to get Gina to confirm it's one and the same. This could be really important. Even without the murder weapon, if we can prove Lenny robbed David, we've got a case. How could we not have seen that straight away? That's what comes of working through the night.'

'Without supper,' Sam added, as she scooped up another mouthful of egg and beans on her fork. 'I told you we should have gone and got something to eat last night. I knew it was a mistake, missing supper.'

'Come on then. We need to see Laura and then –'

'Bloody hell, Geraldine, let me finish this first. It's a sin to waste good food, and besides, a few more minutes won't make any difference.'

Before long they were on their way to David's house. Laura didn't appear surprised to see them. She nodded as Geraldine explained what they wanted, and went to fetch her wedding album.

'He only took it away a couple of weeks ago,' she explained

tearfully as she handed over the album. 'One of the little clasps had worked loose and I wanted to have it fixed so the stone wouldn't get lost.'

Flicking through the pages, Sam selected an image that showed the ring distinctly. 'Can we take this?'

'Yes, if it helps, but I'll get it back, won't I? It's a memory...'

Geraldine and Sam hurried back to the police station to have the image of Laura's finger blown up and enhanced. They now had a reasonably clear image of the ring to show Gina.

Wary at first when she saw them on the doorstep, Gina let out a yelp when Geraldine held up the photograph.

'Where'd you get this?' she asked, snatching the picture from Geraldine.

'Does that look like the ring Lenny gave you?'

'That's it. That's definitely it. That's my ring, so you can give it me now?'

'Look very carefully, Gina. Are you sure?'

'Course I'm sure. Think I don't know my own ring when I see it?'

Inconclusive in itself, Gina's response gave them one more piece of the jigsaw. It was time to question Lenny. With any luck, they had sufficient evidence to put enough pressure on him to make him crack.

'Let's not set too much store by it,' Geraldine said, as they drove back to the police station. 'There's no guarantee Gina would be prepared to testify in court. Even if we subpoena her, she could retract, or say she doesn't remember exactly, she *thinks* it might be the same ring –'

'She'd say anything to get her hands on that ring.'

'That's probably true, but it's not hers anyway, is it? So she won't get it back whatever happens, even if it turns up.'

They agreed it had probably been disposed of through a fence, the diamond sold separately and the gold melted down and reshaped. It would never come to light.

'Our best chance still is if we can get Lenny to confess.'

'That pathetic little weasel won't hold out for long. What's up?' Sam added. 'What are you looking so down about? We've got him haven't we? Whatever he says makes no difference. We know it was him.'

'What happened to innocent until proven guilty? Isn't that the principle we're supposed to be upholding?'

'No. That's for the jury to decide. Our job right now is to get Lenny to admit he shot David Lester.'

'If he shot him.'

'Of course he did. Bloody hell, Geraldine, one night's sleep missed and you turn to jelly.'

Geraldine laughed. 'Well, let's hope you're right and he buckles without any trouble.'

'I am right. You know I am.'

Aware that they were more likely to force Lenny to confess if they approached the interview confident of his guilt, Geraldine didn't answer. As they drove through the London traffic, she tried to ignore her lingering doubts about where Lenny could have got hold of a gun straight after leaving prison, and how he could have disposed of David's leather jacket. There had been no sign of it at his flat, and Gina had emphatically denied ever having seen it. Sam was convinced Gina had sold it, which seemed likely. But they were now in the realms of speculation where it was also plausible that someone else had taken the jacket, a possibility that opened up entirely different theories about David's death.

26

LENNY SAT SLUMPED on his chair, arms folded, eyes fixed on the table, lank hair hanging down over his ears. The harsh lighting of the interview room highlighted a sprinkling of dandruff on his narrow shoulders. His puny figure looked almost childlike beside his brief, who was a large man. As Geraldine gabbled her way through the routine preliminaries, Lenny glanced up and pushed his hair behind one ear with a bony hand, displaying nails bitten to the quick.

'Leonard Parker,' she began. 'Shall I call you Lenny?'

The suspect grunted without looking up. His brief sat beside him watching Geraldine through half-closed eyes. In his early thirties, wearing a tight suit that accentuated his corpulence, he looked smug. Lenny was clearly following his instructions so far.

'Where were you last Monday between ten and eleven pm?'

Lenny shrugged one narrow shoulder.

'Answer the question. Were you in the vicinity of Wells Street between ten and eleven on Monday evening?'

'I dunno the name of the road I was in. I don't go round reading no road names.'

The lawyer frowned.

'So you could have been in Wells Street?'

'My client could have been anywhere,' the lawyer pointed out. 'He's already told you he can't remember the name of the street.'

'But you admit you were out between ten and eleven on

Monday? We know you were in London. Do you remember leaving Oxford Circus station shortly after seven?' She turned to the lawyer. 'We have video evidence.'

'I suppose so.'

'But you are unable to remember where you were between ten and eleven that evening. Is that because you were intoxicated?'

Lenny glanced at the lawyer who was staring at Geraldine.

'I'd had a few pints,' he admitted. 'Nothing wrong in that, is there? I'd only just been let out after eighteen months inside. A bloke's entitled to a few drinks –'

The lawyer cleared his throat loudly and Lenny fell silent.

'Have you seen this before?'

Displaying the blown up photograph of Laura's ring, Geraldine was pleased to see that Lenny looked uncomfortable. For a moment he didn't say anything. Geraldine put the photograph on the table in front of him and waited.

'It's a ring,' he muttered at length.

'A very nice ring,' Geraldine agreed. 'The suspect is looking at a photograph of the engagement ring he gave to his girlfriend, Gina.'

'It weren't an engagement ring –' Lenny broke off in confusion.

Grasping the significance of the ring, the young lawyer promptly came to his client's rescue. 'This is a picture of a very common design of ring, one square solitaire diamond in a plain gold band. Items exactly like this are available in every high street jeweller, pawn shops, markets. It would be impossible to identify a particular ring, and it certainly couldn't be reliably recognised from a photograph.'

Geraldine tried again. 'Did you give a ring like this to Gina?'

Lenny fell back on his earlier response. 'I don't remember.'

'You must have been very drunk if you don't remember whether you gave your girlfriend an expensive diamond ring –'

'Do you have the ring my client allegedly gave his girlfriend?'

Geraldine hesitated before shaking her head. There was no point in lying. The lawyer would only demand to see the evidence.

'I thought as much. Well in that case, you can only speculate as to its value. That looks to me like a cubic zirconia ring that you could pick up for a fiver.'

'We can easily obtain the insurance certificate for the ring stolen from David Lester.'

'Which has nothing to do with my client.'

Geraldine turned her attention back to Lenny. 'You must have been very drunk if you don't remember whether you gave your girlfriend an engagement ring –'

'My client has already told you he didn't give her an engagement ring,' the lawyer replied before Lenny could answer.

'You must have been very drunk if you don't remember whether you gave your girlfriend a ring,' Geraldine said, but by now even Lenny had worked out where she was heading. 'You don't remember where you were, you don't remember whether you gave Gina a ring, you can't remember much about what you did that evening, can you? Fortunately, I can refresh your memory, because we know exactly where you were and what you did. We have evidence that places you at a crime scene in Wells Mews, off Wells Street. You turned in there by mistake, didn't you? All you wanted to do was have a few beers and go home. You never intended to harm anyone. But in Wells Mews you came across a well-to-do man who had also taken the wrong turning. There was no one else around. It was too good an opportunity to miss, so you mugged him.'

'No I never,' Lenny burst out. 'I never mugged no one and that's God's truth.'

He was scared now. His hazel eyes were stretched wide and his face looked pale. He looked sideways at his lawyer in a silent plea, but the other man kept his eyes fixed on

Geraldine, waiting calmly to hear what she would say next. For an instant, Geraldine felt a flicker of loathing for the complacent young lawyer. It wasn't his head in the noose. But he was only doing his job, just as she was. She turned her attention back to Lenny.

'Only for some reason that you can't remember, you shot him in the chest at close range. What happened, Lenny? Were you waving the gun at him to scare him and it went off by accident? If you cooperate with us, your clever lawyer there can make a case that this was manslaughter, and you'll be out in four years, possibly less. It all depends on you. You can make things worse for yourself by deliberately concealing evidence, especially if you've attempted to dispose of it. So if the shooting was an accident and not premeditated murder, you need to tell us now.'

Lenny dropped his head in his hands and refused to respond.

'I need to speak to my client,' the lawyer said quietly.

Geraldine terminated the interview.

'Bastard lawyer knew he'd cave in,' Sam fumed, as they watched Lenny being escorted down the corridor. 'If only we'd had a few more minutes with him we might've broken him. Now that bloody lawyer's going to coach him. Bugger.'

Geraldine still wasn't entirely convinced they had the right man.

'He seems so ineffective,' was all she could say in an attempt to explain her reservations to her colleague.

'Ineffective, useless waste of space and a murderer. OK, I grant you it probably wasn't premeditated, but he was still running around the streets, out of control, with a gun in his possession. In some ways, the fact that he picked on a victim at random makes it even worse.'

'The problem is that all we have against Lenny is circumstantial,' Geraldine said. 'Unless he talks, we can't be sure it was him. He might have just been passing by and somehow got caught up in all this. Yes, I know it sounds unlikely, but it's possible. That's all I'm saying.'

'Let's hope the jury sees what's right under their noses. He's only just come out of prison.'

'For burglary, but never for a firearms offence. This doesn't fit his profile. And there are other questions, like where he got hold of a gun as soon as he left prison, and what happened to David's leather jacket?'

Sam shook her head. 'You can play devil's advocate all you like, but obviously you think Lenny's guilty, and you must have been pretty sure he was armed when we went to pick him up. Otherwise, how could you justify taking an armed response unit, and a helicopter, and all the rest of it, to the lock-up? You'd never have authorised all that if you really thought Lenny was unarmed.'

It was a fair point. Geraldine had stuck her neck out, employing such costly resources to apprehend one man. Unless she had suspected he was armed, she could not possibly justify the expense. She shrugged, resolving to keep her reservations to herself. Adam was already questioning her actions. She had to hold her nerve and defend her decision as robustly as possible.

'We can't be sure,' she said, 'but I had to entertain the possibility he was guilty and armed. Let's just hope he confesses. It would make our lives a whole lot easier.'

She tried to ignore her qualms, but she was not actually convinced they had the right man. And if Lenny was innocent, while they were wasting time interviewing him, they were giving the real killer time to cover his tracks.

27

AFTER A BREAK they tried again. Geraldine hoped a few hours in a cell might loosen Lenny's tongue. He didn't strike her as a strong character, even with a solicitor at his side to guide his responses. At the very least, the cell would have reminded him of his recent stretch in prison, making him vulnerable.

'Are we making you comfortable?'

'At least I can sleep at night. How do *you* manage, knowing you get innocent people locked up just so's you get to keep your job.'

'Bring back memories, did it?' Sam chipped in. 'Plenty more of that where you're headed.'

'If you don't cooperate,' Geraldine added.

'You'll have me banged up whatever I say. I know how this works. You're after a conviction, another box ticked, another target hit. Never mind I'm an innocent man. I been done before so I'm easy pickings. Who's the jury going to believe, police inspector or ex-con? It's all wrong. I done my time. There ain't nothing to put me back inside, only you decide to go after me and here I am, banged up again. Some fucking justice system we got. You're a load of perverts. Guilty once, guilty for any other crime you got. The prison's full of poor sods like me what got caught once and never let off again. Why bother with all this? No lawyer's going to get me off. Once the judge knows my form, I'll be done for.'

Geraldine reminded Lenny that previous convictions were not disclosed to a jury. 'Like you said, you've done your time.'

'So what the fuck am I doing here, talking to you?'

Geraldine went through the evidence that placed Lenny at the scene of the shooting in Wells Mews.

'So I walked past. So what? So did a lot of other people in London that evening. Don't mean I done nothing.'

'You can't convict a man for being in the wrong place at the wrong time,' the lawyer chimed in.

'The wrong time in this case was when a man was shot,' Sam said.

Lenny glanced at his lawyer who gave a nod. Lenny sat forward and stared at Geraldine. 'OK, I'll come clean. I'll tell you what happened, what I was doing there and what I done. I'll tell you the lot, every bit of it. You got to believe me this is God's own truth, so help me, and not a word of a lie. I'll swear it on the Bible.'

'You can do that in court,' Sam said.

'I swear it on my own mother's life.'

Geraldine frowned at Sam to keep quiet and turned her attention back to Lenny.

He cleared his throat. 'This is what happened then. This is exactly what I done. I'm telling you the honest truth now.'

At her side, Geraldine heard Sam heave an exaggerated sigh. Ignoring the sergeant, she kept her eyes fixed on Lenny.

'I come out the bird, right? They give you a wad when you leave, supposed to get you back on your feet a bit. Fine if you got more stashed away, but if that's all you got you're fucked. So I use the travel warrant to get me up to London.'

'Why didn't you just go home?' Sam asked.

Lenny glanced at his brief before answering. 'Look, I just come out the nick, right? I been in eighteen months, for fuck's sake. I was up for a drink, a bit of a good time before going back home. I knew Gina would be on at me if she ever found out, but I deserved a night on the town before going home. Anyone would've done the same.'

'I understand,' Geraldine encouraged him.

'So I'm up town having a few pints and I'm plastered. I ain't been on the piss for that long. Then it starts raining. I gets lost and goes into this lane, and there's a stairs at the end so I think I'll shelter under there, maybe even get a bit of shut eye because I really need a kip. Only there's some other fucker already there, and he's fast asleep under cover, and he's taking up all the space. So I goes up and I gives him a kick to make him shove up and give me some room, but he never even wakes up. He's well out of it. So I think, well if he don't notice when I give him a hefty kick and a shove, he won't notice if I check his pockets. Yeah, I know it was wrong, but I was pissed, right?'

'And you're a thief,' Sam added.

'Back off, bitch, a bloke's got to make a living somehow.'

'What happened next?' Geraldine prompted him.

'Nothing happens. I gets hold of his wallet, and I legs it. That's all there is to tell. And that's the honest truth of it.'

He sat back and crossed his arms.

'Why did you spit on him?'

'The bastard wouldn't shove up and give me any room to get in under cover and it was raining. I told you.'

'What happened to the wallet?'

'Yeah, well, I pockets the cash – nearly a hundred quid and that's the honest truth. And I chucks the wallet down a drain, God knows where. I was lost, I told you.'

'That wasn't all you took, was it?' Geraldine asked.

'What?'

She repeated the question. Lenny looked at his lawyer who merely raised his eyebrows.

'OK, there's this little box.'

'What box?'

'A blue box. I don't know what it is but when I opens it there's a ring inside it.'

'This ring?' Geraldine held up the photograph of Laura's stolen ring.

'Could be. It's just a ring, but I figure it might be worth a bit, seeing as he's a well-dressed geezer, even if he is blind drunk and sleeping it off in an alley.'

'And his jacket.'

'What jacket?'

'You took the dead man's leather jacket.'

Lenny shook his head. 'Look, I never knew he was dead, did I? I mean, it was dark. I couldn't hardly see nothing. And I never took no jacket neither. How the hell was I supposed to get this jacket off of him if he was dead, like you say he was?'

With Lenny insisting he had told them everything, they took a break. The trouble was his account could be true. He had freely admitted being in Wells Mews and robbing David. Until they found the murder weapon, they couldn't prove Lenny had pulled the trigger.

28

STAN COULDN'T BE bothered to go back inside for his coat. The evening was quite mild, and he had only stepped out of the bar for a quick smoke. The sounds of London traffic were muted, but he could distinguish the roar of motorbikes from the general hum of cars on the busy main road nearby. He checked his phone. It was just past midnight. He glanced around as he lit up. The narrow street at the back of the bar was deserted. Closing his eyes and taking another drag, he was aware of a fleeting gust of wind, followed by a dull thud right beside his ear. He opened his eyes. Muttering an expletive he leapt backwards, almost tripping on the kerb. The spliff dropped from his fingers and landed in the road.

A man lay impaled, face down, on the wrought-iron spikes of the fence at the back of the club. For a second Stan stared, stunned into immobility. The spikes were not long enough to have passed right through the man's torso and out the other side. With the ends buried in his body, plugging his wounds, he was not losing much blood. All the same, Stan wondered how severe his internal injuries might be, and whether he could possibly survive such a landing. Mercifully, the poor guy had passed out, but he needed help urgently. With a rueful glance at his half-finished spliff, Stan pulled out his phone.

'There's a bloke here fallen on some railings and it looks real bad,' he gabbled.

As he was speaking, a couple of blokes walked by.

'What the fuck –?' one of them said.

'He's reporting it,' his companion replied, pointing to Stan.

Stan gave his name and number, and the name of the club, but he had no idea what road he was in. The woman reeled off an address which sounded right.

'Yeah, I think that's it,' he said. 'It's called The Road, and it's round the corner from Oxford Circus station, in a side street.' There couldn't be more than one bar with that name in the vicinity.

'The emergency services should be there within fifteen minutes,' the woman said, 'assuming the traffic's moving.'

'Fifteen minutes? He's going to croak by then. I'm telling you, he's fallen on the metal railings. You got to get the fire brigade here right now.'

There wasn't much else he could do. The other two blokes had gone right up to the poor geezer who had fallen on to the railings and were trying to talk to him. Stan guessed they were both drunk.

'Stay with us, mate,' one of them was pleading.

They didn't appear to be getting much of a response. While Stan dithered about whether to join them, or go back inside for his coat, there was a blast of sirens and all at once the street was crammed with people. A couple of police cars drove straight past and parked further along, allowing an ambulance to draw up right beside the injured man. A fire engine stopped at the end of the road, blocking access to other vehicles, and two firemen came running up.

A policeman in uniform shouted out Stan's name. There was no reason for him to feel apprehensive, but his legs were shaking as he walked forward.

'That's me. I'm Stan Bilton.'

He couldn't help glancing down into the kerb to check if his spliff was still there, but he couldn't see it. The policeman asked him a few questions about what he had seen, and why he had been there.

'I just came out for a fag,' he lied.

The policeman wrote everything down and told him he could go.

'Is that it then? I can go home?'

'Unless there's anything else?'

'No, that is, I left my coat in the bar. Can I go and get it?'

The policeman told him to try round the front entrance. Someone was shouting about metal-cutting equipment, a couple of paramedics were standing by the victim with bags and syringes, and there was a general bustle of purposeful activity around the scene of the accident. While all this was going on, one of the barmen burst through the back door of the bar and halted, gazing around in surprise. Tall and dark skinned, he was wearing a smart leather jacket that looked too big for him.

A uniformed policeman ran over to him and ushered him on to the pavement. A moment later, another uniformed policeman disappeared through the door, presumably to prevent anyone else from stumbling through it unawares. Stan and the barman were hustled together to the end of the street.

'I work there,' the barman was protesting. 'I need to get my gear. I got my wages in the till.'

'I left my coat in there,' Stan piped up, realising for the first time how cold he was. 'I can't go home without it.'

The policeman told them that the premises had been evacuated but they would be allowed access through the front entrance, if they explained to the policeman on the door why they wanted to go inside. The back exit was cordoned off and no one was allowed near there apart from the emergency services. Stan followed the barman round the corner. A crowd had gathered outside, people who had been inside the bar and passersby, curious to discover what was going on.

'Hey, Jack! Over here!' one of the bystanders called out.

The barman paused in his stride. 'What's up?'

'What the fuck's going on? Is there a bomb in there or what?'

A burst of excited chatter rippled through the waiting throng.

'Nah,' Jack called back. 'You're all right. Just an accident. Some prat's gone and fallen out of a window. I think he's croaked.'

His friend nodded. 'Thought it must be a stiff. Nice jacket, dude,' he added.

'Is he dead?' someone called out.

'What's happened?'

'What's going on?'

Ignoring the cries, Jack pushed his way through the crowd with Stan following at his heels. Stan knew exactly what had happened, but he was too knackered to deal with other people's morbid curiosity. He was beginning to feel sick and just wanted to go home. Every time he closed his eyes, he saw the bloke lying across the metal spikes, not moving.

'It was horrible,' he said aloud. No one heard him.

29

HAVING SPENT THE best part of the day attempting to cajole or coerce a confession out of Lenny, Geraldine was worn out. Sending the recalcitrant suspect back to his cell, she wrote up her log and cleared her desk. By the time she finished, it was nearly seven o'clock and she was hungry. She went to see Adam. Like Sam, he was convinced Lenny was guilty.

'We know he was there, Geraldine.'

'That's merely circumstantial. It proves nothing.'

'The onus of proof is not on us. We have incontrovertible evidence placing the suspect at the scene. It's backed up by a confession, thanks to your interview. We know he robbed the victim. Who else could have been responsible for shooting him? Are you seriously suggesting someone shot the victim and then left his wallet for Lenny to pick up when he just happened to walk by?'

'Yes, that's exactly what I'm saying. And the onus of proof *is* on us. The suspect is innocent until we can prove him guilty. And we can't. Establishing he was there isn't the same as proving he shot David. If we could be sure no one else was there it might be different.'

There were no functioning CCTV cameras in Wells Mews or along Wells Street. The closest camera was round the corner in Oxford Street. It would have been possible for someone to slip into the mews without being recorded on film.

'I think we have a pretty watertight case against him,' Adam insisted, although he didn't sound very confident. 'The balance of probabilities points to him being guilty.'

Geraldine seized on his uncertainty. 'That's all it is, a probability. And then there's the question of where he got hold of a gun, and what happened to David's jacket.'

Adam shook his head. 'We may never find out what happened to that jacket, but it's hardly germane to the investigation. We're working on the likelihood that Lenny shot him, and the most likely explanation is generally the one that turns out to be true. We just have to work harder to get a confession out of him. Give him another twenty-four hours to stew and we'll try again. You're due a day off. I think you need to step back and get some perspective on all this. It might help you to forget about the missing jacket. That doesn't matter. What's important right now is that we know Lenny was there. Let's focus on that. Organise another viewing of all the CCTV in the vicinity, and come down harder on the suspect to cooperate. I think the CPS will agree we have a strong case.'

Geraldine picked up a takeaway on her way home and sat at her kitchen table eating fish and chips out of the paper with her fingers, while listening to Lenny's second interview again. Although his repeated insistence that he was telling the truth made his story sound dodgy, she couldn't spot any inconsistencies to suggest he was lying. On the contrary, his account was plausible and fitted his history of petty house burglary. As far as they knew he had never resorted to violence in the past, and had never been known to use a gun. In fact, his account of robbing a dead man he had stumbled upon by chance actually matched his profile as an opportunistic thief. It seemed quite possible he was telling the truth.

She had arranged to visit her older sister in Kent the following day. The two of them had been brought up together after Geraldine had been adopted by Celia's natural parents. Not particularly close as children, they had developed a more intimate relationship following the death of their mother a couple of years previously. Geraldine hadn't been down to Kent for at least a month and was looking forward to seeing her sister and her niece again.

It was a relief to be driving away from London and the claustrophobic demands of the case. A fine drizzle began to fall as she drove along the Old Kent Road. It wasn't a bad journey, and she arrived half an hour before dinner. Celia was always pleased to see her and welcomed her with a broad grin. As soon as they were inside, Geraldine looked at her sister appraisingly.

'Not showing yet,' she said, smiling.

It was difficult to tell as Celia's figure was concealed beneath an embroidered smock top. Celia pulled the fabric tight across her belly and Geraldine shook her head.

'No,' she said, 'if you hadn't told me you were expecting, I wouldn't be able to tell.'

Celia laughed. 'Call yourself a detective! The bump is the clue! Come on, I'll show you how we're getting on here.'

Celia was having the house decorated and Geraldine was given a tour of the rooms that had been finished. She traipsed round the house after her sister, making appropriate noises of approval.

'This is going to be the nursery,' Celia said, showing off a room freshly painted in light yellow. A white cot with yellow ducklings painted on the end stood ready. 'I know it's a bit small, but we'll probably move now there's going to be four of us in the family.'

'It's a lovely room.'

'Do you really think so? What about the colour? Do you think the baby will like it?'

Geraldine had to restrain herself from saying what she really thought.

'I'm sure the baby will love it.'

'I can't help feeling scared,' Celia admitted when they were back in the kitchen.

'What are you afraid of? It's not like this is your first.'

'I'm forty-two, Geraldine.'

'So? You've done it before.'

'I know, but I was a lot younger then. The older you are, the more likely there are to be complications, and –'

Geraldine was as reassuring as she could be, given that they were discussing something of which she had no experience.

'What about you?' Celia asked. 'I mean, have you done anything more to trace your birth mother?'

'Well, not really. I called the social worker who was dealing with my enquiry and managed to contact the person who has taken over from the original case worker. She promised to get in touch…'

'So no news then?'

Geraldine shrugged. She had been through this before. Her birth mother had consistently refused to meet her. Celia clearly didn't understand why she persisted in trying to contact her mother. Even Geraldine was no longer sure why she carried on.

'I'll probably give up,' Geraldine admitted. 'She's made it clear she doesn't want to see me.'

'It's sad,' Celia replied, 'but there's no point in beating yourself up about it. At least you tried.'

They had finished drinking tea by the time Celia's daughter, Chloe, returned home from a friend's house. She ran up to Geraldine and hugged her. With Celia looking on, smiling, Geraldine felt a pang of gratitude. She ought to appreciate her family more. Sometimes she felt it was an unfair intrusion on her time, having to go and visit them. Their pleasure on seeing her seemed out of all proportion to what she could offer them. It was chance, not even an accident of birth, that had brought her into their lives at all. If her own birth mother hadn't given her up for adoption, she would never have met Celia. It seemed strange that so random a circumstance had tied them to one another for life. She wondered if David Lester had died as the result of a similarly random encounter with the man arrested for his murder, or whether there was more to the case than anyone yet realised.

30

JACK WHISTLED CHEERFULLY. Even though his room wasn't well lit, he could see how the tailored fit of his new black shirt showed off his toned body. Turning sideways, he examined his profile. At last he stopped scrutinising his reflection and gave a satisfied smile. He had worked hard to achieve the right image. Theo was captivated by the way Jack's mirror tipped forwards and backwards in its polished wooden frame. He loved to stand in front of it, shifting the angle of his reflection.

'You keep playing with my things, you're going to break something,' Jack would shout at him. 'I told you before, stay out of my room.'

Theo would just shake his head, aping Jack's frown. In the end Jack had fitted a lock on his bedroom door to keep Theo out. If Rosa noticed it, she hadn't commented. Absorbed in admiring himself, Jack didn't hear his door open. Without warning Theo's face appeared in the mirror, hovering above Jack's right shoulder.

'Bloody hell, Theo, you give me a fright. What you doing creeping up behind me like that?'

Theo chuckled. 'Bloody hell, bloody hell, bloody hell,' he crooned under his breath. 'Nice, nice, nice shirt,' he added. He patted Jack's arm as though he was petting an animal.

Jack turned to him. 'You know there's times you almost make sense. And yes, it is a nice shirt. A bloody nice shirt.'

'Nice shirt,' Theo repeated, 'bloody nice shirt.'

He put his head on one side as though he was thinking, then

ran from the room to reappear a moment later holding out his anorak. Jack shook his head. Theo always knew when his brother was going out.

'You're like a bleeding dog. Well, I ain't taking you for no walk, not tonight I ain't. I'm off to see my girl and there ain't no room for you. Now bugger off out my room.'

Theo watched intently as Jack finished preening himself, then scurried out of the room after him. While Jack was locking his door and pocketing the key, Theo struggled to put on his jacket. His face screwed up in concentration, he succeeded in thrusting both his arms into his sleeves.

'Come on, come on,' he sang, followed by some tuneless gibberish about Jack.

'You ain't coming along with me,' Jack said, 'and that's that.'

'That that that that that.'

'Shut it, you bleeding parrot.'

Whistling softly, he walked to the front door, Theo still at his side.

'You ain't coming with me, bro.'

He placed a hand flat on Theo's chest and gently pushed him away. Theo stood firm, grinning. Angered, Jack shoved him roughly until he began to whimper.

'Jesus, I said you're like a dog, don't mean you got to make a noise like a bleeding dog. Just shut it, will you? I can't take you out because I'm going to see my girl. Now get away from me, I'm going out. And no following me this time. Oh bloody hell. Leave it out, will you? Ma! Ma!'

Rosa appeared in the doorway of her bedroom, her eyes frowsy with sleep.

'What you want now?' she moaned. 'I'm trying to have a rest. Can't you watch him for a bit? You're never here and I can't shut my eyes for a minute without him running off.'

'Get him away from the door, will you? He ain't coming out with me.'

'Where you off to now?'

'Going to see a friend.'

Rosa called to Theo that it was time for supper but he didn't budge.

'I said get over here. Look what I got for you!'

She shuffled over to the squashy football lying on the floor in the middle of the room and picked it up. 'Here.' She offered it to Theo who didn't move. She dropped it on the carpet.

'Bloody hell, it's lost all its bounce,' she complained. 'And he plays so nice with it. Keeps him busy for hours, only now it's all out of air.'

'I said I'd get him a new one, and I ain't forgot about it,' Jack replied. 'But only if he plays with it. You want a new ball, Theo? You go play with that one then. Let's see how nice you play.'

Theo glanced indecisively from Jack to the ball and back again.

'Come on, then, come and get it,' Rosa coaxed him.

As Theo stepped towards her, Jack was out of the door, double locking it from outside so his brother couldn't follow him. Jack was off to see Sophia, and he was in a good mood. He wouldn't stand for competition. She was his girl, and that was the end of it. He knew it, and soon she was going to know it too. Whatever she thought, she wasn't up for grabs. He leapt into his car and sped out of the side street, heading for her flat. Everything was going to be fine, just as long as she was his girl. That was all that mattered. She felt the same way about him. She just didn't know it yet.

31

GERALDINE RECALLED AS many cases as she could where suspects had held out for hours or even weeks before confessing their guilt. It wasn't unusual. Insisting on their innocence was, understandably, the first defence of the guilty. She hoped that would prove to be true for Lenny. Rigorously, she followed the procedures, aware of Sam fuming impatiently at her side, while the plump lawyer sat silently watching her, his eyes half-closed. If he hadn't interjected from time to time with a laconic reminder that his client had already answered her question, she would have suspected he wasn't following the interview at all. When they took a break, she wasn't surprised that Sam was irritated.

'That wretch is lying through his teeth. We know he was there. He admits as much. Why can't he just come clean and save us all a whole load of bother. Yes, I was there, yes, I already told you I robbed the guy, and yes, obviously I shot him. That's all he has to say. Why drag it out like this? He'll never get off.'

Not for the first time, Geraldine wondered if Sam was in the right career. Gutsy, dogged, and highly intelligent, in some ways she was ideally suited to the job, but she was also impulsive and far too ready to jump to conclusions.

'Like it or not, the burden of proof is on us,' she said, 'and right now we can't prove Lenny shot the victim. Being in the same place as the murder doesn't mean he pulled the trigger.'

They had been over the same ground repeatedly. As Sam

launched into another rant, Geraldine's phone vibrated. It wasn't a work call. If the phone had buzzed while they were in the interview room she would have ignored it. As it was, she glanced at the screen. A caller on an unknown number had left a message. She hesitated, but it was time to go back and have another session with Lenny.

'Come on then,' she said, putting her phone away.

'Let's hope he stops whingeing and starts telling it how it is,' Sam answered, as she followed Geraldine back into the interview room.

After they had finished with Lenny for the day, Geraldine discussed the stalemate with Adam. He agreed to sanction a thorough search of the flat where Lenny lived with Gina and of his mother's home and the car repair yard where he had been hiding. If they found his gun, with his prints on it, the case against him would be watertight. After a quick supper, Geraldine drove to Acton to see how the search was going there. She had a feeling Lenny's mother knew more than she was letting on. Her flat was so crammed with bric-a-brac it would be the perfect place to hide something relatively small like a gun or a ring. Coming across the ring wasn't quite so important, since Lenny had admitted he had stolen one from David. Finding the gun would wrap the case up.

Geraldine could hear a woman screeching as soon as she stepped out of her car. Cynthia was standing by the front door, red-faced with the effort of shouting, thick veins bulging in her neck.

'Bloody hell, she's going to burst a blood vessel if she goes on like that,' a constable muttered to Geraldine. 'She's giving me a ruddy headache. Can't you shut her up?'

'Get on with your job and stop moaning,' Geraldine chided him with a grin. 'Found anything yet?'

'Plenty of dodgy gear, but not what we're looking for.'

'Don't you bloody tell me any of my stuff's dodgy,' Cynthia

burst out. 'It's all been paid for, fair and square. I could do you for all them lies you been saying, ever since you got here. I ain't no fucking thief!'

'Not a thief, just a fence,' someone answered cheerfully.

'Don't you start on again about my boy,' Cynthia retorted. 'He's as honest as the day's long. I know he was framed last time he was sent down, and I know it was you lot what done that to him. I'm getting a lawyer on to you and you'll all go down. Nothing worse than a bent cop. You just wait. All your pictures in the papers, see how you like it.'

'We won't hold our breath, love.'

'Wish she'd hold hers,' another constable called out.

Geraldine eyed up the stout woman shouting obscenities, before interrupting her invective. 'If you don't keep quiet, I'll have you for obstructing the police in the course of their duties.'

Cynthia turned and glared at her. 'Or what?'

'I don't think you heard what I said. If you don't shut up and let my team get on with the job, you'll find yourself nicked for obstruction.'

'You like locking up innocent members of the public, don't you, you self-important cow. Think you're clever, don't you?'

Seemingly delighted to have found a target, Cynthia latched on to Geraldine with a new string of obscenities.

'This is your last warning,' Geraldine said when the other woman paused for breath. 'One more word out of you and I'll have you removed from the property.'

Cynthia grumbled, but quietly this time and Geraldine left soon after. The team had found nothing yet. They would continue all night if necessary, searching outside in the morning. Geraldine was in bed setting the alarm on her phone when she noticed the voicemail that had been left earlier on her private phone. Not recognising the number she listened to the message, expecting it to be a wrong number. The caller introduced herself as Louise who had taken over from Sandra, the social worker who had been in charge of Geraldine's adoption file. Her next words shivered through Geraldine like an electric shock.

'We need to talk about your mother.'

32

THAT NIGHT, GERALDINE lay awake for hours. She tried to focus her thoughts on the case, but it was impossible. Over the years she had learned to accept that it was best to try not to think about her birth mother. Gradually, her raging curiosity had faded until she had become resigned to the fact that she was never going to meet her mother. With the social worker's call, her visceral longing returned, sweeping all her mature deliberations aside in an instant. It was possible her mother was finally willing to meet the daughter she had abandoned all those years ago. Milly had been a teenager when she had given birth to Geraldine. She would be middle-aged now. Circumstances impossible to deal with at sixteen might seem very different with the benefit of maturity. There could be any number of reasons why she might want to meet her daughter after so long.

It was equally possible the social worker had called Geraldine to inform her of her mother's death. That would be hard to bear. Even though Geraldine would be no worse off than she had been with a stranger who steadfastly refused to meet her, she would have lost the hope of ever being reconciled with her birth mother. Not knowing the reason for the social worker's call was agonising. A few hours made no real difference after so many years but, after hearing the message, having to wait a whole night felt unbearable. She wished she had answered her phone when Louise had rung, or at least had listened to the message during working hours, so that she could have returned the call straight away.

After sleeping fitfully, she was up early so she went straight to work, arriving before the traffic built up. It was too early to speak to the social worker but she returned her call anyway, and left a message. 'Please call me as soon as you get this.' Almost in tears, she could hear her own voice shaking. There was nothing more she could do. She turned to her screen and realised that Neil had walked past without her noticing. He was sitting at his desk, watching her curiously.

'Is everything all right?' he asked.

'Yes, thanks. It was nothing to do with work.'

'I don't know if that's a good thing or not. Oh sorry,' he added when Geraldine didn't respond, 'you're telling me to mind my own business.'

'That's OK,' she muttered, keeping her eyes on her screen. 'Now if you don't mind, I need to crack on.'

'Of course.'

Geraldine knew her colleague was only being friendly. It was her own fault that he had overheard her pleading for a quick response. She wondered what he must think of her, and resolved to guard against such unprofessional conduct in future while she was at work. It must have sounded as though she had rowed with a boyfriend. Stifling a sigh, she tried her best to focus on her work. It didn't help that she had to work her way through a list of tedious expenses claims.

Halfway through the morning, her phone rang. Her heart beat wildly, but it was only a call from the mortuary to say the pathologist wanted to see her.

'Why me?' she asked, although she knew Adam was away all day at a meeting. 'Can't he just speak to me on the phone?'

'He said you'd ask that,' the anatomical pathology technician replied. 'He was very insistent that he wants you to come here. He said he has something that you're going to find very interesting.'

'Is it about David Lester?'

'It's a different body this time.'

'Then it isn't my case.'

'He said he wants you to come in person, if possible. That's all I know.'

The technician was beginning to sound impatient.

'Oh all right. I'm on my way. But I don't see what all the mystery is about.'

In spite of her irritation at the interruption, Geraldine was curious. If Miles wanted her to go to the mortuary that meant something was amiss. He liked to play guessing games, but he would never ask her to go and see him unless it was important. Normally, she would have been pleased that some development had come up while Adam was unavailable. Only today she did not want to be tied up at work. She tried Louise's number one more time before setting off, but the line went straight to voicemail. Checking her mobile wasn't on silent, she slipped it in her pocket so she would hear if it rang. In the car, she put the phone on the passenger seat to make sure she couldn't miss a call, and set off.

'This had better be worth dragging me all the way over here for,' she grumbled to the young anatomical pathology technician who opened the door for her.

'Don't blame me,' Jasmine smiled, 'I just passed on the message. Miles is the one who insisted on getting you over here. How are you?'

Geraldine gave an inane reply about things being fine. Nothing could be further from the truth. With a suspect they were unable to nail, and the disturbance about her mother, her life was a mess, her emotions spiralling out of control.

'How about you? How's life?'

'Can't complain,' Jasmine replied, glancing down at a diamond ring sparkling on her left hand.

'You're engaged. Congratulations! When are you getting married?'

Geraldine was afraid her enthusiasm sounded fake, but Jasmine grinned, eager to talk about her future plans.

'We haven't set a date yet, but probably next summer. There's so much to organise.'

Geraldine tried to feel pleased for the young woman standing in front of her, bubbling with excitement. It wasn't that she envied Jasmine's situation, only her happiness. She had felt the same bitterness about Celia's pregnancy. Marriage and babies didn't appeal to her in the slightest. She valued her independence too much to want to compromise with another adult, and loved her job too much to exchange it for baby food and nappies. But she wished she *was* the kind of woman who could bear to share her life and her home with someone else. Solitude wasn't always liberating.

'Miles is expecting you. I told him you were coming.'

Geraldine pulled on a mask and went in, relieved to be back in familiar territory.

Miles greeted her like an old friend. 'How are you, Geraldine?'

'Puzzled about why you dragged me all the way over here, if I'm honest.'

'Well, I hope you'll find it worth the effort.'

He smiled at her in anticipation of her reaction. Curiosity overcame her irritation.

'What have you found?'

Miles pointed to the body of a man. He was lying on his back, his face a livid white mask with dark eyes staring up at the ceiling. Apart from the neat incisions made by Miles, the torso was scarred with four nearly identical small wounds in a diagonal row across his chest.

'He was found impaled on railings outside a bar round the corner from Oxford Street. He'd fallen from an upstairs window.'

'So it was an accident?'

'It certainly looked that way at first.'

'At first –?'

'Well, it's true that he fell on to the railings, but there are a number of intriguing features here. First, and by no means least, is that one of these wounds is not what it seems to be.' He pointed to one of the holes, close to the dead man's heart. 'Unlike the other wounds, this injury here wasn't caused by a metal spike.'

'Miles, what are you talking about?'

'Look closely and you'll see this is, in fact, a bullet wound.'

'You're joking. Bloody hell.'

'Yes, I thought you'd be interested.'

'It's interesting, I'll give you that. But it's not my case, Miles. I'm already working on a case, another shooting, as you very well know.'

'Yes, the body found in Wells Mews, not far from where this victim fell on the railings.'

'Yes. It's the same area, but it's still a different case.'

'Not necessarily. Like I said, things are not always what you might think.'

'For goodness sake, will you stop talking in riddles, Miles, and tell me why you asked me to come here.'

'The bullets match.'

'What do you mean? What bullets? And what do they match?'

'I didn't want to say anything before it had been confirmed, but the same gun was used to kill David Lester and this chap here.'

He tapped the dead man on the top of his head.

'Are you sure?'

'There's no doubt about it. Forensics have examined both bullets and they are positive they were fired from the same gun. I'm afraid we've lost a few days, as the initial assessment concluded this was an accidental death. He was drunk and stoned, and he did fall – or perhaps in the light of what we now know, he was dropped – out of a window and landed on railings. But as it was presumed accidental, we didn't do the post mortem immediately. He was killed three days ago, on Saturday night.'

'Shit. We'll get the crime scene protected straight away, but it will have been hopelessly contaminated by now.' She stared at the body. 'So whoever killed David also had a crack at this poor guy. Presumably he was shot indoors, then chucked out of the window?'

'Or dropped quite carefully to make sure he landed on the railings.'

'Do you think that was deliberate?'

'No, not necessarily. It could have been sheer luck that the shooting ended up looking like an accident.'

'He looks young. Who is he?'

'His name's Luke Thomas. He was nineteen.'

'Oh bloody hell.'

'Indeed. Is that your phone?'

As Geraldine snatched her mobile out of her pocket it stopped ringing. She recognised Louise's number.

'Do you want to take that?' Miles asked.

Geraldine hesitated. Then she looked at the young man lying on the slab in front of her.

'What do we know about him? When did you say he was killed? And do we have the gun?'

150

33

BY THE TIME Geraldine was back, she was pleased to discover that Adam had returned. Quickly she brought him up to speed and he convened an emergency briefing. Having closed the bar where Luke was shot, Geraldine spent the next few hours scanning key statements taken on Saturday night after his death. The body had been found by a young man called Stan Bilton. She reread his account several times. He claimed he had been outside the back exit of the bar, smoking. He was standing right beside the railings, when the body had fallen next to him. His statement said little more than that. Nearly three days had elapsed since then. Geraldine was worried he would have forgotten exactly what he had seen.

'It's hardly the kind of thing you forget,' Sam pointed out.

'I don't know. He was most likely pissed, and probably confused with the shock of it all.'

However good Stan's memory, it was a pity he hadn't been thoroughly questioned on Saturday, but at the time no one had realised they were dealing with a murder. It was extremely annoying, but they had to make the best of the situation. Hoping for the best, Geraldine set out to speak to Stan. She found him at his place of work in a fast food cafe along the Holloway Road. The smell of grease hit her as she walked in. The air was thick with the smell of sausages and bacon. Trying to take shallow breaths, she strode up to the counter.

'What can I get you?'

'I'd like to speak to Stan Bilton.'

'What's that?'

Flashing her identity card, she repeated her request.

'Stan!'

A short man with a sallow complexion turned and nodded. 'What?'

'This cop wants you.'

'What?'

At last Geraldine escaped the stench to stand outside the back door of the cafe with the witness. He offered her a cigarette which she refused.

'Do you mind if I do?'

'Go ahead.'

It was better than the smell inside the cafe.

'Is it about Saturday night?'

'Yes.'

'I thought so.'

Slowly, with frequent faltering, he recounted what he had seen. 'I heard him fall before I saw him,' he finished.

'What exactly did you hear? I'd like to know every little detail. Close your eyes and imagine you're back there, outside the bar, having a smoke. What did you hear? Tell me everything.'

He frowned. 'Like what?'

Geraldine hesitated to put ideas in his head. 'Did you hear anything at all before the body fell? Did any cars drive past, or backfire nearby? Was there any yelling? Anything at all?'

He frowned. 'I could hear the thumping of music from inside the bar. There were no cars and no one walked by, not until after he fell.'

'What did you hear when he fell?'

'There was this kind of whishing sound, and a sort of thump. And then I opened my eyes and saw the poor bugger stuck there. He wasn't moving. I thought he must have passed out with the shock. I didn't know he was dead. I mean, there wasn't loads of blood spurting out everywhere, nothing like that. He just lay there, without moving. He didn't even groan or anything. I didn't think much about it at the time, but it was kind of weird how he just lay there without making a sound.'

'You're sure you didn't hear anything else?'

He shrugged. 'I don't know what you want me to say but that's all I can remember. I mean, I was just there. I didn't see him fall, I just opened my eyes and there he was, stuck on the railings.'

The other two witnesses on the scene before the emergency services arrived could offer even less information than Stan. They had turned up just after the body had landed on the railings, and had neither heard nor seen anything that could help further the enquiry. Geraldine turned her attention to the bar staff. They didn't keep a list of customers; they just checked ID on the door to exclude anyone under eighteen.

'We're very careful about that,' the manager said.

Geraldine had joined him in his small office upstairs. There was a spacious open-plan bar downstairs, while on the first floor there were toilets, a smaller terrace bar and the manager's office. Luke had fallen, or been pushed, from an upstairs window. Scene of crime officers were examining the two windows in the toilets, which were located immediately above the railings, to establish which one Luke had fallen from. As the small window in the manager's office didn't look down on the back of the building, they knew Luke had not fallen from there. The manager's eyes almost disappeared beneath his thick black eyebrows as he glared at Geraldine from behind a small pine desk.

'Now when are you lot going to be finished, only we open in a couple of hours and it's not good for business to have a team of uniformed policemen and women stomping around the place.'

'You won't be opening tonight,' Geraldine replied.

'What? You are kidding me. You can't close us down. We haven't broken any law. We're very strict about who we let in.'

'We're not doing this lightly, or from choice, but we need to examine your premises from top to bottom –'

'Why? Some geezer got pissed and fell out of the window. It's tragic, but it was an accident. The police were here on Saturday and the investigation's over. You had your chance to look around then. We were closed all day on Sunday. You've got no right to even come back here now. If you don't leave right away, and take all your bloody people with you, I'm calling my lawyer. You're not going to stop us opening this evening and that's final.'

'I'm afraid it's not that simple. The post mortem revealed new evidence that's led to the opening of a murder enquiry. We'll be out of here as soon as we can, but you may not be able to open your upstairs bar tonight, and in any case, even if we've finished in there, no one will be able to access the toilets at all for a while. Now, if you're sure there's nothing more you can tell me about Saturday night, I'd like to use your office to speak to your staff individually. You can wait downstairs in the entry hall, but no one is going to be allowed in the downstairs bar until we've finished there. Thank you.'

'I can't allow this –' the manager blustered, but his shoulders sagged in defeat.

'Have you given my sergeant the contact details for your staff?'

'Yes, but –'

'Good. You can send them in, one at a time, as they arrive.'

34

APART FROM THE bouncer on the door and the manager, five people had been working at the bar on Saturday night. There should have been six, two behind the bar upstairs, and four downstairs, but one member of staff had called in sick. The manager grumbled that it wasn't unusual for his staff to let him down at the last minute. So there had been three staff and the manager working downstairs, and the bar upstairs had been manned by two members of staff. The manager wasn't able to say exactly who had been upstairs at the time of what he insisted on referring to as 'the accident'. The staff had taken it in turns to work upstairs. A constable had questioned each of the bar staff in turn on Saturday evening after the incident. None of them had been able to recall for certain which of them had been upstairs at the time Luke had been shot. They wouldn't have been able to see the door to the toilets from behind the bar anyway, so it probably wouldn't have helped to have found out who had been upstairs.

Geraldine had read the initial report from Saturday but she wasn't prepared to leave it at that. She was keen to try and discover who had been working in the upper bar around midnight. Whoever had been there might have heard or seen something suspicious. The first member of staff she spoke to was called Katy. Strolling into the office, narrow hips swaying, she could have been about seventeen, although close up she looked closer to thirty. She had bright pink hair and was wearing silver eye shadow and matching nail varnish on her

155

short nails. She was a pretty girl with good teeth who smiled a lot.

'Yes, I did a stint upstairs,' she told Geraldine. 'We all did. There were two of us.' She smiled. 'Marco goes ballistic when people don't turn up for work but we're cool because he pays us extra to cover.'

She was adamant she had noticed nothing unusual on Saturday evening, just customers having fun. If anything it had been a fairly quiet night, because it had rained earlier on.

After Katy, Geraldine spoke to a young man called Rafe who told her he was twenty-nine. Sharp featured and neatly dressed, he sat awkwardly on the edge of a chair, fidgeting with his cuffs. In answer to every question he shook his head, his bright eyes never moving from hers.

'No, I never heard anything strange that night, and I never seen any arguments. There was nothing going on. It was a dull night, not even busy, especially for a Saturday.'

Geraldine showed him a photograph of Luke and asked if he recognised him. Rafe shook his head.

'I never seen him before in all my life,' he said, so earnestly that Geraldine suspected he was lying.

'Are you quite sure you didn't see him in the bar on Saturday? Look very carefully.'

'I never seen him before,' Rafe repeated.

The third barman looked about twenty. Wearing a smart jacket over dark jeans, he was tall and good looking. By contrast to Rafe, Jack had an air of relaxed confidence that bordered on arrogance. He answered her questions without any hesitation. Like his colleague, Katy, he freely admitted that he had worked upstairs on Saturday evening. Like her, he couldn't remember exactly when he had been upstairs and insisted he had neither seen nor heard anything untoward. The other two barmen were older than the first three. They told the same story. Like Rafe, they had been working downstairs all evening and, like their colleagues, they had noticed nothing unusual at the time of the shooting.

It had been a wearing day. For all her hard work, Geraldine hadn't managed to advance the investigation at all. No one had heard a shot, and no one had noticed Luke arguing with anyone shortly before he was killed. In fact, no one admitted to even recognising Luke from the photograph Geraldine had brought in.

'Someone must have served him,' Geraldine said, as Sam drove them back to Hendon. 'His blood alcohol level was way over the limit. He was completely pissed before he was shot. Why are they all lying about having served him? It doesn't make sense. Do you think Marco warned them not to say anything? And if so, why?'

'To get rid of us,' Sam answered promptly. 'He doesn't want anything to do with this. The less they tell us about any sort of involvement, the sooner we'll leave them alone, or so he thinks. Anyway, Luke may well not have gone up to the bar. Someone else might have been buying, or he could have been drinking somewhere else, and only just arrived there. It's possible he walked in and went straight upstairs to the toilet, and met his killer before he'd even had a drink there.'

Back at the station, Geraldine didn't accompany Sam back inside straight away. She didn't want to make a private call in the office knowing Neil might walk in at any time. She watched Sam stride ahead of her towards the door, before walking back towards the road.

'Geraldine, thank you for getting back to me,' Louise said pleasantly, as though Geraldine was doing her a favour. 'As you know, I wanted to talk to you about your mother.'

'Yes?'

'I know you've been wanting to meet her. You talked about this with Sandra but I see from the file there's been no discussion about it for a while.'

'That's because there was nothing to discuss. My mother refused to have any contact with me.'

'How would you respond if she felt differently about it now?'

'Are you saying my mother wants to see me?'

'She would like to meet you, yes. How do you feel about that?'

Geraldine felt as though she had been punched in the stomach.

'Geraldine?'

'Sorry, it's been so long – I mean, she was so adamant – Sandra said –' She took a deep breath to steady her voice. 'Yes, I'd like to meet her.'

'I have to tell you she's not a well woman.'

'What do you mean?'

'She suffered a coronary and she's in hospital –'

'Is she dying?'

'I don't think it's that dramatic, but she's not well. The hospital are concerned that she should avoid any stress, but she's insisting she wants to see you.'

'When can I see her?'

'Leave it with me. I'll try to fix up a visit tomorrow morning, but I'll need to get back to you to confirm that.'

'I'll be available whenever I can see her. Text me the details first thing in the morning and I'll be there.'

She hung up. She felt perfectly calm, but as she put her phone away, she began to shake so violently she could hardly walk.

35

THAT EVENING GERALDINE and Sam went to speak to Luke's parents. Geraldine struggled to listen to Sam, and in the end her sergeant gave up trying to have a conversation with her.

'I can tell you're not listening.'

'Sorry, I'm just preoccupied.'

She didn't tell Sam what was on her mind. It was easier to let the sergeant assume she was thinking about the case. In the morning, Louise might call to say her mother had thought better of her decision and didn't want to see her after all. In the meantime, Geraldine wanted to put the whole idea out of her mind and concentrate on the case. Easier said than done. Throughout the afternoon her thoughts had kept wandering back to the social worker's words. Louise had been clear that Milly wanted to meet her, which was potentially good news, but her mother had suffered a coronary. Many people survived for years after heart attacks, even quite major ones. Presumably it was her illness that had made her change her mind about meeting Geraldine. In less than eighteen hours Geraldine could be sitting at her mother's bedside.

With difficulty she turned her thoughts to her evening's task. They were on their way to Catford to visit Luke's family. Geraldine had visited families of victims before to break the terrible news of a murder. It was the most harrowing part of her job. This time was different, because Luke's parents already knew he was dead. What they had yet to learn was that his death had not been accidental, as had originally been

159

thought. Information that sensitive couldn't be given out over the phone. In some ways it would be kinder to leave them in ignorance. If an accidental death was shocking to live with, murder was worse. But Geraldine had to find out if they knew of anyone who might have wanted Luke dead.

Mr and Mrs Thomas lived in a terraced house in a side street off the main high street in Catford. They were close to the shops and the bus route, and within walking distance of the station. From there it would be easy for a young man to travel up to Central London for a night out. After parking, they crossed a narrow front yard and climbed two steps to the front door. Sam rapped on the door with her knuckles and they waited. After a few moments she knocked again, as loudly as she could. This time a voice inside the house called out.

'Who is it?'

'Police.'

'What do you want?'

There was a pause then the door was opened on the chain and a woman's face peered out at her. Geraldine held up her identity card.

'Oh yes,' the woman inside called to her, 'they phoned to say you'd be back. What do you want?'

'Can we come in?'

'What do you want?' the woman repeated.

'We need to talk to you about Luke.'

The woman slammed the door shut. Geraldine cursed under her breath, hoping they hadn't driven all that way for nothing. The public's attitude towards the police had deteriorated drastically in recent years, but she wasn't there to arrest anyone. There was no reason for Mrs Thomas to be hostile. As she was wondering whether to knock again, there was a rattling sound and the door swung open.

'Come on in.'

From a dark, narrow hallway the woman led her into an untidy front room where a man was snoring loudly in front of a blaring television. The woman muted it and gestured towards a chair.

'Oy,' the man mumbled, waking up, 'I was watching that.'

'Derek, the police are here.'

Having established that she was talking to Luke's parents, Geraldine asked if they would answer a few questions about their son. Luke's father turned to her, his expression masked by thick grey stubble. Only his bloodshot eyes revealed his misery.

'You going to close that place down?' Luke's mother asked.

'So much for bloody health and safety,' his father added. 'They drive us nuts where I work, you can't hardly move without bloody health and safety breathing down your neck, you can't do this and you can't do that. And then they go and have a window where anyone can just fall out –' He broke off, overcome with emotion. 'He was only twenty. That place should be shut down and the owners looked up. The place was a death trap.'

'We have reason to believe Luke's death wasn't an accident.'

'No, no,' Luke's mother burst out in alarm. 'He never. He was such a happy boy.'

'They're not getting away with that,' his father broke in angrily. 'They're responsible, and I'm going to make damn sure they go out of business.'

Geraldine ignored their interruptions. 'We have evidence that leads us to conclude he was murdered. The fact is your son wasn't killed when he fell on the railings outside the bar. His death was quicker and less painful than that. In fact, we don't think he suffered at all, because he was shot and killed before he fell from the window.'

Luke's parents were shocked into silence for a moment.

'Shot? What do you mean he was shot?'

'Who shot him?'

'I don't believe it!'

'There's no doubt about it, I'm afraid. We're trying to find out what happened. Do you know anyone who might have wanted to harm your son? Did he have any enemies? Had he been in any fights or arguments recently?'

Luke's parents looked at her in surprise. His mother covered her face with her hands, sobbing.

'Luke didn't have enemies,' his father replied.

'Everyone loved him. No one would have wanted to hurt Luke. No one,' his mother agreed, her voice muffled by her hands.

'It's a preposterous thing to say. I don't believe it for one moment. Come on, now, love, don't go upsetting yourself all over again,' her husband said. He turned to Geraldine. 'I think you'd better leave.'

Urging them to contact her if they thought of anything that might assist the police in their investigation into Luke's murder, Geraldine stood up.

'I'm really very sorry,' she added helplessly. 'We'll show ourselves out.'

There was nothing more to say.

36

AFTER A RESTLESS night Geraldine got up early, but she didn't set off for the police station. Instead she sat at home with her phone on her desk and tried to concentrate on work. She decided to give it until ten. If Louise hadn't contacted her by then, she would call to find out what was happening. By nine forty-five the only call she had received was to tell her that Lenny had been released. At five to ten the phone rang. Without any preamble, Louise gave Geraldine the name of the hospital, and the ward, where her mother was staying. As though in a dream, Geraldine scribbled down the details.

'Would you like to see her today?'

'I'll leave right away.'

The Whittington Hospital was probably about an hour's drive away.

'I can meet you there this afternoon –'

'That's OK, there's really no need for you to come.'

'We like to accompany people at initial meetings like this. You and your mother might experience an intense emotional reaction –'

'I understand why you're saying that,' Geraldine interrupted her, 'but it's not as if we're meeting somewhere private. We'll be in a hospital ward. And I am a detective inspector. I'm used to dealing with tricky situations, not that I anticipate this being difficult, I mean, she wants to see me, doesn't she?' She broke off, aware that she was babbling foolishly. 'I mean, of course you're welcome to come along, I just thought you must be busy enough.'

'Well, if you're sure...'

'Absolutely.' Geraldine had never felt less sure of anything in her life. 'We'll be fine.'

After the brief conversation finished, she sat for a moment, staring at the message she had scrawled. If she hadn't written it down, she would have struggled to believe that Louise had actually called and given her the details. Even with the physical evidence in front of her, it felt unreal. As if in a dream she walked to her car and drove to the hospital. In all her fantasies about finding her mother, she had never imagined meeting in a hospital ward, under the watching eyes of other patients and passing staff. She hoped it wouldn't be awkward, establishing a bond in so exposed a place. When she was nearly there, it occurred to her that she and her mother might not feel any kind of connection anyway. Drawing up in the hospital car park, she started to regret having driven there without any last minute preparation. Louise should have been more strident in her warnings. But how could she have prepared herself for this encounter? She had been desperate to meet her mother for so long. The reality was almost bound to be a disappointment. She should never have come. But her mother wanted to see her. How could she have refused? She determined to assume an air of confidence, even though she felt like a frightened child.

Her mother lay in a hospital bed. Tubes attached to her arms connected her to complicated pieces of medical equipment, beeping, pulsing, dripping, keeping her hydrated, maintaining her blood sugar levels, and monitoring her progress. While all that equipment was keeping her physical shell alive, she appeared to be sleeping peacefully. Geraldine hovered near the bed, waiting to be overwhelmed by a wave of affection. When her mother had given her up, Geraldine had been a tiny baby, too young to have registered her mother's face as anything but a blur. Seeing her in the flesh for the first time, she searched her face for any familiàr feature. The photograph of her mother as a teenager looked uncannily like Geraldine herself. There was nothing of that girl in the pale shrunken cheeks and bony chin of the woman lying in the bed. Geraldine wondered if there had been a mistake.

'You here to visit Milly?' a passing nurse asked.

The name coursed through Geraldine like a bolt of electricity. She turned to the nurse. 'She's my – I'm her daughter.'

'Of course you are. You look just like her.'

Geraldine tried to smile at the unlikely comment, which was meant kindly, but she felt tears in her eyes. She couldn't help it.

'Don't fret,' the nurse said, misunderstanding Geraldine's distress, 'she's stable now. The doctor will be round later on. Why don't you sit with your mother for a while?'

Geraldine nodded, unable to speak. Sitting by the bedside, she dabbed at her eyes and waited. After about twenty minutes, Milly's lips twitched. She opened her eyes and turned her head slightly until she was looking straight at Geraldine who stared back into her own large dark eyes. For a moment they didn't exchange a word, but Geraldine knew that her mother recognised her.

Milly smiled weakly and moved her lips. Geraldine leaned forward so she could hear her mother's whisper.

'Can't talk. Such an effort. Sorry.'

It wasn't clear if she was apologising for her feeble voice, or for having given Geraldine away.

'That's OK. All you need to think about is getting well.'

'Someone you have to find. She'll look after you.'

'Go on.'

'Her name's Erin.'

Evidently, Milly was confused. Geraldine wasn't sure whether to explain that Erin was the name on her own birth certificate.

'I'm here,' she faltered. 'I'm Erin. The social worker contacted me about you. Erin's the name on my birth certificate.'

Her mother frowned. 'You're Erin?' Her eyes scanned Geraldine's face as though she was trying to read words in a foreign language. 'I never thought…'

'Don't try to speak any more for now. We can talk when you're feeling better. Just rest. That's all that matters for now.'

'No, no,' her mother shook her head. Her hoarse whisper grew louder and the heart monitor beeped. 'Erin. Help me.'

A nurse came bustling up. 'Come along, Milly, it's time to rest.' She fiddled with Milly's drip, and jerked her head at Geraldine to indicate it was time to go.

'Don't worry,' Geraldine repeated as she stood up to leave.

She hesitated to add the word 'mum'. That would take some getting used to, just as Milly would have to learn to call her by her adopted name. Not knowing how to address one another was understandable, given that they didn't know anything about each other. That first encounter had been a meeting of strangers. In Geraldine's fantasy, she and her mother hugged. As she left the ward, she wished she had at least touched her mother's hand, flesh on flesh. She walked away down a long corridor feeling somehow cheated. It didn't help that Louise had warned her not to expect too much from a first meeting. When she reached the privacy of her car, she dropped her head in her hands and wept for her loss.

37

THE ATMOSPHERE IN the major incident room on Thursday was tense as they waited for the detective chief inspector to arrive. A couple of young constables who fancied themselves as wits vied with one another to raise a laugh.

'Anyone would think someone had died,' one of them ventured.

'Looks like you shot yourself in the foot with that one,' the other one quipped when no one even smiled.

'Oh well, it was just a shot in the dark.'

No one was amused by their clumsy routine. Several colleagues told them to shut up. Even Sam was morose. Geraldine was trying not to think about her sick mother and wondering how to lighten the depressed mood, when Adam strode in. Still energetic, he had lost his air of well-groomed elegance. His shoes gleamed, but his short hair was unkempt and his shirt was creased. His expression looked almost furtive as he glanced around the room.

'You all know we've let Lenny go. He'll be facing a charge of robbery. He admitted stealing property from David Lester's corpse. But we can't make the murder charge stick, not with what we've got. We need to move forward,' he announced.

An impatient sigh rippled round the room at his words. Any hope that the detective chief inspector had summoned them there to tell them something new vanished. This was going to be a futile pep talk. Although they had no proof Lenny had shot David, they knew he had been at the scene. Having admitted as much, he was still the only lead they had. In the absence of any other information, Adam wanted to continue working on the theory that Lenny was implicated in the murder, even if he had not actually pulled the trigger.

He ordered another search of Lenny's and Cynthia's flats, and sent a team into the car repair yard where Lenny had been hiding.

'If the bins have been emptied since Saturday night, we need to search the dump,' he added. 'And what about his mother or his girlfriend? Could they have hidden the gun, or passed it on to someone else?'

Various officers scurried off to carry out the detective chief inspector's instructions with a new sense of purpose, now they had a focus for their efforts. Geraldine hid her dismay that Adam had no news for them. After he left, she waited a few minutes before following him to his office. Not knowing Adam very well, she wasn't sure it would be wise to criticise him, but she had to voice her opinion. Resolutely, she knocked on his door, determined to be as tactful as she could.

'Come in. Oh, it's you, Geraldine. What is it?'

'I just wanted to discuss something with you.'

'Go ahead.'

'Lenny was in custody on Saturday evening,' she began, and hesitated.

'Yes. We know that. What's your point?'

'So the second shooting can't have had anything to do with Lenny, or with Gina or Cynthia, unless one of them went up to London on Saturday evening, taking the gun with them. And that means we're going after the wrong man. I just think we've wasted enough time on this suspect.'

Geraldine took a deep breath, aware that her concerns had tumbled out in a rush. So much for her decision to be diplomatic.

Adam frowned. 'And enough money,' he added sharply.

Geraldine carried on. 'I think we're looking in all the wrong places.'

'Look, Geraldine, if we knew where the right places were, that's where we'd be looking. We haven't got a bloody clue where to look or what to do. You've seen what it's like out there. They're all convinced we're never going to crack this one. We can't just sit around doing nothing. Granted it could be a coincidence that Lenny turned up when he did, just after David was shot. But it seems odd that the killer didn't steal the ring from David himself. We need to rule out the possibility that Lenny was working with this unknown killer. There's still a chance Lenny could be our lead to whoever shot David and Luke. And at least it's a possibility. We can't do nothing.'

Geraldine understood his concern. It never helped when morale among colleagues deteriorated. For that reason she thought it would only hinder the investigation if they expended valuable time and effort in short-term exercises that would ultimately result in a deeper sense of failure. Despite her frustration, she held back from suggesting that Adam's judgement was influenced by his desperation to prove himself in his first case as a detective chief inspector. Instead, she made a positive suggestion.

'Perhaps we should be looking for a link between David and Luke.'

'Other than that they were both shot with the same weapon, you mean?' He didn't add that at any moment they might hear of a third victim, shot by the same gun, and they had no idea where to begin looking. 'Once we give up the search, we might as well write the case off. I'm not going to let that happen.'

'But we're not going to find the gun in Lenny's flat, are we?' Geraldine insisted. 'Even if he did use it to kill David, we know he didn't kill Luke, so if there were two people involved he must have got rid of the gun, passed it on to someone else, or sold it, or chucked it away for the second killer to find. I just think it's unlikely that two different killers would shoot two people with the same gun within five days of each other. So if we think there's one killer, and we know Lenny couldn't have killed Luke, we ought to be focussing on looking for whoever did.'

The discussion ended unsatisfactorily. When Geraldine returned to the incident room she found the rest of the team similarly divided. Some officers thought they should be looking for two people, Lenny and a second killer. The others thought that Lenny had robbed David but not shot him, and they should be looking for just one unknown killer. Geraldine glanced around the room with a sinking feeling. In some ways she could see the sense in Adam's orders. As matters stood, the other members of the team were all over the place. Without firm direction, they might lose their drive. Nevertheless she wasn't happy organising the search teams, which she was convinced were a waste of time. She suspected Adam did too.

Once the work was under way, Sam drove Geraldine to the car repair yard. Neither of them could face listening to another tirade of abuse from Lenny or his mother.

'If he's got nothing to do with the murders, I can understand his feeling aggrieved,' Geraldine said.

'He's admitted to robbing a dead man. David might still have been alive when Lenny found him, unconscious and bleeding to death. It's possible he would have survived if that piece of scum had called for an ambulance straight away. We'll never know. That pariah deserves no more consideration than he gives to others. He's as guilty as if he'd pulled the trigger himself,' Sam said. 'The investigation's a complete bloody mess. We don't know anything. Do you think the DCI has a grip on it?'

'I don't think it's his fault. It's just really complicated.'

What with distress over her mother, and anxiety about the investigation, Geraldine felt drained. She thought she had managed to keep her feelings hidden, but Sam stopped the car suddenly and turned to her, asking if she was all right.

Geraldine nodded. She hadn't told anyone about meeting her mother. The disappointment of that first encounter was too raw. For all her brash impatience, Sam was sensitive enough to know when Geraldine was upset.

'Are you sure? You know you can always talk to me, in confidence, if anything's bothering you. We are friends, aren't we?'

'I'm fine,' Geraldine fibbed. 'I'm just fed up. We're getting nowhere and this case is going to drag on interminably.'

'OK. But you know I'm here if you ever need to talk, about anything. We should go out and have a few beers, and forget about all this for an evening.'

'I don't see how that would help.'

'Well, it might not do much to help the investigation, but it would certainly cheer us up.'

Geraldine smiled. Sometimes Sam made her feel old.

'Why don't you go out with your mates later?' she said.

'You're right. It'll do you good. But I think I'll be more than ready to call it a day after we've been to Alfie's place. I could do with an early night. I didn't sleep too well last night.'

Sam looked at her closely and Geraldine turned away.

'Are you sure you're OK?'

'You just asked me that. I told you, I'm fine.'

She hoped Sam wouldn't see through her lies and take offence, but she couldn't talk about her mother. Not yet.

'Come on now, let's see if they've found anything at the lock-ups.'

'Do you buy Alfie's story that he knew nothing about Lenny hiding out there?' Sam asked as she pulled out into the traffic.

Geraldine sighed, relieved that Sam was talking about the case again. It didn't say much for Geraldine's state of mind that she felt safer discussing a double murder than the circumstances of her own life.

38

THEY GATHERED IN the playground at dusk, just as they did every day. Designed for children, the fenced-off area had a row of tiny box-like swings that even a skinny butt wouldn't fit inside, a seesaw, and a metal slide. The young kids it was intended for never hung out there, because the playground belonged to the gang. That was what TeeJay decreed, and his word was law on the estate. If a mother complained that the gang scared her children away, TeeJay sent a few brothers to put her straight. No one challenged TeeJay for long.

The legend of TeeJay grew out of countless stories of his prowess with a blade, although he boasted that he never carried one.

'No need, innit. No blad's jarring TeeJay.'

Old people on the estate scurried out of their way, eyes averted. Young people were beaten and kicked into submission. If other gangs strayed on to their turf, they were soon chased off, bruised and bloodied. They rarely returned. That was the way of things. No one knew how old TeeJay was, or even where he lived. He was only ever seen hanging out by the playground, whatever the weather.

'Dis ma crib,' he answered, when a gang member had the balls to ask him where he went during the day.

It was a mild evening. More than a dozen youths were hanging out in the playground, standing around or sitting on the ground, rolling spliffs, smoking fags, their faces concealed in the shadows of their hoods. No one spoke. TeeJay watched a bitch deftly roll a joint. Apart from the gentle hum of traffic, pierced by an occasional wail of a siren, all was peaceful. TeeJay acccpted the spliff and lay back on the seesaw, one arm beneath his head, gazing up into the clear night sky.

All at once the silence was disturbed by a burst of laughter from one corner of the playground. A few voices began jeering.

'Tool!'

'Hey, TeeJay, this wanksta's trina beef ya!'

Everyone turned to see what was happening. With a grunt of annoyance, TeeJay heaved himself upright and swung his feet on to the ground. Seeing him scowl, his followers grew quiet.

'Who disrespecting ma space?' he demanded.

'Dat loony wanna cotch wiv us.'

A couple of hefty gang members shoved the newcomer into the centre of the circle, while the others taunted him. By now they had all seen that the cause of the disruption was Theo, a crazy guy who lived on the estate. His curly black hair jiggled every time he moved his head, and his dark eyes stared around in terror.

'Shiv him, TceJay!'

The gang fell silent, jostling one another as they waited for TeeJay to react. Short and stocky, his presence dominated the arena as he took a long drag and dropped his spliff on the ground. A single thread of white smoke rose from it, twirling into the night air. All the time, his eyes never left Theo's face.

At a nod from TeeJay, a lad with a heavy overhanging brow stepped forward.

'Wait till my Jack gets home,' Theo cried out, for the first time seeming to register the danger that was threatening. 'Wait till my Jack gets home!'

At another nod from TeeJay, his chosen follower's Neanderthal features spread in a grin. He raised a huge fist and froze as he caught sight of a gun in Theo's hand. The watchers tensed. TeeJay didn't move a muscle as Theo waved the gun around. At last the gun stopped moving. It was pointing straight at TeeJay. The gang leader couldn't lose face. He kept his eyes fixed on Theo.

'Don't no blad move,' TeeJay said softly. 'Don't no blad make no sound.' He took a step towards Theo. 'Stay cool, brah. Go home. Ain't no blad get hurt. You do us, you mudder croaks.'

As TeeJay was speaking, Theo nodded his head.

'I know where it is,' he said earnestly, 'I know where it is, I know where it is.'

TeeJay's face twisted in a cautious frown. 'What da fuck?'

He glared at the gang members standing behind Theo, but no one jumped the nutter.

'You slow steppin, innit,' he grumbled. 'Listen up, brah,' he turned his attention back to Theo, 'put da shooter way. We gonna smoke.' Theo nodded his head but kept the gun aimed at TeeJay. 'Step off. You think cos you strapped we gonna play nice, innit, but you stuttin. You mudder.'

Something must have registered with Theo because he spun on his heel and darted away. TeeJay wiped his brow on his sleeve before looking round with a forced smile.

'Breathe easy, blads,' he said, clicking his fingers.

Lying back on the seesaw once more, he revelled in the adulation of his tribe. Someone rolled him a spliff and he took a long drag, thinking. No one had leapt to defend him. When they'd had the chance to jump the loony from behind, those losers had just hung around, waiting for TeeJay to sort it. He could have been gunned down, but it had turned out to his advantage in the end. He had stood his ground and, as a result, his credibility had never been so high.

As he smoked, he wondered how a crazy punk like Theo had got hold of a shooter. In the interests of public safety, if for no other reason, TeeJay would have to relieve him of it. If the pigs got to hear about it, they would be all over TeeJay's turf like a dose of the clap. He sat up and beckoned to the gang. When they had gathered round, he sat up and glared around the assembled group. No one was to breathe a word about the gun. Those were his orders. There was a murmur of acknowledgement. Satisfied, TeeJay lay back on the seesaw again, and resumed his smoke. Tomorrow he would think about how to get hold of Theo's shooter.

39

PASSING BY THE main entrance to the compound the next morning, Geraldine saw a convoy of vehicles drive in. She stopped to see what was happening. Several vans squealed to a halt, the back doors were thrown open, and there was a racket as about two dozen young men were hustled into the police station. Aged from early to late teens, the youths were shouting and swearing at the uniformed officers supervising their arrival, making a terrible din. Geraldine walked over to find out what was going on.

A constable was shouting, trying to be heard above the noisy protests. 'Shut it or you'll all be cuffed.'

'You ain't got no business wiv us,' one of the boys yelled back and the rest of them joined in, cursing and issuing futile threats.

The police officers continued to shepherd the group inside. Geraldine abandoned her attempt to talk to one of the constables dealing with the detainees. Instead she went inside and asked the desk sergeant what was going on. He told her that a gang had been rounded up after a resident on their estate had phoned the station that morning. The caller had reported seeing one of the youths threatening the others with a gun the previous evening.

'Of course he couldn't say which of them it was, and of course there's no sign of any gun now,' he added. 'If there really was a weapon yesterday evening, it'll be long gone now. We'll never find it. We'll lean on them for a bit and question them individually and then let them go. Waste of time, really, but we've got to go through the motions. And of course the gang leader's nowhere to be found. It's an established gang. They as good as run the George Berkeley Estate in Camden. Do you know it?'

She shook her head, although the name rang a bell. Looking for a gun herself just then, she knew only too well they were virtually impossible to find.

'So how are you getting on?' the desk sergeant asked.

She shrugged and shook her head.

'It's early days,' he sympathised.

'I suppose so. We're arranging a TV appeal with the parents of the victim shot at Kings Cross so keep your fingers crossed for us.'

'Good idea. You might get a result. It's a busy area, so there should be quite a few potential witnesses about.'

'Yes, you'd think so. Lots of people passing by, but how many of them are likely to see the appeal?'

'You never know.'

They exchanged a rueful glance. There were times when their job seemed pretty thankless, a lot of donkey work for little or no return. Geraldine continued on her way to her office where she had to make the arrangements for the broadcast.

'Someone must at least suspect who shot him,' Geraldine had suggested to Luke's parents.

She didn't necessarily believe her own words. It was possible that no one knew who had pulled the trigger, apart from the killer himself. Even if someone else knew, and happened to watch the appeal, they would still have to be willing to share that information. Not everyone was prepared to help the police, whatever the circumstances. Still, she had to pursue any possible avenue and hope for the best, and Luke's parents had agreed to participate, which would make the appeal more effective. Checking everyone was in the right place, and ensuring the bereaved parents understood what was required of them, occupied most of her morning.

The first time Geraldine had seen Luke's mother, she had been wearing a shapeless grey jumper and baggy leggings that could have been pyjama trousers. Now she was dressed in a smart well-fitting navy trouser suit. Her hair, which Geraldine remembered as greasy and unkempt, looked glossy, as though it had just been washed and straightened. Mr Thomas had also made an effort for the television cameras. He was dressed in a dark suit and tie, and his thinning hair was plastered to his head with some kind of hair product.

'What if I cry?' Mrs Thomas asked.

Geraldine told her it wouldn't matter. The parents of a murder victim displayed the human side of such a tragedy. She didn't add that a display of grief could help persuade viewers to pick up the phone if they were in two minds about whether to come forward or not. Shortly before the appeal was due to begin, Geraldine's phone rang. She glanced at the screen and recognised the social worker's number. Excusing herself, she stepped out of the room where Mr and Mrs Thomas were seated at a table, ready to make their appeal. They were due to begin in just over five minutes.

'Geraldine?'

'Yes. How is she?'

'The hospital called to say there's been a minor complication –'

'Oh my God. How is she?'

'She's stable.'

'That's good, isn't it?'

'She suffered a minor setback an hour ago –'

'What does that mean, a minor setback?'

'She had a second heart attack –'

'Oh my God. Should I go there? Is she all right? Why didn't you phone me straight away?'

'I only just heard. But they said she's stable –'

'So you keep saying, but what does that mean? Is she all right?'

'It means she's not in any immediate danger. It's not critical. But you might like to go and see her later today. Give her a few hours to rest first. They said she's sleeping, and that's the best thing for her right now.'

'OK. I'll be there later. And Louise –'

'Yes?'

'Can you ask them to call me if there's any change? I do appreciate your help, you know, but I'd rather hear directly from the hospital. Tell them I'm her next of kin.'

'I'll tell them. And don't worry. She's in good hands.'

Feeling slightly shaky, Geraldine returned to the parents waiting to talk about their murdered son. Although she tried not to think about her own mother, sick and possibly dying in hospital, she struggled to maintain her professional detachment when Mrs Thomas broke down in tears.

40

THEO OFTEN WOKE up early. His sense of time was erratic. It gave Rosa a brief respite when he overslept, even though it meant he would probably be up late at the end of the day. This morning she had enjoyed the luxury of breakfast on her own. As she cleared the table she hummed softly, enjoying the temporary peace. Theo still wasn't stirring. Determined to make the most of it, she busied herself tidying the small living room. Once Theo was out of bed, chaos would return. For now she could imagine her home as it might have been without him. But however destructive her son's presence, she could never allow them to take him away. No one else would care for him like she did.

When he still hadn't appeared by one o'clock, she began to wonder if he was sick. There was no response when she rapped at his door. Cautiously, she pushed it open. It was tricky stepping into the room. The floor was covered with clothes, pages ripped from magazines, old children's toys, and odd items of bric-a-brac he had scavenged on his rare excursions outside: a broken umbrella, a wooden spoon, a man's scuffed leather shoe, various items of underwear – clean and soiled seemingly interchangeable – and several woolly scarves Rosa had knitted for him in different colours. On his bed, along with his scrunched up duvet and pillow, were a tiny red patent leather shoe and a grubby pink woollen pig. Theo wasn't there.

She checked the bathroom. It was empty. She looked in the cramped kitchenette. That was empty too. Panicking, she dashed round the flat, calling his name. The only place she couldn't check was Jack's bedroom. His door was locked. She banged furiously on the door. Theo must have managed to lock himself in there, although Jack kept the only key. When there was no response to her shouts, she checked the front door. It wasn't locked. She was always careful to secure the door to prevent Theo running off, but she must have overlooked it. She hadn't seen Theo for about seventeen hours. He might have slipped out at any time since then. He could be anywhere. Trembling with shock, she flung herself down on a chair in the living room and tried to work out a course of action. She didn't really have much choice. Theo had to be found. He could be lying in a gutter, dying from a severe beating.

On the point of calling the police she thought better of it and rang Jack instead. He wouldn't thank her for contacting the police. Besides, there was a chance Jack had accidentally locked his brother in his room before going out, or he might even have taken Theo out with him. He did occasionally take him out for a walk, although he had never kept him away for longer than an hour. Her hopes were dashed when Jack answered his phone. He had no idea where Theo was. As she had expected, Jack insisted it would be a mistake to invite the police to poke around in their business.

'I ain't letting no one take my bro away. They gonna say you ain't able to take care of him. They'll take him away from us and bang him up. They ain't good to loonies, ma. You know it.'

'Your brother ain't no loony.'

'We know it, but you know what they gonna think.'

Jack offered to come straight home, and made her promise not to do anything before he arrived.

'We gonna find him, ma. He ain't gone far.'

'You better be right.'

Jack was as good as his word. Within an hour he was home, breathless and stressed. He had seen no sign of Theo as he had made his way across the estate and up the stairs. Rosa begged him to go back out and search for his brother again, but he seemed more interested in searching Theo's room.

'What you wanna look in there for? You ain't gonna find nothing in there. It's fulla junk. You need to get outside and find your brother. He ain't gone far, you said so yourself. You gotta find him.'

Jack glared at his mother. 'Fuck off telling me what to do. Ain't no one tells me what to do. I gotta find something in my bro's room so get outa the way, will ya? There's something in Theo's room I gotta find, and you don't need to know no more.'

Rosa was really frightened now. 'What he got in there that you so keen to find? What you been giving him? What you got in there?'

'Fuck off. I ain't given nothing to my bro. I look out for him.'

He pushed past her and she heard him swearing as he rummaged around in his brother's room.

'Theo don't like no one messing with his stuff,' she muttered, wondering what Jack was so desperate to find in there. 'You stashed weed or crack in there, you as good as killed your brother.'

Jack didn't answer.

41

THE TELEVISION APPEAL took longer to record than anyone had anticipated. For a start, Luke's father refused to speak on camera.

'He's shy,' his wife explained, while he shrugged, red-faced and awkward.

Luke's mother was keen to participate, but kept breaking down in tears. Her crying was only natural, but she quickly became incoherent. What with his silence, and her hysterics, the filming dragged on. There was little Geraldine could do to speed it up. She had to remain seated at the table making sure all of the key points were included. At last they finished and she arranged for a patrol car to take Mr and Mrs Thomas home.

'Do you think a witness will get in touch with you after this?' Mr Thomas asked, finding his voice now the recording equipment had been switched off.

'Let's hope so,' Geraldine replied. 'These appeals sometimes help to jog someone's memory, or it might prompt a witness to come forward when they've been in two minds over whether to get involved.'

She didn't add that it was anyone's guess whether they would receive useful information as a result of their afternoon's work, or just the inevitable barrage of deluded and mistaken responses.

'One day one of our regulars is going to come up with a genuine lead and no one's going to pay any attention,' Sam said, referring to the cranks who contacted them every time an appeal was made. 'My money's on Psychic Sue,' she added, with a grin. 'Imagine her excitement if she witnessed a real murder.'

'Imagine her giving evidence in court,' a constable added. 'She'd insist on taking her crystal ball with her. She'd start by telling the judge all about her past life as a hangman, and then she'd predict his future with an exotic stranger –'

'But if she witnessed a murder she wouldn't know it was real,' another constable interrupted. 'She can't tell the difference between the real world and the world that goes on inside her head.'

'What if a killer disguised as an alien committed a murder in front of Annie?' someone else added. 'Has anyone actually kept a note of all her sightings? Who would have thought so many aliens would want to prowl around the streets of Hendon!'

'Why would a killer disguise himself as an alien?'

'I don't know. A fancy dress party?'

'This speculation is all very entertaining, but can we please focus on the job in hand,' Geraldine interrupted the chattering. 'And as for you, DS Haley,' she went on, addressing Sam with mock severity, 'you should know better than to encourage your constables to waste their time like this.'

'Yes ma'am,' Sam replied, with a grin.

A young constable new to the job glanced anxiously from Geraldine to Sam and back again, before visibly relaxing on realising the reprimand wasn't serious.

It was growing late by the time Geraldine finally left her office. Stopping off at a garage en route, she realised she had no idea of her mother's favourite flowers, or whether she preferred red or white grapes. Hoping she had inherited her mother's taste she selected what she herself liked, a small bunch of brightly coloured freesias, splashes of bright purple and orange. Prevaricating, she picked up a plastic punnet of grapes, half white and half red. Armed with these inadequate offerings, she drove to the hospital.

'I'm here to see Milly Blake.'

The nurse on the desk glanced up at a clock.

'Are you a relative?'

'Yes, I'm her daughter.'

'Go on in then, but don't disturb her if she's asleep, will you? She didn't pass a good night.'

'Oh, OK. I wouldn't wake her up anyway, but what does that mean, she didn't have a good night? Is she all right? She seemed to be making a good recovery and then I was told she had another coronary.' It was a struggle to keep her voice even.

The nurse shook her head. 'It's nothing to worry about, she just had a minor setback, but it's important she rests as much as possible.'

Geraldine couldn't help feeling disappointed when she found her mother asleep. Childishly, she had been waiting to see her mother smile on seeing the flowers she had brought. They could hardly establish a relationship based on a preference for the same flowers, but somehow Geraldine felt as though that would help. At least it would give them something to talk about. On her way to the hospital, she had imagined the conversation. It would begin with her mother smiling at the flowers.

'They're lovely! How did you know I like freesias?'

'I didn't. They're my favourites.'

'Mine too!'

'The colours are so vivid.'

'Exactly.'

Their eyes would meet in mutual understanding and Geraldine would feel a connection to the woman she had never known, deeper than any other, a bond forged in blood and flesh. Instead she sat gazing at dry skin stretched taut across sunken cheeks.

'I'm here,' Geraldine whispered. 'I'm here, Mum.' A word

so often used with her adoptive mother to express annoyance, or make a demand, the term had become a plea. The sleeping woman didn't move, but the green line on the monitor progressed with quiet regularity across the screen, reassuring an observer that the patient was alive, at least. Geraldine waited for about fifteen minutes before putting the flowers and grapes down on the table beside the bed. She wished she had thought to buy a card and wondered if her mother would even find out she had been there. She rummaged in her bag and tore a page from her notebook.

'Get well soon, love Erin,' she wrote, then shoved the page in her bag and tore out a second sheet of paper. This time she omitted the word 'love' from her message. It seemed a bit presumptuous to use it with the mother she had only met once. But she added a kiss.

'Tell her I came to visit,' she called to the nurse at the desk. 'I left some flowers and grapes. I'm her daughter, Erin.'

'Erin,' the nurse replied, smiling. 'She was talking about you and Helena.'

'Who's Helena?'

The nurse looked surprised. 'No, I must be getting her confused with someone else. But she was definitely talking about you today. She'll be pleased you came by. I think she was expecting you earlier.'

'Yes, I meant to get here before now but I couldn't get away.'

'Not to worry. There's always another day.'

'I'll be back tomorrow.'

'I'll tell her that.' She smiled. 'It's good to give her something to look forward to. Mind you don't let her down again.'

42

ON SATURDAY, GERALDINE decided to spend the morning visiting her mother. She was due some time off. Going to the hospital before work meant she couldn't be sidetracked into going to see her mother later than she intended. If Milly was asleep when she arrived, Geraldine could wait at her bedside until she woke up, even if it meant staying at the hospital all day. It wasn't as if the investigation would grind to a halt without her. For the first time in her adult life she was putting someone else before her work. It was liberating but frightening, acknowledging that another person was so important to her.

She finished a late breakfast and set out for the hospital. On the way she stopped off to buy a large bunch of flowers, almost a bouquet, and more mixed grapes. As she laid the flowers carefully on the passenger seat, her work phone rang. Glancing down she recognised Sam's number. She ignored it and drove off. The phone shrilled again. When it rang for the third time, she answered it.

'This had better be important.'

'The gun's turned up.'

'What?'

'The gun we've been looking for. It's turned up.'

'What? Where? Are you sure? How do you know it's the same one?' Her hospital visit temporarily postponed, Geraldine made a quick turn and headed towards Hendon. 'I'm on my way right now. Tell me everything you know. I just want the facts.'

Sam told her that a young man had been apprehended somewhere in Central London. As far as Sam knew, he had been either blind drunk or else high on drugs, or possibly both. He had been seen threatening passersby with a hand gun. The street had been cordoned off and the armed response unit summoned.

'They threw the whole lot at him, as you can imagine, but in the end it seems he gave up quietly and it was all over pretty quickly. A bit of a non-event really, except that when they examined the gun, some bright spark in ballistics matched the idiosyncrasies on the barrel to the bullets that were used to shoot our victims, and there it is. We have the gun and what's more, we've got the guy who was running around town with it! Looks like we've got our killer, just like that. I knew we couldn't go on much longer without any sort of a break. Two people shot dead. No one does that and gets away with it.'

Geraldine wasn't convinced the case would be quite so easily wrapped up.

'We've got the weapon, anyway,' she agreed.

'Oh for goodness sake, Geraldine, even you can't pour cold water on this. What else do you need? A signed confession in triplicate and video evidence of him shooting the victims? I'm telling you, we've got him.'

'All right. Where is he?'

'They're bringing him over to Hendon right now. He should be here in about half an hour.'

Geraldine glanced at the time. 'Don't let Adam start without me!'

'Well, I'll do my best, but it's not exactly my shout.'

Geraldine grunted. It was typical that the killer would be picked up just when she was away from her office.

'So, back to the facts. Who is he? What do we know about him?'

On that point Sam was less forthcoming. It seemed no one

had yet managed to discover the suspect's name, or anything much about him. All she could say was that he was around twenty, and he refused to say anything. Neither his prints nor his DNA had ever been entered on the system so they had no way of identifying him yet.

'The arresting officers think he might be a bit odd,' Sam added.

'Odd in what way?'

'I don't know.'

'Oh well, I guess we can make up our own minds about that. See you soon.'

Geraldine put her foot down and reached Hendon ahead of the suspect who was still being processed out of the London police station where he had been overnight, prior to his transfer. The paperwork was going to take a while, which gave Geraldine time to study the report on his arrest. Sam's summary had been accurate, as far as it went. The suspect had been picked up on Thursday night and the station in Hendon had only been notified on Saturday when the gun had been identified as linked to their case. Other than that, the account of his arrest seemed to confirm that he had been spaced out when the police picked him up, too far gone even to speak.

She smiled, reading the report. It was a massive step forward. They had been searching for the murder weapon for days without getting anywhere and now it had just dropped into their laps together, hopefully, with the killer himself. There was an atmosphere of elation in the incident room that contrasted with the deflated mood last time Geraldine had been there. Some of the officers were beaming. For others, the enormity of the breakthrough was only just beginning to sink in. Even Adam was smiling as he greeted her.

'Looks like we've got him,' he said, echoing Sam's words.

Geraldine nodded. 'Let's hope. What time will he be here?'

They discussed the practicalities for a while. Adam wanted

Geraldine to accompany him in the interview. She agreed with alacrity. The excitement in the team was infectious. Within an hour or two they expected to secure a confession, after which they would start to prepare a case to present to the Crown Prosecution Service. The end was near. While they waited for the suspect to arrive, Geraldine read through the account of his arrest again. As Sam had told her, the actual event had been low key once the police had arrived on the scene. The suspect hadn't resisted arrest, and had handed over his gun without demur. The whole time he had refused to utter a word.

At last the message came through that the suspect was waiting, along with a brief. The interview could begin.

'Come on then,' Adam muttered, 'let's see if we can make him talk.'

'I don't really see how he can hold out now,' Geraldine replied. 'He was caught virtually red-handed, with the gun in his possession.'

'Yes, he was holding it, waving it around, so he can't spin some cock and bull story about it being planted on him without his knowledge. He must at least tell us where he got the gun, if he wants to claim it wasn't him shooting people with it a week ago. Either way, we're home and dry.'

Geraldine nodded. She hoped he was right. Adam opened the door to the interview room and stood aside for her to enter first. With a terse smile in appreciation of his good manners, she walked in and faced the man accused of shooting two people dead.

43

AGED AROUND TWENTY, the suspect looked faintly oriental. Beneath a mop of curly black hair, a pair of wild, dark eyes stared round the room from a thin pale face. His shoulders jiggled as the tips of his bony fingers tapped out a rhythm on the table. His demeanour suggested he was high, although it was difficult to tell whether his pupils were dilated, because his irises were almost black. As soon as Geraldine began to talk he sat perfectly still. Only his eyes roamed all around the room, as though he wasn't listening to a word she said. Probably he was familiar with the preamble to a police interview.

With worried blue eyes and a snub nose, the lawyer at his side looked about fifteen. When he leaned forward his sandy-coloured fringe flopped over his high forehead. He spoke rapidly in a low voice as though he didn't want to be overheard. 'In my opinion my client is not in a fit state to answer any questions. I haven't been able to get a single word out of him. We don't know how old he is. If he's under age, your attempt to interview him is illegal, as you well know.'

Geraldine studied the suspect who stared back at her. 'What is your name?'

He didn't respond. She turned to the lawyer and asked for his client's name.

'I've no idea who he is.' He sounded like a sullen adolescent. His studies had not prepared him for this circumstance. 'I just told you, he refuses to say a word to me, although I've explained very clearly that I'm here to help him. He just won't speak to me.'

'That's going to make it difficult for you to represent him.'

The lawyer shrugged. 'If he won't speak to me, I'll have to withdraw. I've tried my best. He doesn't seem to understand any known language.'

While this exchange was going on, the suspect fixed his attention on Geraldine and sat silently watching her, his mouth slightly open.

'He looks pretty out of it,' Adam admitted.

The lawyer mumbled under his breath as Adam attempted to persuade the suspect to state his name. 'If you think you can get out of this by simply refusing to speak to us for long enough, you're mistaken,' Adam went on, turning to threats in his efforts to loosen the suspect's tongue. 'We may struggle to get anything out of you, but we're not letting you go until you tell us your name and where you live –'

'My client appears to be deaf mute or mentally challenged,' the lawyer interrupted, 'which makes any attempt to interview him inappropriate as well as a waste of time for everyone concerned. It is my considered opinion that he needs a psychiatric assessment, not legal representation.'

'And it's my opinion that he's either spaced out on drugs or else he's putting up a good show of being off his face. We'll adjourn this interview to allow your client time to sleep it off. After that we expect him to stop messing about, and start talking.'

In the absence of any further information, there was little point in pressing on. They agreed to take a two-hour break while the suspect was returned to his cell. He was led away, still silent. Geraldine followed the custody officer and watched the suspect shuffle into his cell and sit down on the hard narrow bunk. He didn't protest as the door clanged closed behind him. Observing through the peephole, Geraldine saw him lie down and close his eyes.

'It's just a matter of time now,' Adam was saying when she returned to the incident room. He glanced up as she entered. 'We've got nothing on him yet,' he told her.

It was frustrating that the suspect had been carrying no form of identification when he had been picked up. Going through his pockets they had found a handful of coloured elastic bands, a packet of chewing gum, a penny, a broken biro, and a single button that didn't match any of his clothes. Without money, credit card or Oyster card, or even a bus ticket, it was impossible to guess where he had come from. He was unlikely to have been mugged, given that he was armed; he didn't look as though he had been sleeping rough, and he appeared to be well fed.

'There's definitely something wrong with him,' Geraldine said.

'Like he kills people,' Adam replied. 'We need to get him to talk.'

Geraldine didn't respond but she was inclined to agree with the lawyer that the suspect was suffering from mental problems of some sort, and was perhaps deaf as well.

'It's odd that he doesn't seem frightened,' she said.

'He's too high to know where he is or what's going on,' Adam replied.

A team was watching CCTV footage taken near both murder scenes, searching for a sighting of the suspect. His prints and DNA had been sent to the forensic laboratory where they were hunting for evidence that he had been in contact with either or both of the murder victims. There was nothing more for them to do now but wait for the results. There wasn't enough time for her to visit the hospital, so Geraldine returned to her desk to reread some of the statements they had received. The atmosphere of elation that had greeted the arrest had faded. The case continued to frustrate them. To begin with they had arrested the wrong man. Now their second suspect was proving awkward. There was nothing to suggest he could be innocent, but unless he spoke it might be difficult to establish the truth. Lies were easier to confound than silence. They had nothing to work with. All they had was the gun, and that might not be enough to secure a conviction.

Two hours later they reconvened. According to the custody sergeant, the suspect had slept peacefully on his bunk throughout the break. He looked dazed, as though he had just woken up, and sat yawning while Geraldine initiated their second interview.

Geraldine leaned forward. 'What's your name?' she asked softly. 'You don't have to be afraid. Just talk to me. You can trust me. What is your name?'

The suspect's pinched face broke into a grin and he nodded his head. 'Theo,' he said, in a curiously high-pitched voice.

'Theo what?'

He grinned. 'Theo what?' he echoed.

Geraldine held his gaze. 'Where do you live, Theo?'

'Where do you live, Theo?' he repeated, parrot fashion, imitating her intonation perfectly. On his lips the mimicry sounded weird rather than impudent, as though he was incapable of producing words of his own.

'Oh Jesus,' Adam muttered impatiently.

'Do you live with your mother?'

The suspect nodded his head and his curly hair bobbed up and down. Geraldine wasn't sure if he meant anything by it.

'What is your mother's name?'

'Mum, mum,' he intoned anxiously.

'You live with your mother. What's her name?'

Theo dropped his gaze and began singing quietly to himself, as though the conversation was over. 'Around around de garden, around around around around.'

'What is this?' Adam burst out. 'Stop singing and answer the questions.'

The lawyer interrupted. 'I must insist my client be accompanied by an appropriate adult before he continues with this interview, and that his parents or legal guardians are informed. We don't know how old he is, and his mental capacity hasn't been assessed. I insist we stop this now.'

'We're trying to find out who's responsible for him,' Adam snapped. 'Has it escaped your notice that we have absolutely no idea who he is? We don't know where he comes from, and we don't know who's responsible for him. Someone's been taking care of him so let's start by checking the mental institutions.'

'We have a first name,' Geraldine pointed out. 'That gives us something to work on.'

'He's like a child,' the lawyer said. 'He doesn't seem to understand anything. He can't make any decisions or give instructions, and I can't be expected to take responsibility.'

Geraldine thought about her niece who had been trained to trot out her name and address from a very early age. She turned back to Theo.

'Where do you live? Tell me your name and address.'

'Theo Bates George Berkeley House St Pancras Way Camden London England,' he replied promptly.

'Why the hell didn't you tell us that in the first place?' Adam burst out. Sounding exasperated, nevertheless he was smiling.

44

GERALDINE AND ADAM drove straight to George Berkeley House, a large council estate on St Pancras Way in Camden, near Central London. On the way, Adam told Geraldine what he knew about the estate. All sorts of criminal activities were rumoured to take place there, mainly involving hard drugs and gang warfare. The two problems were closely interrelated. Although the police had been summoned on more than one occasion to investigate reports of gun crimes, no one living on the estate had been convicted of any such offence. There had been many busts over the years, but now the police largely left the place alone.

'It's a question of containment,' Adam explained. 'As long as they keep their problems behind closed doors, the drug squad just keep an eye on the place; keep things under control as far as possible.'

When Geraldine expressed her indignation at his resignation, he laughed.

'Don't be naive. This isn't the Home Counties. You're in London now. It would take more resources than we can ever hope to throw at the place to clean it up completely, and then the problem would only move elsewhere. At least we know where they are and can keep on top of things.'

'But are we keeping on top of it?'

He shrugged again. 'Speak to the drug squad.'

'But –'

'Let's focus on what we've come here to do. I don't want to hang around here any longer than is necessary.'

They drew up outside an ugly concrete building constructed on seven floors, all identical, with narrow windows in its dirty grey walls.

'I can see why you don't want to stay here long,' Geraldine said. 'It's not the sort of place you want to hang around.'

'I wasn't referring to the place. I was talking about the occupants.'

No one answered the door at the first couple of flats they tried. At the third one, a very old woman opened the door on the chain.

'Pigs,' she spat and closed the door again.

Adam and Geraldine exchanged a glance, wondering how the woman had been able to identify them without even seeing them properly.

'Do we smell different or something?' Geraldine muttered.

'More likely we're different because we don't smell,' he replied. 'Come on.'

The next door was opened by an old man who scowled up at them.

'What? Theo? The nutter what lives upstairs?'

'Yes, that's the one. Can you tell us where he lives?'

'Upstairs,' he repeated and slammed the door in their faces.

Everyone seemed to know Theo the nutter. Finally a young girl told them he lived at number sixty-seven, on the sixth floor. The metal lift stank of urine. By the time they stepped out on to the gangway on the sixth floor, Geraldine felt sick.

'I'm glad we didn't get stuck in there,' she said, inhaling deeply.

She followed Adam past a row of dirty front doors, stopping at number sixty-seven.

'Here we are,' he said, and knocked.

A woman opened the door.

'Where you been –?' she burst out and stopped in mid-sentence, seeing Adam and Geraldine.

She made to close the door but Adam stepped over the threshold.

'Does Theo live here?' he asked.

'What? Ain't none of your business. Get off out of it.'

'We need to talk to you, Mrs Bates,' Geraldine interrupted quickly.

'Who you calling Mrs Bates?'

'I'm sorry, I thought that was your name.'

'You ain't got no business thinking about my name. Ain't nothing to you. Now piss off. You got no right poking your noses in here.'

'Don't you want to know where Theo is?' Geraldine asked her.

The woman hesitated. She was thin and scraggy, with a sallow complexion, and would have been quite pretty if her face hadn't been all out of proportion. Emphasised by her greasy hair being tied back in a rubber band, her high forehead dwarfed her small nose, tiny mouth and pointed chin.

Her cheeks suddenly flushed red. 'What you done with my Theo?' she demanded. 'Where is he?'

She glanced up and down the walkway as though expecting to see him.

'I think you'd better come with us,' Geraldine said gently.

'Did someone hurt Theo? Oh my God, if anyone hurt my kid, I swear, I'll kill him.'

'Mrs Bates, or whatever you call yourself, we want you to come with us right now,' Adam barked suddenly. 'We need to get moving.'

'What's your hurry?' she asked, crossing her arms and leaning back against the door frame, sensing she might somehow have the advantage. 'I ain't in no hurry.'

'If you want to see Theo again, you need to come with us right now,' he said and turned away.

'Wait!' she cried out, alarmed. 'I'm coming. I never said I

wasn't coming. Just wait while I get my coat, will you?'

She disappeared into the flat to re-emerge a moment later clutching a large brown handbag and a dirty pink mac. 'I'm coming, I'm coming. Where we going anyway? What happened to my Theo?' She pulled on her mac.

On the way down, Geraldine explained that Theo was being looked after at a police station after he had been picked up in possession of a hand gun. She refrained from adding that Theo was a suspect in a murder enquiry.

'Is Theo your son?'

In the lift, the sallow-faced woman told them her name was Rosa. Theo was her son who lived with her. When they had Rosa safely in the car, Geraldine explained that they were having difficulty persuading Theo to answer their questions.

'He doesn't seem to be frightened, but we're not quite sure how well he can hear us, and how much he understands of what he does hear.'

Rosa nodded without speaking. They drove for a few moments in silence before Geraldine tried again.

'We haven't been able to persuade Theo to cooperate with us. If this continues, we will need to recommend him for a psychiatric assessment. Does he suffer from any medical disabilities? Is he on any medication?'

'You leave my boy alone!' Rosa snapped.

She seemed insanely defensive about her son, but at least they had a responsible adult to sit in on his interview.

'We need the name of Theo's doctor,' Geraldine added.

'We don't need no doctor. I take care of him,' Rosa said fiercely.

'I see.' Geraldine sighed.

Theo's situation was even sadder than she had realised. Although the young man clearly needed some kind of treatment or support, it appeared his mother wasn't prepared to allow him access to medical attention.

'Is he under any medical supervision at all?' she asked.

'We don't need no doctor interfering with him,' Rosa repeated. 'I can take care of my son. You leave him alone. Ain't no one taking him away from me.'

'We're not trying to take your son away from you,' Geraldine reassured her. In the mirror she saw Adam raise his eyebrows at her statement, but he didn't contradict her.

The justice system would take Theo away from his mother and place him in care; whether in a secure mental institution or a prison cell was for the courts to decide. Either way, his mother wouldn't be taking him home with her. Geraldine stared straight ahead and didn't say any more. Rosa was guilty of letting her son roam freely in the community, posing a danger to himself and others. What had happened had been inevitable. Rosa's misguided motives had led to the deaths of two innocent victims and the incarceration of the son whose liberty she had been so desperate to protect. Despite her evident distress, Geraldine felt little sympathy for her.

45

LENNY SETTLED IN again, like he had never been away. Glued to the football on the telly, he didn't look up when she entered the living room.

'Get us a beer.'

'I ain't your skivvy,' she grumbled, but he ignored her.

Muttering under her breath she went to the kitchen. The fridge was empty.

'We ain't got no beers,' she told him, sitting down.

'Go get some,' he replied, without taking his eyes off the game.

'Go yourself.'

'That's a bloody nice welcome home, after all I been through, can't even get a beer. Fucking hell. Might as well still be banged up.'

'You got me.'

Someone scored a goal and he yelled in chorus with the supporters on the screen. 'Get in there!' He turned to her. 'Go get us some beers.'

'I ain't got no cash.'

'Get it on the card.'

'I got no credit.'

'Fucking hell.' He reached into his pocket and fished around, finally pulling out a twenty quid note. 'Here. Get us some fags an' all.'

She took the money. 'Where you get this?'

'Mind your own fucking business. Now for fuck's sake go

and get us a beer. The bloody game'll be over before you move your lazy arse.'

Hiding her anger, Gina hurried off to the corner shop. The more aggrieved she felt, the more determined she was to get what was hers. There was no point running off with nothing. Lenny had given her a ring that could be worth thousands of quid. Impatient to get away from him, she wasn't leaving without it. That ring could set her up nicely. If he would only tell her where he had taken it, she would go and get it herself, but he was keeping his cards close to his chest. If she tried to wheedle it out of him, he only clammed up and snapped at her to mind her own fucking business.

'It is my business,' she had protested. 'You give it me. It's mine. I only want what's mine.'

'It's yours when I say and not before.'

He wasn't even grateful when she got back with his booze and fags. 'About bloody time. It's nearly half-time, you dozy bitch. I been watching without a beer or a smoke.'

By the time the game ended he was pissed. She laughed at him for slurring his words.

'Don't take much to get you wrecked.'

'You try being inside for months. Shame no one bangs you up, it might shut your fucking face. Give me some peace for a while.'

Shaking with sudden rage he jumped up and swung his fist at her, but she wasn't smashed and easily dodged out of his way.

'Get over here.'

'What? So you can hit me?'

'I'll teach you, fucking bitch.'

He made another attempt and lost his balance. This time, one of his flailing arms whacked her on the side of her head, knocking her off her feet. She yelled in alarm. Luckily she landed on the sofa where she lay still for a moment, stunned.

'Get up, I'll teach you!' he bellowed.

For a second she thought about staying where she was, not moving a muscle. With luck he would think he had really hurt her. But she was afraid he was too far gone to worry about that, and if she didn't move out of the way fast, she would be an easy target. With a screech she flung herself off the sofa and made a dash for the door. She wasn't fast enough. He got between her and the door and stood, fists raised, poised to hit her. Terrified, she began to cry real tears

'Don't hurt me, Lenny, don't hurt me no more. You really hurt my head.' She put one hand to the side of her head and winced. 'It's gonna be a real big bruise there. Don't hurt me no more. How about I roll you a joint and we have a smoke? I ain't nothing but a friend to you, Lenny. Didn't I come to see you every week all the time you was inside?'

Wisely she held back from adding that Cynthia hadn't been to visit him in the nick once. Best not to risk antagonising him. He could be touchy about his mother. To her relief, he dropped his hands and his shoulders drooped.

'I dunno what gets into me,' he muttered. 'You ain't a bad girl. Come here.'

Trembling, she approached and he put his arms round her and pulled her very close, whispering in her ear.

'I know it don't mean nothing,' she said. 'Let's have that smoke.'

'You're a saint, what you put up with,' he said. 'I dunno why you stay with me. A girl like you ought to find yourself a decent bloke, someone what'll take care of you and not give you hell and get banged up. You deserve better than what I can give you, baby.'

There wasn't going to be a better time.

'What you talking about? You're good to me. You give me that lovely ring.' She kissed him on his slobbery lips. 'What you done with it, Lenny? When you giving it to me? It's mine, because you give it to me, and you got no right taking it off me again like you don't want me to have it after all, like you decided to give my ring away to someone else.' She bit her lip, aware it would be dangerous to bring his mother into it. 'It's like you said, Lenny, I been good to you, ain't I? I deserve to get my ring back, don't I?'

'Tell you what, baby,' he said, 'that shop ain't open tomorrow but first thing Monday I'm going back there to get it back for you.' He kissed her. 'You're gonna have it on Monday. Now let's get up to bed.'

For once, she had a genuine excuse because her head ached where he had hit her, but she didn't want to annoy him now. Until Monday she was going to put up with him and then she'd be off.

46

QUESTIONING THEO IN his mother's presence yielded no new information. Although he seemed willing to speak in front of her, what he said made no sense.

'Who's Jack?' Adam asked, after Theo had repeated a phrase about waiting until Jack came home.

Rosa denied knowing anyone called Jack. Geraldine thought she was lying, but Theo was incapable of explaining what he meant.

'Who's Jack?' Adam asked him again.

'Wait till my Jack gets home,' Theo repeated in his curiously high-pitched voice. 'Wait till my Jack gets home!'

The interview dragged on all afternoon and through most of the evening, with frequent intervals. It was impossible to determine whether Theo was unwilling or unable to say who had given him the gun, or what he had been doing wandering around the streets of London with it. When Adam asked him point blank if he had been present when the two murders were committed, he babbled inconsequentially about a squashy football.

'He don't know what he done today,' Rosa interrupted the questioning at one point. 'He ain't gonna tell you what he done any other day. Leave him alone with your questions. Let him come home.'

At last the lawyer looked at his watch and announced the interview was over for the day.

'Thank Christ we got someone here talking sense,' Rosa

said. 'Theo's knackered and he needs to come home.' She stood up, hands on hips, and stretched her back. 'We been sitting too long. Come on, kid. You don't look like you slept last night no more than what I did.'

No one else budged.

Geraldine spoke up as gently as she could. 'I'm afraid that won't be possible.'

'Jesus, what now?'

'Theo can't go home yet. It's just not possible.'

'What you talking about? Theo, you get on up and walk right outa here. Ain't no one gonna stop you. He ain't done nothing.'

When Adam explained that Theo was helping them with a murder investigation, Rosa flew into a temper, insisting her son had nothing to do with any murders. He was harmless, she claimed, and the police were out of line if they thought they could use him as a scapegoat.

'Pick on the weak ones,' she ranted. 'You loada bastards!'

'Pick on de weak ones,' Theo echoed cheerfully. 'You loada bastards!' He seemed to enjoy repeating everything his mother said.

'What's your bleeding murder gotta do with my kid? Nothing, that's what!'

'Nutting, dat's what!' Theo shouted gleefully.

Ignoring Theo, Adam explained to Rosa that her son had been apprehended in possession of a gun that had been used to shoot two people dead.

'He picked it up,' she replied dismissively. 'He picks up all sorts of things, anything he can get his hands on.'

'This was a gun,' Geraldine said.

'Don't mean he used it. You got no proof. Theo ain't no killer.'

'So you're telling us he is always in control of his actions?'

'What?'

'Do you mean Theo knows what he's doing?'

'Don't you go putting words in my mouth. I never said that, did I?' She turned a scared face to the lawyer. 'I never said nothing.'

Theo appeared to have no inkling that he was suspected of murder. His mother, on the other hand, grew increasingly strident in her rage. Seeing Theo was becoming upset by her shouting, Adam directed that he be returned to his cell, and stood up to accompany the escort himself.

'You leave him be!' Rosa screeched. 'You ain't got no right touching him! Theo, get over here. You coming home with me.'

Theo turned to his mother and began to whimper.

'Get him out of here,' Adam barked.

Two constables promptly stepped forward and took Theo's elbow, guiding him from the room. 'Come on, son, there's a nice dinner waiting for you back in the custody suite.'

Theo went with them quietly. Left alone with Rosa, it took Geraldine some time to quieten the angry mother. Furious that Theo was being held in custody overnight, being told that he was going to be assessed by a mental health expert did nothing to appease her rage. She insisted that she was the only person who understood her son, and she alone was fit to take care of him. They didn't need strangers interfering in their lives. Only by resorting to threats was Geraldine able to persuade her to go home.

'You'll be no use to Theo if you're taken away and locked up for obstruction. He's going to need you when he gets home. Who's going to look after him if you're in prison?'

At last Rosa left, still protesting. 'He don't need no strangers. I'm his mother.'

With a rush of guilt, Geraldine remembered her own mother. In all the frantic activity surrounding Theo, she hadn't thought about her since the morning. She dithered over whether it was too late to call the hospital. It was probably too late for a message to reach her mother that evening. In any case, what could she possibly say that would make amends for her negligence? As far as she knew, she was the only person supporting her mother but, despite her good intentions, she had been too busy to manage a visit.

Before she went to sleep she took her mother's photograph out of the drawer beside her bed. Staring at it, she tried to connect her memory of the sick woman she had seen in hospital with the girl gazing up at her from her own face. The changes wrought by time were hard to grasp. The girl in the photograph, young enough to be her own daughter, had been her mother in another era. She wondered how close they would have been if she had grown up as Erin Blake. Relationships between mothers and daughters were often fraught, but her mother had cheated her out of having any relationship with her at all. Pricked by sudden anger, she replaced the photograph in the drawer. She wasn't the one who should be feeling guilty. She would go and see her mother the next day. In the meantime, if she allowed herself to become upset, she would never get to sleep. But when she closed her eyes, she saw Rosa's distraught face. Theo couldn't be easy to look after, yet Rosa was frantic at the thought of losing him even for one night.

47

THE NEXT MORNING a constable working in the borough intelligence unit reported that Rosa had two sons, Theo and Jack. Theo had gibbered about Jack. It wasn't clear why Rosa had lied. Geraldine double checked the tape.

'I don't know no one called Jack,' Rosa had insisted.

She might have fallen out with her other son, perhaps over frustration about Theo, but it was possible she had a more sinister reason for trying to conceal Jack's identity from the police. Geraldine took Sam with her to George Berkeley House in Camden to see Rosa. They left early, hoping to catch her before she set off for the police station.

Rosa came to the door straight away.

'Where is he? What you done with him?' she demanded, her eyes flicking past them along the corridor.

Geraldine explained that they hadn't brought Theo home. He wouldn't be released until he had undergone a psychiatric assessment, and even then there was no guarantee he would be allowed out into the community again.

'Into the community?' Rosa snarled. 'Some bleeding community they are. I'll get my coat.'

She flew into a temper when Geraldine told her they wanted to look round her flat before taking her to the police station.

'I'm afraid we have a search warrant.'

Rosa stood in the doorway, arms crossed, shaking her head. 'You got no right.'

'Rosa, your son was found in possession of a gun that has

been used to kill at least two people. I hardly need to point out we are conducting a serious criminal investigation – a murder investigation. If you attempt to hinder us in carrying out our duties, I will arrest you and you will be prosecuted for obstruction. Under these circumstances, that will carry a custodial sentence. And you won't be able to help Theo if you're in prison. Now move out of my way.'

Rosa hesitated. Geraldine and Sam pushed past her into the flat. The front door opened into a small living room, furnished cheaply but comfortably, and dominated by a large television screen attached to the wall. A sliver of daylight lit the room through a slit in grubby yellow curtains that hung at the window. Geraldine checked the bathroom. There was no evidence of a third person living there. She tried one of the doors off the living room and found it locked.

'You leave it alone,' Rosa shouted.

'Open this door.'

'Well that's tough shit because I ain't got a key.'

'If you don't open it for us, we'll break it down.'

'I told you, I ain't got a key. He don't give me one.'

'He? Do you mean Jack?'

'Who's Jack? Just because Theo says a name it don't mean nothing. There ain't no one called Jack here. You got it all wrong.'

'You have until we've checked the rest of the flat to open this door.'

Leaving Sam to keep an eye on Rosa, Geraldine took a look in the next room. Rosa's bedroom was tiny, with barely enough space to walk around the bed. A heap of clothes in one corner seemed to be all she had. Geraldine flicked through it, but found nothing either incriminating or interesting. Anything worth discovering was likely to be concealed behind the locked door. The next room was a complete jumble. There was a bed, barely discernible beneath piles of clothes, broken toys, a rolled-up carpet, and random pieces of trash.

'Is this Theo's room?' she called out, although the answer was self-evident.

After looking around the kitchenette, only the locked room remained. Geraldine nodded at Sam who kicked the flimsy internal door open to reveal a third bedroom. By contrast to the other two bedrooms, it looked as though it had recently been decorated. The largest of the rooms, the walls and ceiling were painted white, and there was a double bed with a navy cover and matching pillow cases. Fitted white wardrobes ran the length of the wall opposite. Geraldine saw herself reflected in a full-length, free-standing mirror that stood beside the bed. Over her shoulder in the mirror she could see Rosa's shocked face.

'What you done?' Rosa whispered. 'You broke his door.'

The room they had broken into looked out of place compared to the relative squalor of the other rooms.

Geraldine turned to Rosa. 'Whose room is this?'

Rosa shook her head and mumbled about it being a spare room. She was obviously lying. Geraldine took a look around. The wardrobes were stuffed with men's clothing most of which looked new, including several different raincoats and pairs of leather shoes. Although there was nothing in the room to identify its owner, it could only be Jack's room.

'Where is Jack?' she asked.

Rosa just shook her head. She looked terrified. Geraldine turned back to the wardrobes and began to search through the garments hanging there.

'What you looking for?'

'A leather jacket.'

'There ain't no leather jacket in there. He ain't got no leather jacket. What you trying to frame him for?'

Ignoring Rosa's protests, Geraldine continued methodically working her way along the row of clothes. She had nearly come to the end of them when she saw a dark brown leather jacket. Pulling on gloves, she removed it, still on the hanger, and laid it on the bed.

'I ain't never seen that before,' Rosa blustered. 'Must be new.'

Carefully, Geraldine checked the pockets. They were all empty.

'Ralph Lauren,' she read the label aloud. 'Very nice. Must have cost a few quid.'

'If it was new,' Rosa said quickly.

'Whose is it, Rosa? Who sleeps in here? This is Jack's room, isn't it? Your younger son, Jack. We know all about him, Rosa, so there's no point in denying it. Where is he?'

With a sigh Rosa hung her head and her shoulders drooped. 'Must be at work now.'

'Where does he work?'

'Thought you knew all about him.'

'Come on, Rosa, the game's over. We'll find him so you might as well just tell us. Where does he work?'

As Rosa mentioned the name of a bar, Geraldine saw Sam's eyes widen. Both of them had recognised the name of the bar where Luke had been shot. It could hardly be a coincidence.

'It's a bar up in London somewhere, up in Central London,' Rosa added vaguely, 'but I couldn't tell you where. He earns good money there, and that's all I know.'

Sam left the bedroom and Geraldine could hear her talking rapidly on the phone in a low voice. Before long Jack would be picked up. Then they would find out which of the two brothers had shot David and Luke. At the moment, Theo was the main suspect, but it was possible that Jack was responsible for the murders. After using the gun he could have asked Theo to hide it in all the clutter in his room. No one was going to suspect Theo, or find the gun in his untidy room, and Jack would not have bargained on Theo running around the streets waving the weapon around, with no idea of what he was doing. Either brother might be guilty but at the moment only one of them was in custody.

48

WHEN GERALDINE RETURNED to the station with Sam, she was gutted to learn that Jack had not yet been apprehended. A patrol car had been despatched straight away to pick him up, but he was not at the bar where he worked.

'He's not at work, and he's not at home, so where the blazes has he got to?' Adam asked.

Geraldine could tell the detective chief inspector wasn't really worried. They knew where Jack lived, and where he worked. It could only be a matter of time before they caught him. Still, it was an aggravating delay. As far as they knew, Jack was due at work the following day. No one who worked there was aware that the police were looking for him. A female constable was watching Rosa to make sure she couldn't warn her son. Unless something went wrong, they would arrest Jack the following day. Apart from that, all they could do was hope a patrol car would happen to spot him somewhere.

In the meantime there was work to be done. Geraldine called David's young widow, Laura, and asked her to come in and look at the leather jacket they had found in Jack's wardrobe. She arrived at the station late on Sunday morning. Geraldine took her straight to an interview room, where they waited for a constable to bring in the jacket. Laura had dressed smartly for the occasion in a knee-length black skirt, a crisp white shirt and a navy jumper. Her hair was well groomed and her make-up neat. She looked like a professional woman going to work. After a few minutes' polite conversation, the jacket was brought in, enclosed in a protective plastic covering. Geraldine watched the young widow's face closely as the constable laid her burden on the table and stepped back. Laura's eyes narrowed. Geraldine waited.

'Can you take it out of the plastic so I can get a proper look at it? I want to be sure.'

'No, I'm sorry, we need to keep it sealed until it's been for forensic examination, fingerprints and so on.'

'Oh yes, of course. I'm sorry. Well, the thing is, David did have a leather jacket like this, a really nice Ralph Lauren one, but I don't know if I can be positive it's the same one. I mean, leather jackets are all pretty similar, aren't they, and it's difficult to be sure, especially with it in that plastic.'

'Was your husband's jacket brown?'

'Oh yes, it looked just like this one. It could be the same one, but I can't be sure.'

'Thank you.'

Laura's reservations were understandable. As she pointed out, David's jacket wasn't unique. It was possible that Jack had coincidentally got hold of a similar, or even identical, jacket. But such coincidences were rare. Jack worked at the bar where Luke was killed with the same gun that had shot David, whose leather jacket had disappeared. And now an identical jacket had turned up in Jack's wardrobe. All the evidence pointed to Jack, and it was beginning to look conclusive.

She thanked Laura for coming to the police station.

'I wasn't much help, was I? I'm sorry.'

'On the contrary, you've been extremely helpful. Now we know that this could be your late husband's jacket, we'll have it sent off for urgent forensic examination. If we find traces of your husband's DNA on it, then we'll know for certain it was his, and that will give us invaluable evidence against the man we suspect of shooting your husband.'

Laura's eyes opened wide and her hand flew up to her mouth.

'Does that mean you know who killed him? Oh my God. He was such a kind man. Who would do that to him?"

The widow's composure crumbled. Tears slid down her cheeks, leaving faints streaks in her foundation. A tiny drop settled, twinkling, above her upper lip.

'Tell me everything,' she pleaded. 'I need to know what happened. Please.'

Geraldine explained that nothing was certain. They were following a strong lead. She could say no more than that, but she promised to let Laura know as soon as they had proof of the suspect's guilt. She didn't tell Laura that the suspect hadn't even been arrested yet.

'But you've found David's jacket,' Laura protested. 'Surely that's enough evidence?'

'Assuming it *is* your husband's jacket then it could be enough, but we need to be certain. You said you couldn't identify the jacket with complete confidence, and in any case we'd have wanted to check for DNA before we could be sure.'

Laura blew her nose. 'I'm sorry,' she said. 'I know it won't make any difference. Nothing's going to bring him back. But I need to know what happened. It's driving me crazy, not knowing who killed him. Why would anyone do that? I mean, why David? He never did anything bad in his life. He didn't deserve that. He was a good man.'

After sending the leather jacket to the lab for examination, Geraldine set off to visit Celia.

'You're seeing a lot of your sister these days,' Sam said, as Geraldine was leaving.

'Yes, well, she's pregnant.'

'You don't have to justify it. I think it's great.'

Geraldine didn't mention that going to see Celia gave her an excuse to postpone visiting her mother in hospital. She wasn't sure why she hadn't felt able to tell anyone about finding her mother, but she needed to sort out her own feelings about her new situation before dealing with other people's reactions to the reunion. Celia would treat the news with suspicion, worried that Geraldine's attention would be snatched away from her and Chloe. Sam was bound to be enthusiastic about it. Geraldine could just imagine her response.

'Oh my God, that's fantastic!'

The trouble was, Geraldine wasn't elated by the thought of the sick pale woman lying in hospital, barely conscious. Her mother remained untouchable.

49

GERALDINE'S BROTHER-IN-LAW ANSWERED the door. Tall and slim, he gave her a characteristically distracted smile.

'Hi Geraldine. Good to see you.'

He leaned down and pecked her on the cheek with soft dry lips.

'Celia's in bed. I'll call up and tell her you're here.'

Geraldine felt a stab of fear. 'No, don't get her up. What's wrong? Has the doctor seen her?'

As she was speaking, Celia appeared on the stairs. 'I'm pregnant,' she laughed. 'I'm not ill for goodness sake. I don't need a doctor. I was just having a rest before you came. I get tired, that's all, and it's good to rest.'

'My wife likes to take things easy,' Sebastian smiled.

Celia reached the bottom of the stairs and came forward, arms outstretched for a welcome hug. Feeling the warmth of physical contact with another woman, Geraldine felt like crying.

'I was just worried about you, that's all,' she muttered into her sister's hair.

'I feel like a hippopotamus,' Celia said, pulling away.

'You look great. It doesn't even show yet.'

They sat in the kitchen with a pot of tea while Sebastian went to collect Chloe from a friend's house. Celia chattered about her pregnancy, pausing only for reassurance that she wasn't boring Geraldine.

'No, no, of course not,' Geraldine lied. 'It's amazing what a complicated business it all is. I mean, it's a natural process but there's so much you have to prepare and do.'

'Yes. I can't believe women used to just squat down and drop it, and then carry on working in the fields,' Celia gave a rueful smile. 'I tell you what, Geraldine, if you're thinking of ever having a family, you seriously need to get on with it. The further you go past forty, the more tiring it is, really.'

'I need to find myself a man first, and I can't see that happening any time soon.'

'Did you look at that online dating agency I mentioned?'

'I looked at it, but I really haven't had time to do anything about it. In any case, my job's bound to put men off, isn't it?'

'Why?'

'Well, I spend most of my time going after criminals –'

'It's what all the youngsters do these days,' Celia interrupted her impatiently. 'Three of the girls at my antenatal class met their partners online. Seriously, Geraldine, you should at least give it a go.'

'Did you say you're going to antenatal classes?' Geraldine asked, seizing the opportunity to divert the conversation back to Celia and her pregnancy.

'Yes, I know this isn't my first, but it's such a long time ago, I've forgotten just about everything. I've no idea what to do.'

'I think it'll happen anyway,' Geraldine said and they both laughed.

'Now,' Celia said when they had discussed her pregnancy some more, 'enough about me. How're things with you?'

'Since last week, you mean? Well,' Geraldine hesitated, 'we think we've cracked the case. We just need to pick up the suspect and hopefully it's all sorted. It should go without a hitch from now on.'

'You don't sound very confident.'

'Unless you have credible independent eye witness accounts, ideally more than one, or CCTV evidence, and a plausible confession, it is difficult to be confident. And even then it's not always cut and dried. There's always room for doubt.'

'Surely no one can disprove a confession? Don't you record everything?'

Geraldine smiled. 'You wouldn't believe the number of false confessions we get.'

'No way! Why would anyone do that?'

'Protecting someone else, nutters, pathological liars – we had one old boy who used to come in on a weekly basis to confess to some crime or other, it didn't seem to matter what. Always on a Thursday. He hasn't been in for a while, now I come to think of it. I wonder what happened to him.'

'That's nuts.'

'The people I deal with in my job aren't always what you might call normal.'

She smiled at Celia. It was a relief to visit her sister and take a break from all the crazy people who inhabited her own world. She sometimes wondered if she was one of them. She wanted to say something to Celia, tell her she was sorry about all the time she had wasted resisting a relationship with her adopted sister. They had never been close when they were growing up together. Now Geraldine was beginning to realise that their shared memories were unique. Before she could think of the right words, Chloe came running in.

'Mum! Mum! Guess what! Lucy's having a disco for her birthday. I have to go! I have to!'

'Chloe, look who's here.'

Celia smiled apologetically at Geraldine. Chloe was nearly a teenager. A visit from her aunt was no longer as exciting as it had once been.

'We must go shopping,' Geraldine said. 'I don't know what to buy you any more.'

'Oh that's OK.' Chloe turned back to her mother. 'I can go, can't I? I told her you'd let me go.'

Geraldine helped Celia clear away the tea things. It was nearly time for supper.

'I can't stay late,' Geraldine said. 'I have to visit someone in hospital on the way home.'

'Nothing serious I hope?'

Geraldine hesitated. Celia had her back to her, checking something in the oven.

'No.'

'Anyone I know?'

'No.'

That, at least, was true. Before she could become embroiled in any more lies, Chloe and Sebastian came in asking when supper would be ready, and they all sat down at the table. The conversation moved on to Chloe who had given up dancing and was now desperate to own a pony.

'Why not? Lucy's got one.'

'Lucy's parents have got a lot more money than us,' Sebastian said.

'It wouldn't cost much,' Chloe pleaded, 'and I'd look after it.'

'A pony is not like a kitten,' Celia said.

'Well, d'uh!' Chloe retorted.

Celia turned to Geraldine. 'See what you're missing?'

Geraldine raised her eyebrows, trying not to smile.

When they finished eating, she stood up and explained once again that she had to go.

'But you've only just got here,' Chloe protested. 'I've hardly seen you.'

'I'll come back next week,' Geraldine promised.

She was too late to visit her mother but called in at the hospital anyway to leave flowers.

'Milly's asleep,' the nurse told her, 'but she wants to see you. She was asking for you this afternoon.'

Geraldine left, promising to return the next day.

50

LENNY WAS UP early on Monday, intending to leave before Gina was stirring so there was no risk of her insisting on accompanying him to the jewellers. He was dressed before she woke up.

'What you up so early for?'

'Jesus, you made me jump. What you doing, creeping up on me like that?'

'You're the one what's creeping around. Where you off to?'

'I'm going to get your ring, like you wanted.'

'Wait up. I'm coming with you.'

'No time now. You should've thought of that before. I'm going now.'

'You better do right by me, Lenny, after all I done for you. You better get me my ring and I don't want no crap.'

She was still railing at him when he slipped out and banged the door shut. Hurrying along the corridor, he was out of the building and away up the street before she could even get dressed. So far so good. Now he had to see what was happening with the jeweller.

Nearly two weeks had passed since his former cell mate, Berny, sent him on what had seemed to be a wild goose chase that had started in East London and ended in a dank basement flat in Dalston. He struggled to remember where it was. At last, after walking for hours, he found the right place.

A skinny man opened the door a fraction and squinted up at Lenny. In the darkness behind him, a dog let out a deep throated growl.

'What you after?' he asked in a hoarse voice, and coughed.

'It's me, it's Lenny. You remember me. It was Berny what sent me.'

Des opened the door just wide enough to admit his visitor. Lenny entered, glancing nervously at the dog.

'Shut it, Bonnie!' Des snapped, and bent double in a fit of coughing.

The dog retreated, still growling.

'You remember me? I brought you a ring to fix.'

The other man nodded his head. 'What you after?' he repeated, and was shaken by another fit of coughing.

'Can't you stick that dog in the bedroom like you done last time?'

'I got company in the bedroom. She don't like Bonnie.'

Lenny didn't believe him, but he was in no position to argue. He knew dogs could sense fear and did his best to hide his nerves as he explained that he had come to collect the ring he had left with Des.

'You was going to do a little job on it for me. I don't want to hassle you or nothing, only my bird's driving me nuts to get her ring back and I could do with the dosh right now anyway. I been cleaned out.'

It was difficult to make out the expression on the jeweller's gaunt face. One of his eyes was permanently half-closed, so that he looked as though he was sizing Lenny up. Apart from that, it was very dark in the room. Little daylight penetrated the dark curtains at the windows.

'You want me to give you back your ring and you want me to hand you over some dough?' Des rasped.

Lenny went through the whole thing again. He had already explained it all to Des when he had given him the ring in the first place. Des had agreed to do the work, claiming it would be easy.

'You can't have forgotten,' Lenny concluded, struggling to

hide his desperation. Something stank, and it wasn't just the dog.

Des walked over to the far end of the room and switched on a lamp to illuminate a workbench covered with a hotchpotch of tools: pliers, files, hammers, saws, a soldering torch, lengths of delicate wire, tweezers, goggles, batteries, pots and brushes. He opened a drawer and pulled out a tangle of gold and silver chains. Putting them aside, he took out a handful of rings, some of them sparkling with gems. In the light of the lamp, he picked through them, searching.

'I forgot your face, but I remember the ring,' he muttered. 'Nice little piece.'

In his relief that Des remembered, Lenny babbled on about what he wanted, the diamond removed and paid for, replaced with a replica piece of glass. Des nodded as his fingers deftly sorted through the rings. At last he picked one out and held it up for Lenny to see.

'This one yours, innit?'

Lenny stepped forward. 'Looks like it.' He didn't add that they all looked the same to him. 'It had a bloody big diamond, anyway. Must be worth a good few grand.'

Des cackled, and began coughing again. 'A few grand? You're having a laugh,' he gasped when he was able to speak.

'What you on about?' Lenny demanded, although he knew well enough where this was heading. 'That's a bloody big rock and I want what it's worth. I could pawn it and buy a cheap one with all the cash they'd give me, and still be better off without you.'

'Your bird would know the difference. Them birds, they always know. You try and trick her, you got to do it clever or you won't get away with it.' Des paused to cough. 'You need it done proper or you're in deep shit.'

'So can you do it?'

'Ain't nothing I can't do.'

'I need it now. And how much will you give me for the rock?'

Des stared at the ring for a moment, then he studied it carefully through an eye glass. 'Looks like a decent stone. I'll give you a grand for it.'

'Make it five.'

Des put the ring down and shook his head 'A grand, or you can take your ice and walk. It ain't worth no more to me. In fact, the honest truth, it ain't even worth that much, what with all the work you want done. It's a skilled job, that. I must be mad, offering you so much. But I know what it's like to have a bird on your back. You got my sympathy, Lenny, that's the honest truth of why I'm giving you such a good price. You'd be mad to walk away. Tell you what, I'll throw in the work for nothing. A grand in your pocket and you walk away with a new ring and she won't never know the difference. I'll put a nice bit of zirconia in a gold-plated ring and it's going to look the business. Even another jeweller won't know, not unless they test it.'

Des put the ring back in his drawer. The dog growled.

Lenny shrugged helplessly. 'When can I come and get it?'

'I'll have it ready in an hour.'

The dog growled again, and Des shouted at it to be quiet. Lenny nodded. He knew when he was beaten. Still, a grand was better than nothing, and on top of it he was being paid to get Gina off his back. He was sorry he had come to see Des. He should have just pawned the ring and walked away with the proceeds, and to hell with Gina and her demands. He'd be better off without the whining bitch. A pawnbroker might give him more than a grand for a rock like that.

'We got a deal?' Des asked.

Lenny hesitated. He would have liked to ask for his ring back, but Des had already closed the drawer and there was no way Lenny could get past him, not with the dog's eyes fixed on him.

'You better make it look good,' he muttered.

'Come back in an hour and your bird won't know no different. Ain't no one else in the whole of London would do a job half as good. Lucky for you, you come to the right bloke.'

51

A PAIR OF plain-clothes constables waited outside the bar on Monday to arrest Jack. They contacted Geraldine to advise her that the suspect hadn't turned up for work that day.

'No one knew you were waiting for him?'

'No one.'

Geraldine went to the bar herself to find out what had happened. Recognising her, the manager sighed when she entered his office. He didn't get up but sat peering at her from the other side of his desk, his thick eyebrows lowered.

'What can I do for you this time, Inspector?'

'It's just routine,' she lied. 'I need you to think very carefully. Can you remember anything about the night of the shooting that you haven't told us yet? Is there any detail that came back to you after it was all over? It's not unusual for people to remember details later on, once the shock has worn off. Is there anything more you can tell me, however small?'

'All I can remember about that evening is that your lot turned up, went stomping all over the place, and chucked all my punters out. Until then, as far as I was aware, it was no different to any other night.'

'We'd like to speak to all your bar staff who were here on the night of the shooting.'

The manager checked a list pinned to the wall 'Well, two of them aren't here, but you can speak to the rest if you have to.'

'Who isn't here?'

'Rafe and Jack.'

'Is it their day off?'

'Yes and no.'

'Don't play games with me.'

'It's Rafe's day off. Jack just hasn't turned up. It happens.'

'Is Jack unreliable?'

'No, not as a rule, but you know how it is with youngsters nowadays. It's good for business to have young, good-looking staff, but they tend to please themselves. Some are worse than others. Jack's generally reliable but he acts like he thinks he's the boss, you know – cocky.'

Geraldine nodded, wary of letting it slip that she was looking for Jack. The manager might alert him deliberately, or he might happen to mention the police visit to someone else who could warn Jack. Whatever happened, Jack mustn't be scared off before they had a chance to question him.

'I'll send a constable in for a quick word with the staff who are here, and you can give me addresses for the two who aren't.'

She would send a couple of constables along to ask the staff if they had remembered anything else. It wouldn't take long, and would scotch any suspicions her visit might otherwise arouse. The manager printed off a document and handed it to her.

'I'm not sure I'm allowed to give you their addresses...'

'We can easily get hold of them anyway,' she reassured him. 'This just saves us time, and of course it's an opportunity for you to show that you're willing to aid us in our enquiries.'

'Of course,' he said quickly. 'We are careful to keep well within the law here.'

'I'm sure you are.'

Sitting in a corner of the restaurant, Geraldine sorted through the statements, trying to piece it all together. Two men who worked at the bar both reported independently that Jack had a close relationship with Katy, who worked behind the bar with them. Geraldine read their statements thoughtfully. The first one had seemed reluctant to voice his suspicions.

'He and Katy had a thing going on.'

'What do you mean, "a thing"?'

'Relations.'

'You mean they were having sex? How do you know?'

'You can just tell, can't you?'

It was very vague. The constable had been under instructions not to appear particularly interested in Jack so the conversation had moved on, leaving nothing resolved.

The second man had been more forthcoming. According to him, Katy was aggressive in her pursuit of Jack.

'Were they having sexual relations?'

'I couldn't say, but she's always mooning around, asking for Jack. She's got the hots for him all right.'

Geraldine decided to speak to Katy herself. She began with the same wording that had been used with all the staff.

'This is just routine. Take your time and think carefully before you answer. Is there something about the night of the shooting that you haven't told us?'

She was surprised when Katy gave a guilty start. 'What the fuck do you mean?'

'Is there any detail that occurred to you, when it was all over? It's very common for witnesses to recall things after the event, once they've got over the initial shock of it all. Can you tell me anything else? Anything at all? You were working upstairs, weren't you? Are you sure you didn't notice anything unusual?'

Katy insisted she couldn't remember noticing anything out of the ordinary that evening. Geraldine approached the next question cautiously, feeling her way.

'One of your colleagues suggested you might be particularly friendly with Jack –'

Katy interrupted her angrily. 'Particularly friendly? What

the hell's that supposed to mean? Who told you that anyway? They're a bunch of busybodies here. Makes me sick.'

'More than one of them appears to be under the impression that you and Jack are very close.'

'Look, I don't know who's been saying what, but it's a load of malicious crap. Sure I like Jack, and he likes me. Nothing wrong with that, is there? But that's all it is.'

'So you're not his girlfriend?'

'Bloody hell, no. Anyway, he's already got a girlfriend.'

'That's not what I heard,' Geraldine said quickly, hoping to draw her out.

'Are you sure?'

'Of course I'm sure.'

'What's her name?'

'Sophia,' Katy responded promptly.

Geraldine really didn't want to sound as though she was interested, but she had to know. 'Sophia what?'

'I don't know.' Katy shrugged. 'What does it matter, anyway?'

'Oh, it's nothing. We're just trying to build a picture of what happened that evening.'

'Well, Jack's girlfriend wasn't here. He never brought her here. But he talked about her. She was doing his head in, poor bloke.'

Geraldine wondered if Katy was hanging on, hoping Jack's relationship with Sophia would come to an end. She wouldn't be the first girl to live in hope like that. Asking the manager to let her know as soon as Jack turned up at work, Geraldine left.

52

BACK AT THE police station, Geraldine went straight to the borough intelligence unit where she spoke to Tom, a burly, good-natured sergeant she had worked with on a previous case. With a large, bald head and finely freckled face, he looked like a speckled brown egg.

'I need you to find a woman for me.'

Tom pulled a face, pushing the corners of his mouth downwards. 'Batting for the other team, are you? So much for my chances then.'

Smiling at his banter, Geraldine continued. 'Her name's Sophia.'

'Sophia? I don't suppose you can tell me her surname?'

'Afraid not.'

'I suspected as much. How about where she lives?'

'If I knew that, I wouldn't be asking you to find her, would I? All I know is that she's called Sophia and she's the girlfriend of our elusive suspect, Jack Bates.'

'Aha.'

'So she's likely to be young as he's only twenty, and probably good looking – and she probably lives somewhere in or around Camden, near him, although that's a guess.'

The borough intelligence officer shook his head. 'You don't give much away, do you? What d'you think we use here? A crystal ball? Oh well, leave it with me, but it might take some time.'

'Thanks.'

'No promises, mind.'

'As quick as you can. We need to find her boyfriend.'

Leaving Tom to look for young women called Sophia, Geraldine returned to her own office. Neil was sitting at his desk, doodling.

'Busy?' she asked him.

He looked up with a grin. 'I hear you've already got the case all but done. That's pretty good going.'

Geraldine was momentarily surprised by his comment. It felt as though the investigation had been dragging on for months. In fact, only just over two weeks had passed since David had been found, shot dead in the mews. She shrugged.

'We haven't actually found our suspect yet, and it's been quite costly so far, getting an armed response unit out to arrest the wrong man.'

Neil laughed. 'All in a day's work. But from the sound of things you've got it pretty well wrapped up.'

Geraldine nodded. She hoped his optimism would prove justified. Apart from questions about the expenses she had sanctioned, the media were whipping up a furore about the unsolved murders in Central London. There had been some flak from restaurants and bars in the area claiming in the news that their takings were down. Even the government was apparently taking notice. At a briefing, Adam had mentioned pressure on the commissioner to resolve the case before tourists were discouraged from visiting London.

'That's ridiculous,' Geraldine had burst out. 'As if we're not already doing everything we can.'

'What the hell do they think we do here?' someone else agreed. 'We're not a PR office for London's tourist trade.'

Geraldine smiled ruefully at Neil. 'I hope you're right about that. Anyway, how's things with you?'

'Oh, nothing much going on today,' he replied. 'Paperwork for the last case is done, and now I'm on call. I dare say something will come in soon. This is London.'

He sounded cheerful but Geraldine sensed his frustration. It was one of the most difficult aspects of the job, flipping between hanging around waiting and full-on adrenaline-charged activity, often with more than a spice of danger thrown in. But Neil was right. Life in London was rarely dull for long.

'Apart from your investigation there doesn't seem to be much going on,' he added. 'I should be pleased it's all quiet out there.'

'You're in the wrong job if you want a quiet life.'

'True. But it won't last.' He paused. 'What are you doing for lunch?'

They went to the nearby pub for a sandwich. Neil had a beer.

'There has to be some consolation for not being on a job,' he said.

'Bearing in mind you could be called at any time.'

'Yes, ma'am.'

It made a pleasant break, popping out for a relaxed lunch with a colleague. They exchanged a few yarns about previous cases they had each worked. After a pleasant half-hour, Geraldine thanked Neil.

'It's been nice to get away for a bit, but I need to get back.'

He nodded. 'Well, I think I'm going to push off. Best of luck with finding your suspect. I'm sure the guys will come up with an address for his girlfriend soon.'

'We haven't given them much to go on, have we?'

'Leave it to the borough intelligence officers. They can find anyone.'

Geraldine hoped he was right, although she doubted they would be able to get anywhere on the strength of a first name. She was sitting at her desk, staring idly at paperwork, when Tom called. With a rush of excitement, she hurried along the corridor to see what he had come up with.

'So far, we've got five women who fit your profile.'

'How the hell did you find them?'

He grinned and tapped the side of his nose. 'Call it genius.'

'Or he could tell you we've all been flat-out, tracing school records and following up anyone called Sophia to see where they're now living,' another VIIDO office said.

'We ruled out a couple because they're mingers,' another constable added.

Tom looked anxious. 'You did say she was pretty, didn't you?'

'Well, we don't know anything about her other than her first name, so we can't rule anyone out, but let's start with the girls who might attract a good-looking young man, yes.'

'So far we've found five who are tolerably attractive, two of them living within a mile of George Berkeley House. One of them lives right there on the estate, on the ground floor.'

'We'll start with her. This could be it. Thanks, Tom.'

'Do you want us to keep looking?'

Geraldine hesitated. 'Yes. Until we find him, we can't let up.'

'Righty ho.'

Geraldine took Sam with her to visit Sophia Dexter, a thirty-year-old woman who lived in George Berkeley House. It was mid-afternoon but Sophia came to the door looking as though she had only just got out of bed.

Geraldine held up her identity card. 'Sophia Dexter?'

'Oh bloody hell. Yes, I'm Sophia. What do you want?'

'Do you live here alone?'

'Wish I did. No. I've got three kids and a boyfriend, when he's around.'

'Is he here now?'

'Yes.'

'We'd like a word with him.'

'Why? What's he done?'

Geraldine explained tersely that he hadn't done anything, but they thought he might have witnessed a crime they were investigating. Sophia laughed.

'I don't think so.'

'What do you mean?'

'He's blind as a bat.'

As she spoke, a man in dark glasses appeared behind her, feeling his way along the wall with one hand. Black and podgy, he couldn't have been less like the fit, young barman they were looking for.

'Who is it?' he asked, leaning forward and inhaling, as though he was trying to identify the visitors from their scent.

'It's the pigs. They come here asking for you because they think you witnessed a crime.'

'Does anyone else live here?' Geraldine interrupted her impatiently.

'My three kids.'

'How old are they?'

Sophia frowned. 'Ten, eight and three. Do you want me to tell you their shoe sizes and all?'

'Who the fuck is it?' the blind man repeated. He sounded tetchy.

'Do you know someone called Jack?' Sam asked in desperation.

'No. Now bugger off, will you?' the woman said, as she closed the door.

Geraldine and Sam turned to Tom's list to see who else lived locally. It was going to be a long job.

53

IT WAS GONE seven by the time Geraldine left work. It would take about half an hour to reach her mother's ward, allowing for traffic and finding a parking space. The hospital visiting policy was fairly relaxed, but they didn't like anyone to stay beyond eight o'clock. She put her foot down, and didn't stop to buy flowers or fruit on the way. Making good time, she arrived in the corridor outside the ward at twenty to eight. Out of breath, more from anxiety than exertion, she stopped for a moment to calm herself, before going in through the large swing doors.

The atmosphere of muted bustle along the corridor contrived to be both restless and soporific. Geraldine found it faintly disturbing. Celia claimed she didn't understand how anyone could work on murder investigations. Geraldine felt exactly the same about hospital staff who dealt with sickness and physical suffering, day in day out, hour after hour. At least Geraldine didn't have to spend all her working week in the company of the worried and the bereaved. As for the victims in her cases, they were beyond suffering. Hospital staff faced a constant battery of human anguish and pain.

'Not everyone dies,' Celia pointed out, when Geraldine said she thought nursing must be a more difficult job than police work. 'People go to hospital to be cured, not to die. In your job, the victims are dead before you even begin.'

Forcing a smile, Geraldine pushed open the door to her mother's room. It was quiet inside. One old woman lay surrounded by visitors who were getting to their feet, preparing to take their leave. They all looked up as Geraldine entered, as though surprised to see someone arriving so late. She walked past them to her mother's bed. It was empty. Frowning, she walked slowly back to the door, looking around the room as she went. The other beds were all occupied by strangers. With growing dread she approached the desk, where a nurse was talking on the phone. After a moment, a second nurse appeared and Geraldine called out to her.

'Excuse me, I'm here to see Milly Blake. Can you tell me where she is? She's been moved.'

'What's that?'

As Geraldine repeated her request, the woman on the phone ended her conversation and looked up. She was young, and she spoke in a friendly manner that inspired confidence.

'Are you her daughter?'

'Yes. Where is she?'

'Oh dear. You didn't get the message?'

'What message?'

The young nurse hurried out from behind the desk and spoke to her gently. With a tremor, Geraldine recognised the hushed tones she herself used when breaking the news of a death. Sounds floated past her. She knew straight away what they meant, before she even registered them as words. The nurse's face seemed to wobble slightly, peering closely at her and receding again.

'I'm so sorry, I'm afraid your mother died three hours ago.'

'What? But she wasn't – I mean, her condition wasn't critical. She was recovering.'

'This woman was a stranger to me,' she thought fiercely. 'I won't cry for someone I didn't know.' But she felt tears prickling the corners of her eyes.

'I'm so sorry. We did all we could. Would you like to say goodbye?'

'Thank you,' she whispered. 'I don't need to see her. I'll just leave.'

'Before you go, she left a letter,' the nurse said. 'She said it was for her daughter. I just need to check your name?'

'Geraldine. My mother called me Erin,' she corrected herself. 'My name is Erin Blake.'

For an instant, she thought the nurse was going to demand to see some kind of identification before handing over the letter. She had her birth certificate at home, together with all the adoption papers, but nothing to prove she was her mother's daughter apart from an old photograph of her mother which looked exactly like her. If the hospital staff refused to believe her, she might never read her mother's parting words to her – almost her only words to her. As these confused thoughts whirled through her mind, the nurse fished out an envelope from behind the desk.

'Here you are,' she said, with a practised air of sympathy. 'It's from your mother.'

Geraldine glanced at the envelope. It was addressed to Erin Blake, in shaky handwriting.

'Thank you.'

She turned and walked quickly out of the ward where she had seen her mother twice, and heard her voice just once. Driving home she tried to recall what her mother had said to her during their one conversation. Milly had been finding it difficult to speak. Almost all she had said was that she wanted Geraldine to find Erin. That had been one more disappointment because clearly she hadn't recognised her daughter at all, mistaking her for someone else, a nurse perhaps, or the social worker. It was a bitter realisation.

Her mother would never let her down again. She had died before Geraldine had a chance to ask her all the questions that now crowded her head. She would never know who her father was; never learn how her mother had felt on giving her up for adoption; why she had refused to see her lost daughter, or whether she had even cared. As she drove, stony-faced, she realised her eyes were streaming with tears.

'I won't cry for a stranger,' she muttered, angrily wiping her eyes on her sleeve.

The first thing she did on reaching home was open a bottle of her favourite red wine. She had been avoiding alcohol in a futile attempt to clear her brain as she sifted through contradictory evidence, while every few days Adam seemed to latch on to a different suspect with an alacrity that hardly inspired confidence, as though he thought the truth would be obvious, once they spotted it. His air of cool detachment was a sham. At the same time, Geraldine realised that her emotional confusion over her mother had been making her hypercritical of all her colleagues. Steering clear of alcohol hadn't helped her to see her way clearly through any of the mess.

'Sod it,' she thought, as she poured herself a large glass. She held it up, admiring the beautiful crimson hue. It didn't make her feel any better. Half an hour later, she was in tears again. She wasn't crying over the death of a woman she had never known. She was crying for her own solitude, and for what might have been.

54

EVERYONE TOLD ALISTAIR he was lucky to be partnered by PC Ned Allsop, an experienced police officer close to retirement.

'Ned knows the ropes,' they all said, 'and he's a good bloke, salt of the earth.'

Alistair gazed gloomily out of the window at pedestrians hurrying by. He had been looking forward to careering along Oxford Street, siren wailing, blue light flashing, weaving in and out of the London traffic at speed while other vehicles darted aside to let them pass. He did his best to hide his impatience because he didn't want to offend his partner. Ned was a decent guy, but crawling in traffic beside an old bloke like him wasn't much fun.

'I wish something would happen,' he said.

'It will. Sooner or later, something's going to kick off, and we'll be called in to pick up the pieces for which we'll get no thanks, just abuse. I'll be glad to get out,' Ned admitted. 'Everything's changed. I remember belting along, no need for sirens and flashing lights. Other drivers just moved over to let us pass. Respect. That's what we used to have. Deference.'

The radio crackled out a message. A fight had broken out in a side street nearby.

'Calling all units in the vicinity of Marylebone Passage off Margaret Street and Wells Street.'

'We're one minute away. How many people are involved?' Ned snapped as he swung the wheel.

'Two youths, IC1 male, one or possibly both carrying knives. Back-up is on the way.'

Ned turned to his young companion. 'There's two of them got into a fight, one or possibly both armed with knives. You wanted to see some action, didn't you? We should be first on the scene.'

'I'm up for it! Let's go! Shall I put the siren on?'

Ned nodded and Alistair turned on the siren, grinning as they nudged their way through the dense traffic. It was still slow going, but at least they were making their presence felt.

'This could be bloody, you know,' Ned warned his companion. 'Someone's likely to get hurt. Make sure you don't do anything stupid.' He broke off at a sudden thought. 'You remembered your stab vest, didn't you?'

'Of course.'

They pulled up in a side street, jumped out of the car, and ran towards a small crowd that had gathered to watch two young men. Alistair glanced around, apprehensive now they had arrived. He and his colleague were the first officers on the scene. There were about a dozen onlookers, mostly male, all in their twenties or thirties. If they turned on him and Ned, he and his colleague wouldn't stand a chance. As they drew near to the fracas, he heard sirens approaching. That must have been the cue Ned was waiting for, because he broke into a trot.

'Break it up now,' Ned called out, as he sprinted forwards.

Two men were facing one another, one fair haired, the other dark. As Ned pushed his way into the centre of the circle the blond fighter staggered and fell to the ground, bleeding from a gash on his arm. The dark-haired one stood, knees bent, knife in hand, glaring at Ned as though daring him to approach. For a second no one moved. Alistair was relieved and, at the same time, irrationally disappointed to see two more patrol cars arrive to block both exits from the street.

'Put the knife down before someone gets hurt,' Ned said calmly.

The armed man slashed the air with his blade. 'Back off, pig.'

With a burst of anger, Alistair barged through the watching crowd, and dashed to Ned's side. With two police officers standing firm against him, the knife-wielding thug didn't stand a chance. It was over. Shaking with relief, Alistair kept his face immobile.

Without warning, the dark-haired youth leaped across to his victim who was still lying on the ground, moaning. Seizing the injured man round the neck, the armed man held the point of his knife at his opponent's throat.

'Back off or he croaks.'

'Don't do anything rash, lad,' Ned said quietly, taking a step forward. 'This is just a scrap that's got out of hand. You don't want to be done for murder. With so many witnesses, there's no way you'd be pleading manslaughter. There's no getting away from it. You're surrounded. Do yourself a favour and drop the knife, and let's get that bleeding stopped or you might still be had up on a murder charge.'

The man with the knife hesitated. All at once his shoulders dropped and the knife clattered to the ground. As soon as he let it fall, the blond man sat up and socked him on the jaw. They wrestled for a moment.

'You take the dark guy, I'll take the blond one,' Ned snapped.

Alistair and Ned pulled them apart and handcuffed them.

The wounded man began to groan. 'I need a doctor.'

'All in good time,' Ned assured him. 'You're not going to die.'

'Get these fucking handcuffs off me now. You can see I'm bleeding. This is fucking police brutality. Get them off me!'

'Don't overdo the gratitude,' Ned said. 'Wc only saved your life.'

'I would've had him if you hadn't interfered,' the blond man snarled. 'This ain't over, Jack.'

'Like fuck it ain't,' the other man retorted.

'Well, your gratitude makes it all worthwhile,' Ned said. 'I just saved your life, and saved you from going down for murder, and all you can do is complain.'

'Too bloody right I'm gonna complain. You got no right interfering in my business,' the dark-haired man spat. 'I'm gonna get you.'

'Come along now, Jack, is it? You're coming with us. If you want to add threatening a police officer to the list of charges we've got against you, that's up to you.'

55

As usual, Geraldine went into work early the next morning. She spent a couple of hours reading through Theo's statements, failing to make any sense out of them. Ready for a break, she was relieved to be summoned to the incident room. Anything was better than kicking her heels at her desk, reading nonsense that made her head ache with frustration.

'It sounds like something important's come up,' Neil said. 'The DCI wouldn't be calling everyone together just for a pep talk.'

'Have you worked with Adam before?'

'No.'

Geraldine just grunted before leaving the room. She understood that Neil was trying to be encouraging, but until she heard what Adam had to say, she wasn't going to get her hopes up. The case so far had been full of disappointment. Like her life. Doing her best to shake off her depressing thoughts, she made her way along the corridor to the major incident room. On the way, she heard Sam calling her name. Reluctantly, she slowed down and allowed the sergeant to catch up with her.

'What's going on?'

Geraldine shook her head. 'Search me. We'll find out soon enough. Come on.'

'I don't mean about this meeting. I mean you. Are all right?'

'Yes. Why wouldn't I be?'

Sam frowned. 'I don't know. It's just that – well, you've just been looking so down lately, I just wondered if something was wrong. If it's me, if I've done something to piss you off, I'd rather you just told me, only you seem to be avoiding me.'

'Don't be ridiculous. It's just this bloody investigation doing my head in.'

They reached the incident room and Geraldine hurried in ahead of Sam, keen to avoid her questions. If she *was* feeling distressed, that was no one else's business. She would talk about her mother when she felt ready. They didn't have long to wait before the detective chief inspector arrived. He strode in, looking more cheerful than Geraldine had seen him for a while.

'Good morning everyone.' There was a faint muttering in response. 'We've had a stroke of luck,' he went on loudly. 'At last, things are going our way. Two men were apprehended last night in a knife fight, not far from Oxford Circus station. They were taken to the local station where it was discovered that one of them is our suspect, Jack Bates.' He looked around with a triumphant grin. 'Thank Christ for the stupidity of criminals. Here we are chasing around all over the place trying to find the bastard, and he turns up and as good as hands himself in!'

A murmur rustled round the team. Someone cheered. The atmosphere in the room changed. Officers who had walked in looking weary and disgruntled appeared transformed.

'He'll be here shortly,' Adam went on, 'so let's be ready for him. The duty brief needs to be called, so that we can get started as quickly as possible. Well done, everyone, for all the hard work that's gone into this. I know we've been running around like blue-arsed flies, but it's all been worth it. We've got him.'

'He's not the one who's been running around,' Sam muttered to Geraldine.

'It's more through luck than hard work that we've found him,' Geraldine replied.

'It's as good as over,' Adam went on. 'The suspect's safely

in custody and with so much evidence stacked up against him, a conviction is a stone-cold certainty. Now, let's get going and wrap this up.'

'Typical,' Sam complained, grinning broadly. 'All our leg work gets us nowhere and then some patrol car just picks him up, just like that. I wonder who'll get all the glory?'

'This job isn't about glory,' Geraldine retorted sharply. 'In any case, let's not count our chickens.'

'What do you mean?'

'He was carrying a knife, wasn't he?'

'I know. That's why they took him in, isn't it?'

'Doesn't it strike you as odd that he was carrying a knife, not a gun, when a gun seems to be his weapon –'

'That's because we've got his gun!' Sam's round face creased in a broad grin. 'Look, are you sure you're OK? I mean, you don't seem exactly pleased we've got him...'

'Of course I'm pleased. I'm just a bit preoccupied...'

On the point of admitting that she had found her mother, only to lose her again, Geraldine hesitated. It was a complicated situation to explain in the few minutes they had together, walking along the corridor. It wasn't the right setting. They could be interrupted at any moment. But this was not the right time to take a break. She needed to prepare the interview.

'Thinking about your questions? Sorry. I'll leave you to get ready.'

Sam turned away. Wanting to call her back and talk to her, instead Geraldine stood silently, watching her colleague walk away. There was something robust and frank about Sam that Geraldine found reassuring yet unaccountably intimidating at the same time. With a sigh she returned to her office, resolving to tell Sam all about her mother when the case was over. It was looking as though that wouldn't be long now.

'Well?' Neil asked her, as she sat down at her desk.

Although she had only just learned that their suspect had

been apprehended, it seemed surprising that her colleague hadn't yet heard about the latest development. Under normal circumstances she would have enjoyed passing on the news. But this was not a normal day. Her mother was dead. Her back to Neil, she told him they had caught the suspect.

'Now, if you don't mind, I need to get ready.'

'Of course.'

Without turning round she couldn't tell if he was offended by her curt response, but she didn't care. Struggling to cope with the loss of the only blood relative she had ever met, she had to focus on Jack Bates and the fall-out from the deaths of more people she had never known.

56

'How DID YOU get your hands on David Lester's leather jacket?'

The young man glared sullenly straight ahead, refusing to look at her. He had classical good looks, with a long face, high cheekbones and a thin, straight nose.

'I dunno what you're on about. I never had no leather jacket.'

For the tape, Geraldine described the exhibit that was being brought to the table.

'We found this in your wardrobe at your home in George Berkeley House. It has your DNA and prints all over it indicating that you wore it before you hung it in your wardrobe.'

'So what? It's mine. It's my jacket, innit?'

Geraldine paused, wondering how to deal with such stupid lies. If the suspect continued to contradict himself so freely, they would have no trouble getting him to implicate himself. The interview had barely started and he had already managed to undermine his own credibility. The duty lawyer stirred in his chair but said nothing. Geraldine wondered what he was up to, allowing his client to drop himself in it so completely. It was obvious Jack had taken David's jacket. It was too far-fetched to claim the suspect owned a jacket exactly the same as the one the victim had been wearing the night he was killed, especially as the victim's jacket had unaccountably disappeared when he was shot.

'This jacket, which was found in your wardrobe, was identified by the victim's wife as identical to the one her husband was wearing the night he was shot.'

'Is this jacket unique in any way?' the lawyer asked.

'Other than yielding DNA from both the victim and your client, you mean?'

The lawyer scowled at her. She returned her attention to Jack.

'Are you sure this is your jacket?'

'Is what I said, innit?'

'Where did you buy it?'

He shrugged. 'I dunno.'

'Come on, Jack, you must remember where you bought it. It's a Ralph Lauren, must have cost you over a thousand quid. Surely you can't forget a purchase like that. Where did you get it?'

'I got it off a mate, all right? I never paid no grand for no fucking jacket.'

'What's your mate's name?'

'What?'

'The mate you bought this jacket from.'

'I never bought no leather jacket. I never seen it before.'

'Jack, stop playing games. This jacket was in your wardrobe.'

'Says you.'

'You admitted a moment ago, on tape, that it's yours. So let's try again. When did you get it?'

'I ain't saying nothing about it.'

'What if he did steal it?' the lawyer chipped in, 'that has no bearing on this case. My client hasn't been arrested for theft.'

'I never nicked nothing. Jesus, man, I thought you was supposed to be on my side.'

Seeing Jack was rattled, Geraldine continued.

'A leather jacket identified by the first victim's widow as identical to the one her husband was wearing the night he was shot was found hanging up in your wardrobe. The dead man's jacket has disappeared. The evidence is beginning to stack up, and it's not looking good for you, Jack. Why don't you do yourself a favour and tell us what happened that night in

Wells Mews? You never meant to shoot anyone, did you? You were only out to mug him. Bloke in expensive gear, must be loaded, you chanced upon him when he was pissed and lost in a dark alleyway. It was too good an opportunity to miss. It's a nice jacket, isn't it? You only meant to take his jacket off him, but then it all went wrong and you shot him. Why? What happened? If you cooperate with us the court will be lenient. Your clever lawyer there will convince them it was all a mistake. Manslaughter. You never meant to shoot him, did you? You only wanted his jacket.'

'Which appears to have no blood stains,' the lawyer said, 'despite its wearer being shot in the chest.' He shook his head. 'You'll have to come up with something better than this, Inspector.'

Jack grinned and clicked his fingers. 'That's my man.'

Geraldine suggested David had handed over the jacket before he was shot.

Jack's lawyer robustly refuted her theory. 'You're making this up as you go along. You've no proof against my client. And luckily for him, your version of events doesn't add up. If all he wanted was the victim's jacket, why would he have shot him after he had got what he wanted? You know perfectly well someone else came along and robbed the victim.'

Jack turned to the lawyer. 'You mean the guy what shot him?'

Now Geraldine was confused. 'What guy?' She leaned forward. 'Tell us what guy you're talking about.'

Unexpectedly, Jack caved in. 'All right, all right, I'll tell you what happened. Only stop going on at me. You're driving me nuts.'

According to Jack's garbled account, David had been to the bar where Jack worked. He hadn't stayed long and had gone leaving his jacket behind.

'This leather jacket?'

'Yeah, that's what we been talking about, innit?'

As he was collecting glasses, Jack had seen the jacket, grabbed it and rushed after the customer, hoping to catch up with him. He didn't think anyone else had noticed the jacket in the corner, and he didn't stop to tell any of his colleagues, who were all busy behind the bar. Outside in the street, he had caught sight of the man who had left the jacket behind and had run to catch up with him.

'I went after him out of the goodness of me heart,' he added. Following as far as Wells Mews, Jack had just turned the corner when he heard a gunshot up ahead. He turned and fled, with the jacket still over his arm.

'It was a nice jacket, so I kept it.'

'When you entered Wells Mews you heard a shot?'

He nodded.

'What else? What did you see?'

'Nothing. I didn't look or nothing. I legged it.'

'Why didn't you call the police?'

'What for?'

'Police, ambulance, someone had just been shot.'

'Nothing to do with me. I never even saw nothing.'

'You could have saved someone's life.'

'Landed myself in a heap of shit more like.'

'You mentioned he was shot by a man.'

'I never saw nothing.'

'Let's talk about the gun that was used in a shooting in Wells Mews, and subsequently in another shooting in the bar where you work, the gun that your brother, Theo, had in his possession.'

At the mention of Theo's name, Jack's demeanour altered. He sat up in his chair and his expression changed from sullen to openly hostile.

'You leave my bro outa this,' he said, after which he sat in obdurate silence.

At the lawyer's insistence, Geraldine drew the interview to a close for the day and went back to her office. She was writing up her report when the detective chief inspector summoned her.

'Oh shit,' she muttered.

'Trouble?' Neil asked.

She just shrugged. Adam wasn't going to be any happier than she was at the way Jack's interview had gone.

'Let's just say we haven't got a confession yet.'

'Are you deliberately setting out to look for problems? Reg warned me about you.' Before Geraldine had a chance to react to the reference to her previous DCI, Adam laughed. 'Don't look so aggrieved. There's nothing worse than people who don't think for themselves, especially in this job. A colleague who never challenges anything might as well not be here at all. But you don't need to feel duty bound to challenge *everything*. The fact is, we have Jack Bates behind bars, and there's no question that he's guilty. All the evidence points in his direction – compelling physical evidence. OK, there's nothing specific that places him, gun in hand, at Luke's shooting, but we know he was in the bar, working upstairs, and it's his gun, and we know he used it to kill David. You can't argue with the facts, Geraldine.'

Geraldine refrained from pointing out that it was only a week since the detective chief inspector had been convinced Lenny was their killer. In his determination to wrap the case up promptly, she was afraid he was rushing to conclusions. He was an able superior officer, but he wasn't much older than her and this was his first case as a detective chief inspector.

'What about Lenny?' she couldn't help asking.

A disgruntled expression crinkled Adam's youthful face, making him look older. 'What about him? We know he was here when Luke was shot so he can't be the gunman. I'm no happier about it than anyone else, but we can't go after him any more, not for these shootings anyway, and his account of his presence in Wells Mews is credible, at least.'

'As is Jack's explanation of how he came to have David's leather jacket hanging in his wardrobe.'

'And the gun? I know it was Jack's brother who was found with it on his person, but he's hardly a credible suspect, and how could he have got hold of it anyway? Luke was shot in Jack's presence –'

'We don't know he was actually there when the shooting took place –'

'With Jack in the building, and next thing we know the same gun pops up in Theo's hand one week later. How the hell did he get hold of it, if not from Jack?'

'I don't know.'

'First thing in the morning we lean on Jack and get him to talk. Now you get off home and make sure you're here early tomorrow.' He grinned, bright eyed. 'We're this close to securing a conviction. Let's not screw it up. That's all that matters right now.'

57

GINA HELD HER hand up. The diamond didn't seem as sparkly as the first time she had seen it, but she supposed that was because the ring wasn't so new. It must have been handled while it was being resized.

'They could've given it a clean while they·was at it,' she grumbled.

'What you complaining for, woman? Always complaining. It fits, don't it? First it's too big, then it's not clean enough for you. If that bloody great rock ain't good enough for you, I can give it to my mum. She won't drive me nuts complaining about it, that's for sure. What you after, anyway? The bleeding crown jewels. Come here then, I got something else for you.'

He lunged at her, grabbed her hand, and put it on his cock. She smiled nervously and snatched her hand away.

'Give over, Lenny. It's a lovely ring. I'm real pleased you got it to fit right, course I am, and I won't never take it off now we're engaged.'

Lenny jumped up out of the armchair where he was lounging. 'Jesus, will you stop saying that. It's only a ring so don't you go running off with your fancy ideas. As if I'm gonna get hitched to you! What the fuck would I do that for? What you got?' He forced a laugh. 'You win the lottery and then we'll talk. Look, it's a ring, right. A bloody nice ring and all. And I ain't saying as you don't deserve it, because you do. That's why I give it you. Jesus, I coulda sold it and not had none of this. It's a ring, baby. Get over it. That's all it is. Bloody hell. Why would I want to get hitched? What the hell for?'

Gina was shocked. 'How can you be such a shit? After all I done for you. I done more than anyone in her right mind would ever do and I done it because you and me – look!' She held up her hand. 'What the fuck is this if it ain't an engagement ring? And what the hell's that if it don't mean I'm gonna be your wife? What the fuck, Lenny? What's wrong with getting married anyway? You said. You promised me.'

He sat down again and put his head in his hands. 'Well, maybe I said stuff,' he admitted, 'but then again maybe I was drunk when I said it.'

'Then you can bloody well get drunk when you marry me. You promised me, Lenny.'

'Well I ain't gonna do it so you can just shut the fuck up about it. You hear me? Shut the fuck up, woman! Oh fuck you, I'm going out.'

'Running back to your ma?'

'I can go where I like. I ain't in prison no more and you ain't my screw.'

'Well, you can just fuck off then.'

Lenny stormed out of the house. She was glad to see the back of him. It was the last time she was going to put up with his lies. She had offered him one last chance to be good to her and he had given her his answer. Bawling, she went upstairs to the bedroom. While he was out of the way she had a chance to pack her bag and leave. She had suspected for a long time that it would end like this. The ring had given her the chance to get away and she wasn't going to blow it this time. Such opportunities didn't come twice. She would pawn the ring, and head off. Anything would be better than this. With cash in her pocket, she could please herself. Lenny had tried to deny it afterwards, but he had let slip that it could be worth tens of thousands. If she couldn't have him, she would at least get her hands on the dough. Money couldn't lie.

Sobbing, she packed her clothes into his big suitcase on wheels. His bitch of a mother ruined everything. If Lenny died while he had some dosh, or some gear that was worth something, Gina would get fuck-all because she wasn't his wife. After she had lived with him for so long, looking after him when he was sick, waiting for him when he was banged up, she would have to watch Cynthia cop the lot. Not that Lenny had much to leave, but anything was better than nothing, and it would be typical of him to have a big win on the horses just before he croaked. Well, if he was so keen for his mother to get her hands on everything, he could go fuck himself for being such a prick. She'd find someone who would look after her properly, someone who didn't have a mother out for whatever she could get. She must have been an idiot to stay with him for so long.

The first jewellers she went to on the High Street didn't do valuations.

'We can send it away for you,' the heavily made-up shop assistant said, tapping Gina's stone with a long red nail. 'It's a nice ring. Nice design. When are you getting married?'

'I ain't sending it away no place,' Gina replied, pulling her hand away. 'I want someone as can value it and give me my money straight away.'

'You're better off going to Hatton Garden.'

'Oh right.'

It was the same in the first three shops she went in. She was growing desperate by the time she entered the fourth jewellers. With a narrow shop front and dingy interior, she expected the same brush-off but the old man behind the counter smiled and nodded when she asked if he could do a valuation there and then.

'Depends what it is,' he replied.

Gina held up her hand, displaying her ring. The old man scrutinised it and asked her to remove it.

'You ain't taking it away no place.'

'Don't worry, I'll just take a look at it right here, where you can see me.'

She took off the ring and handed it to him. The old man pushed an eye glass into one eye and switched on a bright light so that he could examine it. Turning it one way, then the other, he held it up to his lips and breathed on it before studying it again. Finally, he returned it to her.

'Zirconia.'

'What?'

'I thought as much when you first showed it to me on your finger. It doesn't reflect any colours, you see. It's a pretty enough design made to look reasonably authentic, but it's only a bit of zirconia.'

'What do you mean?'

'This isn't a diamond. It's zirconia. The band is worthless too, I suspect, although I'd need to check to be sure.'

Gina snatched her ring and replaced it on her finger. 'You telling me this ain't no diamond?'

'I'm afraid that's exactly what I'm saying. Diamonds reflect colours. Look, you can see it doesn't even sparkle when you hold it up to the light. If it was a genuine diamond, you'd be able to see different colours reflected from it, even with the naked eye. Especially one this size. Even a flawed diamond would show some colour. And this hasn't got any visible flaws, which is another indication that it's fake. If it was a real diamond it would be worth a fair few thousand.'

'Could it be your shit light?' she asked uncertainly.

'Hold it up in the sunlight you'll see the same. Tell you what, you can test it for yourself. Breathe on it. Go on. A diamond doesn't retain heat so if the stone looks at all cloudy when you breathe on it, you know it's a fake. Go on, try it.'

'What will you give me for it? I mean, you could sell it as if it was real, couldn't you? So it don't make no difference, not really. No one would know. You said it'd be worth thousands.'

The old man shook his head at her. 'You're nuts, lady,' he said. 'I got a reputation. I'll give you a fiver for it, and that's a good offer.'

58

THE NEXT MORNING Geraldine was called by the desk sergeant who told her Rosa Bates had turned up and was causing a scene. With a sigh, Geraldine went along to see what was happening. On the way she took a detour down to the custody suite.

'Your suspect's quiet as a lamb,' the custody sergeant told her with a grin. 'We don't get many happy chappies down here.'

She took a look through the peephole at Theo who was sitting on his bunk. His lips were moving as though in prayer.

'He slept like a baby, and he's been singing to himself ever since he woke up for his breakfast,' the sergeant said. 'Not right in the head. I don't think he knows where he is.'

Thanking her colleague, Geraldine went to find out what Theo's mother was complaining about. The desk sergeant was a large, red-faced man who leaned forward earnestly, lowering his booming voice as he explained that on Rosa's arrival he had assured her new information had come in which meant Theo would be released. According to his account, Rosa had insisted on taking Theo home straight away. The sergeant had advised her to be patient. Nothing moved swiftly at the police station; due process had to be followed, and so on. He had assured her that he was sure it wouldn't take long but she had flown off the handle once again, screaming about justice for her son.

'But your son's out of the frame,' the sergeant had protested. 'What's your problem?'

He hadn't been able to quieten her ranting and had summoned

a female constable to take her to an interview room and watch her. Before she left the custody sergeant, Geraldine told him that the new suspect was also Rosa's son.

'What? She's got two sons and first one now the other is a suspect for the same murders?' he repeated in a low voice. 'I wouldn't want to be around when she's told why this one's being released. She's going to go apeshit.'

Reluctantly, Geraldine went to the room where Rosa was being looked after and told her Jack had been apprehended fighting in the street. Already distraught, Rosa leapt to her feet and launched into a hysterical tirade accusing the police of targeting her sons.

'You couldn't make nothing stick against Theo, so now you gone and started on Jack. What is it with you people? My boys never done nothing wrong. We ain't done nothing to you. Go and get my boys right now or I'm going to the telly, and I'm going to tell everyone what you done. You got no right to lock my boys up. All Jack done was get in a scrap with another lad. You got no business victimising my family like this!'

Geraldine let her rave for a few minutes, waiting for her to run out of energy. When it seemed that she was only winding herself up even more, Geraldine interrupted her firmly.

'You need to sit down and listen to me.'

'You need to let my boys go.'

All at once, Rosa slumped down on a chair and burst into tears. Quietly, Geraldine assured her that Jack would receive appropriate legal support.

'The last thing we want to do is send a case to court that isn't going to stand up. If there's any doubt that Jack is implicated in the recent shootings, he will be released. But as things stand, the case against him is compelling.'

'Bullshit. He got in a fight, that's all.'

'We think we can prove he was involved in the shooting of two men. That may not be what happened, but we have to proceed on the basis of the evidence. We're still analysing the data and talking to witnesses. Until we finish conducting our investigation, Jack will be staying where he is, in custody. He's being well looked after, and you can visit him, but he's not going home and there's nothing anyone can do about it. When we've concluded our investigation, if we still think Jack is responsible, it will be up to the Crown Prosecution Service to weigh up all the evidence and decide whether or not to go ahead with a prosecution. There's nothing you can do to stop this, Rosa. Two men have died. We have to take our investigation seriously and I'm sure you can understand that.'

'I understand you been fitting up my son.'

There was nothing more Geraldine could say. In a multiple murder enquiry there was no prospect of bail. All she could do was encourage Rosa to take Theo home. There was no question of her seeing Jack straight away as he was seeing his lawyer, after which he was going into an interview.

'So when *can* I see him?' Rosa wailed as Geraldine stood up to leave.

Geraldine turned to the constable who was sitting with Rosa. 'Look after this, will you? Get her another cup of tea and send her on her way.'

'I'm not going without my boys!' Rosa shrieked as Geraldine left the room.

Jack was even more sullen than he had been the day before. To begin with he refused to answer any questions.

Adam challenged him about his arrest. 'There's no point in trying to deny it. What were you fighting about? Why did you stab him? Think carefully. Remember we have witnesses who saw exactly what happened. We know you started the fight.'

'Him getting jiggy with my bitch so I shank him.'

Geraldine held out a photograph of a naked girl they had found on his phone. 'Is this your girlfriend?'

'What you doing with my gear? You got no right to look at

my phone. I never give you permission. It's private. You got no right looking at that.'

'Where did you get the gun from?' Geraldine asked, putting the photograph away.

'What gun? I never had no gun.'

'We're talking about the gun you gave to your brother, Theo.'

'What you talking about? I never had no gun.'

Adam leaned forward. He spoke very softly. 'You mean Theo got a gun all by himself?'

Jack looked worried.

'Theo was arrested with a gun in his possession, a gun that was used to shoot two people dead. We thought maybe you might know something about that. But if you didn't give your brother the gun, then it seems he's guilty after all.'

'Guilty? What you mean he's guilty? Theo ain't done nothing.'

Adam replied that if Jack hadn't shot two people and given the weapon to his brother to hide, then Theo must be solely responsible for what had happened.

Jack glared at the detective chief inspector. 'What you on, man? Theo ain't never done nothing to you.'

'No,' Adam leaned forward, sensing his advantage, 'but he shot two men and they're dead. He's going down for a long time. He may never come out. I can't see him surviving long behind bars.'

Geraldine thought of Theo singing happily to himself in the cell, and said nothing.

'Man, you full of shit.'

'The gun was found in your brother's possession. A jacket belonging to one of the victims was found in your locked room. The other victim was shot at the premises where you work, while you were there. What happened, Jack? Was it you or Theo who shot those men? You can't continue to pretend you know nothing about it. Who was it, Jack? You or your brother?

Or were you in it together? Come on, Jack, you need to give me an answer,' Adam insisted.

'We need to take a break,' the lawyer said. 'I have to talk to my client.'

59

'DAMN IT,' ADAM fumed, 'we had him. He was about to confess when the bloody brief interrupted. You saw it on his face, didn't you? I'm not imagining things. We had him.'

'We'll be back on it soon,' Geraldine replied.

'We have to keep the pressure up. Did you see his face when I pinned him down? He knew the game was up, and his blinking brief knew it too. That's why he was so quick to insist on taking a break. It was him or Theo, it had to be one or other of them.'

Geraldine wondered if Jack was guilty or just concerned about his brother, and whether Theo would be capable of using a gun, but she didn't contradict her superior officer.

'One more minute in there and we'd have had him,' he insisted, glancing at his watch. 'We need to get back on it as quickly as possible.'

When they sat down again, the lawyer spoke first.

'My client would like to confess. He found the gun at his place of work after the shooting took place. That was the first time he had ever been in possession of this or any gun. He deeply regrets that, instead of handing the gun in to the police as he now recognises he should have done, he took it home with him. He is adamant that he never had any intention of using it. The gun was to be used for self-defence only.'

Behind his mask of composure, Geraldine sensed Adam's disappointment. Pressing his lips together, he nodded.

'I never done it,' Jack muttered. 'Whatever you said, I never done it.'

'You need to be more specific,' Geraldine said.

Adam glanced at her then repeated her words. 'Tell us exactly what happened.'

'I never done it. I never shot them two geezers, like you said I done. I lifted the old guy's jacket and legged it outta there, just like I told you. I heard a shot, but I never seen nothing. The other geezer what was shot in the bar, I never shot him neither. I only found the gun and took it home. But it weren't me what shot him and it weren't Theo neither. And that's all I gotta say. My blad, he ain't never used a shooter in his life. He wouldn't know what the fuck to do with no shooter. So you leave him alone. This ain't nothing to do with him. He don't even know what a gun is. He don't know nothing, I'm telling you.'

'So you found the jacket in the bar on the night its owner was shot, and then a few days later you found a gun there after another man was shot. A jury might find that hard to believe,' Geraldine said, 'so let's try again and this time you need to answer our questions truthfully.'

'My client has nothing more to say,' the lawyer replied.

Persuaded that Jack wasn't going to add anything to his statement, Adam stood up and gathered his papers together as the suspect was escorted from the interview room.

'He gave a neat explanation for having the gun without saying anything that implicates him in the shootings,' he burst out when he and Geraldine were alone. 'I'm not convinced by his account, but a jury might swallow it. I'm just saying – it's something we need to consider. He confessed he took the gun, Geraldine, but we need more than that.'

'What if it was Theo all along?'

Adam sat down again abruptly. 'The thought did occur to me. To be honest, Geraldine, I've no idea whether it was the nutter or the wide boy, or if they were both in on it together, but whichever one of them it was, he has to be stopped. And if Jack's statement's a lie, and that comes out, then he might be lying about the shooting too.' He shook his head, but he was smiling. 'It has to be one or other of them. So if we're not ready to break open the champagne yet, we can put it on ice.'

He jumped up and held the door for Geraldine. She couldn't help returning his smile, although she felt his triumph was a little premature.

'Champagne, eh?' she replied. 'It was a pint of bitter with my previous DCI. Things are looking up!'

'That's more like it. I was beginning to think you suspected we'd arrested the wrong bloke.'

Geraldine didn't point out that it wouldn't be the first time that had happened on this case. First Lenny, then Theo, and now Jack, had been accused of killing David Lester. She hoped they had the right man at last.

'We need Jack to make a full confession. We know what he did with the gun afterwards, now we need him to own up that he shot both men.'

As Adam strode away, Geraldine checked her phone and saw a missed call. There was no message. She went outside to call back.

'Hi Louise, it's Geraldine – that is, Erin – Milly Blake's daughter. You phoned?'

'Yes. We wondered if you would like to be involved in the funeral arrangements?'

'What?'

'For your mother. Would you like to discuss it? We can make the arrangements for you, if you prefer not to be involved.'

Geraldine's breath caught in the back of her throat so that she couldn't speak for a second. 'It's not something I've really thought about. I mean, I've no idea what she would have wanted.'

'It's up to you, as her next of kin. But if you'd rather not be involved, you don't have to be. You just have to say the word.'

'Can I think about it?'

'Of course. And did the hospital give you a letter from your mother? Only the ward sister mentioned it –'

'Yes, they gave it to me.'

As they were talking, Geraldine walked over to a row of silver birches growing beside the car park. She was dimly aware of the faint rustling of the wind in the leaves above her head.

'Oh good. And I take it there was no mention in the letter about what she wanted at her funeral?'

Geraldine hesitated to admit that she hadn't opened the letter yet. She had put it in the drawer beside her bed, along with the one old photograph she had of her mother.

'I'd like to think about it,' she repeated. 'When do you need to know by?'

'There's no rush. Shall we speak tomorrow?'

'Tomorrow?'

'Yes.'

'OK. I'll call you tomorrow.'

She hung up. Having met her mother just once, she had until the following day to decide on the kind of funeral Milly might have wanted. Hysterical laughter bubbled out of her. She wasn't even sure if she was laughing or crying. With a sharp intake of breath she pulled herself together. Her mother's funeral would have to wait until she had read the letter at home that evening. In the meantime, she had a job to do.

60

THAT NIGHT, GERALDINE opened the drawer beside her bed and took out the photograph of her mother, and the envelope on which 'Erin Blake' had been written in shaky capital letters. She took them into the living room and placed them side by side on the coffee table. Then she went into the kitchen and poured herself a glass of red wine. Returning to the living room she sat on the sofa, sipping her wine and studying the letter. It was sealed in a cheap white envelope that her mother must have been given in the hospital.

With sudden resolve, she gulped the rest of her glass of wine. Snatching up the letter she tore the envelope open, removed the sheet of paper, and stared at the words scrawled on it. The writing sloped downwards on the right hand side of the page and it looked messy, but the words were easy to decipher. Having scanned through it, she poured herself another glass of wine and read the letter again carefully, struggling to cope with her shock.

Dear Erin

I'm sorry we never talked. It's my fault. Forgive me. I never should have left it so long for us to meet. Now it's me that's waiting for you. I hope you come back to the hospital in time for me to see you. If you don't, the nurse promised to give you this letter. Please forgive me if you read this. It means we never got to talk, not properly.

When the social worker said you wanted to meet me, I was

so happy. But then she told me you're a policewoman, and I knew it was better for you to know nothing about me and my life. You would be ashamed of me, and I couldn't bear that. God knows I've done more than enough hurt to you already.

I never wanted you to be punished for my wickedness. Please don't hate me. I only wanted what was best for you. It broke my heart to lose you but I didn't know what else to do. I think about you every day.

When you were born, they told me Helena was going to die. But she didn't. And then time went by and I couldn't give her away. It sounds bad, but nothing I ever did went right. Now I'm gone, you need to find Helena, and help her. God knows, I tried.

I wish I'd kept you as well but what happened was better for you. The social worker said the family you went to were good people. It would have been better for Helena if she'd gone with you but she was sick and they said she wouldn't live.

I can't help Helena but you can, if she's still alive.

I'm sorry. Please forgive me.

Milly

your mum

When Geraldine finished reading, she touched the page gently with one finger. Her dead mother had written to apologise for never knowing her. Tears trickled down her cheeks. Too emotional to think clearly, she understood only that, through some bitter irony, her career with the police had prevented her mother from wanting to meet her. Reading the letter again, she gathered that she had a sister, Helena. Her sister had been expected to die when Geraldine was born, but she had survived. It sounded as though Helena might be her twin.

She gazed around her neat living room with a sense of unreality. She had no idea what her mother had done that could be so shameful. Whatever it was, Geraldine would have done her best to help her. She was devastated to learn that her mother had died believing Geraldine might not forgive her. The fact that her mother had been reluctant to meet her once she had learned her daughter worked for the police suggested that Milly had lived on the wrong side of the law. But that did not excuse her refusal to give Geraldine a chance to help her.

'I forgive you,' she whispered to a sheet of paper with words scrawled over it. 'I forgive you.'

Her bout of crying over, she went to the kitchen and returned with the wine. She knew she ought to eat something before finishing the bottle, but this was not the time for being sensible. She wanted to get so pissed she would care only about her hangover in the morning, and not even think about her mother. Or her sister, Helena. Putting her feet up on the sofa, she poured herself another glass of wine. Thinking about the letter, she started to feel angry. It was true her mother was dead, and she would never have the chance to try to build any sort of relationship with her. That was sad, but it was her mother's fault. While she had been alive, Milly had refused to have any contact with her. Now it seemed she had only written to her out of concern for her other daughter, Helena. Her letter was not a genuine apology at all but an attempt to persuade Geraldine to take responsibility for the sister she had never known about, the sister Milly had been unable to part with.

No longer sure she could forgive her mother, Geraldine stood up and was surprised to find herself a little shaky on her feet. She hadn't had that much to drink. Going into the kitchen, she popped some frozen bread in the toaster and took a packet of cheese from the fridge. Tea and toast shouldn't be beyond her in her sozzled state, and it would soak up the alcohol. Tomorrow she needed to get back to the job that had scared her mother away. At least that had never let her down. As for Helena, Geraldine didn't even know if she *was* her sister. Thinking about the way her mother had treated her, she could not see why she should care. She had lived all her life so far in ignorance that she had a biological sister. Only now it would be Geraldine's decision if she turned her back on her sister. Knowing changed everything.

She carried her mug and plate back into the living room on a tray. Catching sight of the letter and photograph lying on the table, she trembled. Miserably, she munched her toast, telling herself she was just tired, hungry and tipsy. All she needed was a good night's sleep and she would be fine. She touched the signature where Milly had written her name, followed by the word 'mum', as though Geraldine might not realise who she was. Knowing she could never reply to her mother's letter, she broke down in tears at the finality of that silence.

61

GROGGY FROM TOO much wine and too much sleep, it took Geraldine a moment to come to. Then, in a rush, she remembered her mother's death, and the letter that suggested she had a twin sister. The lifestyles of twins who were brought up apart were supposed to be uncannily similar, but from Milly's letter it seemed that Geraldine and Helena were very different. Geraldine had worked hard to become a successful professional woman, owning her own flat in a relatively expensive area of London. Her twin sounded dysfunctional. Drugs and crime might play a part in her life. Geraldine didn't intend to rush blindly into a relationship with a stranger who might turn out to be a parasite ready to fleece her. If what Milly had written was true, Helena's life might demonstrate what Geraldine would have been like if she had been brought up by her birth mother. She thought about it as she lay in bed. There was nothing to stop her tracing her sister and observing her from a distance; a stalker driven by benign curiosity. She would help Helena if she could.

She had put her mother's letter and photograph away in her bedside cabinet. With the help of another photograph, Jack's girlfriend had been identified. Before driving to work Geraldine wanted to speak to Sophia, to see if she could add anything to what they already knew about Jack. Sophia worked in a clothes shop in Camden, not far from where she lived. The shop was close to Camden Town station so Geraldine took the train there. It was sunny and warm as she strode along Camden High Street in early summer. The pavement was crowded with young people of different ethnicities. She overheard snippets of conversations from the other pedestrians as she walked by, a world away from Milly Blake's sorry history.

She found the shop where Sophia worked without any difficulty. The window displayed an eclectic mixture of vintage Indian cotton gathered skirts, Afghan coats and fake-fur bomber jackets, together with a couple of pairs of ankle boots, some odd hats and tasselled pashminas. The interior of the shop was dark. Almost every inch of yellow wall was covered in rails of clothes, and shelves packed with hats, bags, shoes and boots. Colourful dresses hung from hangers suspended on hooks in the ceiling. The shop assistant behind the till looked up and nodded a greeting. Geraldine recognised her from the photograph on Jack's phone.

'Are you Sophia?'

The girl was mixed race, beautiful in a sensuous way, with full lips and large, dark eyes. Above the counter Geraldine could see her curvaceous body, and long lean arms.

'Is your name Sophia Laramie?' Geraldine repeated.

'What do you want?' The girl glanced towards a second shop assistant who was tidying dresses on a rail and called out, 'Shaz, can you get over here?'

The other assistant was older than Sophia, dressed in a long flowery skirt and a brightly coloured tasselled shawl, her middle-aged face heavily made up.

'I'm the manager. Can I help?'

'I'd like a word with Sophia. Is there somewhere we can talk?'

The manager glanced at Sophia. 'Is this customer a friend of yours?'

'I'm not a customer, and I'm afraid I'm not a friend either.' Geraldine held out her identity card. 'Now, is there somewhere we can talk in private?'

'Go on.' The manager nodded at Sophia. 'I'll take over here.

You'd better go downstairs. You won't be long,' she added, as though the duration of the interview was up to her.

'Follow me,' Sophia said.

'She's not in any trouble, is she?' the manager asked. 'Only if she is, I'd like to know about it.'

After reassuring them that Sophia wasn't directly involved in any police enquiry, Geraldine followed the girl down a spiral staircase past two changing cubicles, through a low door which Sophia unlocked. It led to a small office with a battered desk and an old computer. Sophia sat behind the desk and gestured to the one other plastic chair in the room.

'I'd like to ask you about Jack Bates.'

'What about him?'

'Do you know him?'

Sophia wriggled uncomfortably on her chair and nodded.

'Is he your boyfriend?'

'He thinks he is.'

'You know Jack was arrested on Monday evening for stabbing another man?'

Sophia's eyes widened, but she didn't say anything.

'What can you tell me about the incident?'

Sophia replied that she hadn't been there. At first, she said she knew nothing about it, but then admitted she knew the man who had been injured in the fight, insisting he was just a friend. When Geraldine asked if Jack was violent, she denied the allegation.

'That ain't it. Jack ain't bad. He'd never hurt no one. He's gentle. You should see the way he is with his brother, who's like a kid.'

'We know Jack's violent. He was arrested for stabbing another man. And that's not all. As well as using a knife, we believe he shot two men.'

Sophia looked scared. 'Nah. Not Jack. Someone's fitting him up.'

Geraldine pressed her point, but the girl refused to budge, insisting that Jack would never hurt anyone, and he must have been provoked into using a knife in self-defence.

'Ain't a guy allowed to take care of himself? Where was you lot when he was assaulted? That's supposed to be your job, protecting people, innit?'

Geraldine changed her approach. 'You told me Jack would like to be your boyfriend, and you also said you knew the man he attacked.'

'He never attacked no one.'

'You said you knew the other man involved in the fight.'

'Whatever.'

'Is it possible Jack stabbed him in a fit of jealousy?'

Sophia pouted. 'You go putting words in my mouth, I'm gonna deny ever saying a word. I ain't got nothing more to say to you. I need to get back to work. Shaz is up there all on her own. Now you gotta go.'

Geraldine followed Sophia back up the spiral staircase. The visit had been a waste of time.

62

LENNY WAS OUT when Gina returned home from the pawn shop. She waited for hours, fuming. It was late when he finally turned up, blind drunk. He had money enough to get himself pissed when he wanted, which was most evenings, unless he was feeling ill. He staggered into the living room too drunk to take in a word she said. When she tried to talk to him seriously, he collapsed on to the sofa laughing hysterically, only to fall off it making a grab for her.

'Get over here, baby,' he called out, using the arm of the sofa to pull himself up on to his knees. His speech was slurred.

'Get off me,' she snapped. 'You're pissed. I'm going to bed.'

She could hear him snoring on the sofa all night. By the time he woke, Gina was already up and dressed. When he came into the kitchen, she was waiting for him, hands on hips.

'Get us a cup of tea, babe.'

For answer, she held out her hand, wriggling her ring finger at him.

He grinned. 'Very nice.'

'What happened to my diamond?'

'It's a beauty,' he replied, but he didn't sound quite so enthusiastic now.

'What happened to my diamond?' she repeated, her voice rising in anger.

Lenny blinked at her, his mouth hanging open. 'What you yelling at me like that for, woman? Jesus, I only just woke up. Get us a cup of tea for fuck's sake. My head's killing me.'

Gina waved her hand in front of his face. 'I know this ain't the same as what you give me. I know it. This ain't the same as what you give me. I got eyes. I ain't no idiot. I can see when something's different and this ain't the same. It ain't got the real colours like what you see in a real diamond. You think I'm an idiot. I seen it when you first give it me, and it was all shiny and it had colours in the diamond what you could see with your eye. And now they ain't there so I know it ain't the same.'

'You're not looking at it right.'

'I know what you done,' she shrieked, 'you gone and sold my diamond and given me some shit fake crap instead. I want my diamond back! You fucking cheapskate, I want what's mine or –'

Lenny knew when the game was up. He took a step towards her.

'Or what?' he interrupted her.

'Or you'll be sorry.'

'Don't you threaten me!' he yelled.

Beside herself with fury she seized a saucepan off the hob and raised it above her head. Lenny lunged forward and grabbed her arm, jerking it downwards with a sudden wrench. The pan fell from her grasp, landing on the floor with a loud clatter. She screamed.

'Let go! You're hurting me!'

'Don't you ever raise your hand against me again, you fucking bitch!'

Lenny swung his free hand and slapped the side of her head. 'After all I done for you! I took you off the street and put a roof over your head. If it wasn't for me, you'd still be in the gutter, you piece of filth.'

He let go of her and she retreated out of reach, sobbing. 'I only wanted what was mine. I only wanted my diamond, the one what you give me. It was mine. You said so.'

'Whatever you got is because of me. Whatever you got is

mine. You got nothing. Nothing! Now get lost for fuck's sake. No, forget it, I'm going out.'

'Where you going?'

'Down the pub. Anywhere I don't have to see your fucking face and hear you bloody moaning all the time. Ungrateful bitch. You're lucky I don't throw you back in the gutter where you come from.'

Afraid of provoking his anger again, Gina didn't dare move or speak but waited in the kitchen, trembling, until she heard the front door slam. Then she ran into the bedroom and flung herself down on the bed where she gave way to a fit of sobbing. As she wept, she pummelled Lenny's pillow, wishing it was his face. At last she sat up and went to the bathroom to study her face in the mirror. Her left temple was still red from the impact of his slap. She was lucky he hadn't given her a black eye. If he had used his fist, he might have knocked her out. It wouldn't be the first time. She considered her options but without the diamond, her choice was limited. She was getting too old to go back on the street. Her pimp wouldn't be interested in her any more, if he was even still alive. Younger women would have come along to take her place. In any case, even living with Lenny was preferable to the dangers of getting in strangers' cars. He could be a vicious brute but she knew what she was dealing with and, to be fair, he hadn't put her in hospital yet.

He would stagger home later, blind drunk, and come on to her as though they hadn't fought earlier on. In his own way, he was fond of her. They had been together for years, like an old married couple. It wasn't unreasonable, expecting her to take a few beatings in exchange for a home, and she didn't really mind the occasional bruises. They soon faded. The problem was, she hated him, and that was never going to fade.

63

BACK AT HER desk, Geraldine decided to contact Louise after writing up her report on her interview with Sophia. Neil was at his desk and any one of her other colleagues might come into her office at any moment. Geraldine went outside so no one could overhear her conversation. Walking past the row of silver birch trees, she made the call and was invited to Louise's office to discuss the funeral face to face. Geraldine agreed at once. She would happily have finalised the arrangements over the phone, but she had her own reason for wanting to meet the social worker in person.

Geraldine arrived on time and Louise took her straight up to her small office where they sat on either side of a small desk, gazing solemnly at each other.

'So, have you thought about your mother's funeral?'

The social worker was in her late twenties. She had a kind face and a gentle voice, but her eyes looked anxious behind her gold-rimmed glasses. Geraldine didn't want to be unkind, but she couldn't help feeling let down by the lack of support she had received. She had met her mother only to bury her.

'I want a dignified cremation.'

'A cremation?' Louise echoed. 'That shouldn't be a problem. Is that what your mother requested?'

'To be honest I don't know what she wanted. As far as I know she never thought about it or if she did, she never mentioned anything about it to me. We never even discussed it. We never really had a chance to talk about anything. There wasn't time.'

'Did she say anything about it in her letter to you?'

'No. I've no idea what she wanted but this is what I want, a nice quiet send off. I'll pay for everything.'

'There's no need for that –'

'I want to.'

Geraldine hadn't intended to offer to pay for her mother's funeral, but the words slipped out before she thought about it. She didn't regret her offer. She could afford it, and however absent she had been as a mother, Milly Blake had given birth to her. Geraldine owed her a decent funeral.

'Is there anything else?'

Geraldine nodded. 'Yes, there is something else I want to ask you before I go.' She took a deep breath. 'How well did you know my mother?'

There was a pause before Louise admitted she had never met Milly Blake. 'I took the file over from Sandra. You met her, didn't you? She left some notes on the file about you, and how you'd requested a meeting with your mother several times. It's a pity she left it so late to agree to see you.' She sighed. 'Your mother remained adamant she didn't want to meet you, right up until she suffered her coronary. I'm so sorry. It was only when she wanted to see you that I became involved at all really. Before that there was nothing for us to do.'

Geraldine hardly dared ask her next question. 'What about – what about my sister?'

'What sister?'

'My mother's letter mentioned she had another daughter, Helena. Did you have any contact with her?'

Louise shook her head. 'No, like I said, I'm afraid I never even met your mother. I didn't know she had another daughter. Are you sure?'

Geraldine shook her head. 'It doesn't matter.'

'No, I'm sorry, I'll see what I can do –'

They both knew that, if Milly had produced another daughter,

Geraldine was as likely to trace her as Louise.

'I'm sorry for your loss,' Louise repeated. 'I'll do what I can, and get things in motion for your mother's cremation. As far as your sister's concerned – Milly's other daughter – I'll do my best to find out what I can for you. I'll try and contact Sandra and find out if she knows anything. There was nothing on the file, but I know your mother spoke to Sandra, and she might have mentioned something. I'll let you know straight away if Sandra can remember anything. And if there's anything else I can do, let me know. If there *is* another daughter, she'll need to be notified of course as I'm sure she'll want to attend her mother's funeral –'

Geraldine forced a smile. 'Thank you very much. I'm sure you'll do what you can. Thank you for your time, and all your help.'

Louise blushed. 'I didn't really do anything.'

Geraldine stood up without contradicting her, the legs of her chair scraping noisily on the floor. She did her best to hide her disappointment. The social worker didn't know anything about Milly's other daughter. If Milly had spoken about Helena to Sandra, the retired social worker was unlikely to remember in detail after such a long time. Thoroughly fed up, Geraldine returned to the police station, sorry she had taken the time to visit Louise's office when they could just as easily have spoken on the phone. Neil wasn't at his desk but Geraldine's relief at finding herself alone was short lived. She had hardly sat down when Sam put her head round the door.

'I was hoping to catch you on your own,' Sam said, going in and closing the door. 'I wanted a word with you –'

'What about?'

Sam frowned and looked down at the floor. 'Actually, about you, Geraldine.'

'It'll have to wait. I'm too busy to chat right now.'

'That's OK,' Sam answered quickly. 'My flatmate's out tonight so I thought maybe we could go for a drink and a bite to eat. We haven't gone out together in ages.'

'Thanks, Sam, but like I said, I'm busy at the moment.'

'You still have to eat,' Sam protested. 'Or is it just that you don't want to spend time with me? Geraldine, are you sure I haven't done anything to piss you off? You don't seem comfortable with me any more, not like we used to be. I thought we were friends.'

Geraldine put down her iPad and turned to her colleague. 'Look, we've already had this conversation, Sam. You haven't done anything, it's me. I've got something I need to sort out and I'm just a bit preoccupied, that's all.'

'Is it about your mother?'

'I really don't want to talk about it.'

She hadn't yet told Sam that she had met her mother. Even Celia didn't know that she had finally found her, only to lose her again. It was over. Now Milly was dead it would be even more difficult to share the news that had somehow turned into a secret. Thinking about it, Geraldine wasn't sure she wanted to tell anyone about her mother – or her missing sister. It would serve no purpose. The most sensible course would be to accept that her search for her blood relatives was over, and put the past firmly behind her, where it belonged.

64

THEO RUSHED ACROSS the room, spun round and ran back again, waving one arm above his head and shouting. His curly hair bobbed up and down, and his eyes glinted with maniacal laughter as he pretended to shoot Rosa.

'Bang! Bang! Bang!'

The neighbour next door thumped on the wall. 'Shut it!'

Theo laughed and pointed his make-believe gun at the wall. 'Bang! Bang! Bang!' he yelled. 'Bang! Bang! Bang!'

His chant changed. 'Shut it!' he called out, mimicking the neighbour's voice. 'Shut it! Shut it! Shut it!'

He darted over to the wall and began hitting it repeatedly with the flat of his hand, yelling all the while. Although his high-pitched voice was thin, it was piercing. It grated on Rosa's nerves. It would easily penetrate the thin internal wall between the two flats. Recovered from her rage at the way the pigs were treating her boys, Rosa was growing anxious. The neighbours must have seen the recent flurry of activity centring on her flat, with so many police coming and going. The detectives were relatively discreet. There was a chance they might have escaped notice. But when uniformed officers had turned up to search the flat, there was no disguising their presence.

The residents on the estate were always on the alert. Once word got around that Jack had been taken away, Rosa and Theo would be sitting ducks. Jack had done a good job of protecting them, but he hadn't stopped to make friends in doing so. The old geezer next door was not the only one who had a score to settle with her family. The minute Theo stepped outside the front door, anyone Jack had terrorised would be targeting his brother, and Rosa had no way of keeping him safe. The pigs were supposed to protect people. Instead, they swept around like a self-righteous army, leaving devastation in their wake. They had no idea of the harm they caused to vulnerable people.

There was a knock at the front door. Rosa froze. It hadn't taken long for hostilities to kick off. She stole over to peer through the peep hole. If it looked like trouble, she would send Theo to his room and tell him to stay silent. He was a good boy. He would do what he was told, provided she offered him sufficient inducement. With Theo out of sight, she would tell whoever was calling that she was at home by herself and suffer the consequences. Any amount of beating was better than seeing Theo hurt. At least she understood what was going on.

She recognised the detective inspector standing outside the flat. As far as Rosa could see, she was on her own. Cautiously she opened the door on the chain.

'Hello, Rosa. Can I come in? I'm by myself. I just want to talk to you.'

'Is it about Jack?'

'Not exactly. Can I come in, or will you at least open the door so we can talk?'

Rosa hesitated, but they had Jack behind bars anyway. It could do no harm to talk. She opened the door and let the inspector into her front room where nothing matched. There was a threadbare armchair for Theo that had originally been bright red, a relatively smart black leather chair where Jack sat in state, as the man of the family. Rosa had an old yellow kitchen chair, the only one left from a set she used to own in better times, before Theo was born.

'Why you don't get a better chair?' Jack had asked her, but she liked her chair. It had sentimental value for her. 'Why not get sentimental over a nice chair?'

By contrast, the inspector looked immaculate in dark grey trousers ironed on the creases, a white shirt, and a tailored blue jacket. Her shoes gleamed, and her short hair lay flat on her head like a glossy black helmet. Rosa pushed a straggly lock of her own hair behind one ear, scowling as she perched on her own seat while the inspector took the leather chair.

'I've come to talk to you about Theo.'

Theo must have been listening from the kitchen because he ran into the room as soon as his name was mentioned.

'Bang! Bang! Bang!' he yelled, pointing a pretend gun at the detective.

'Shut it!' the old man in the next flat shouted.

The inspector gazed at Rosa, a visor of fake concern plastered over her face. 'I'm here to discuss Theo –'

'We don't need no one poking around in our business. You leave my boy alone!'

'Leave my boy alone!' Theo repeated, grinning and nodding his head. 'Leave my boy alone!'

'There are places where Theo could receive appropriate help,' the inspector insisted. 'Rosa, you need to think about what's best for him.'

'You ain't taking him away.'

'He would still live here with you. No one wants to take him away from you. But he would learn how to take care of himself, and you'd get a break –'

'He's fine as he is. And I don't need a break from my own flesh and blood. He's my son.'

Jack's chair creaked softly as the inspector leaned forward. 'You have to think about Theo. You can't take care of him all by yourself.'

'He got a brother. That's all we need, our Jack back home. He takes care of Theo. We don't need no one else.'

'Rosa, I'm going to chase social services about Theo. They can help you take care of him, but sometimes they're so overworked that things get overlooked. Staff change, social workers move around or leave, and details can get lost when people retire, important details –'

'I got no idea what you're on about. Leave us alone.'

'We need to think about Theo.'

'I am thinking about him. I don't think about nothing else. He ain't nothing to you, but he's my son. He won't last a day without me. I take care of him. Now fuck off out of our lives and give us back my boy. That's what Theo wants. Like you care about him, about any of us. We're just the dregs to you. Well, we don't want you neither, so you can just piss off and don't you never come back here.'

With a sigh, the inspector stood up. 'A social worker will be in touch,' she said.

'Bugger off and leave us alone. We was all fine until you come along.'

65

THE MANAGER LOCKED up the front and went, leaving Rafe and Katy to finish tidying upstairs. As soon as he had gone, Katy made for the optics behind the bar. Rafe watched her nervously, fidgeting with a button on his shirt. Her pink hair was a mess, and her make-up was smudged as though she had been rubbing her eyes. Without her habitual smile, he decided she was actually quite plain, and looked considerably older than the twenty-five years she admitted to.

'Shouldn't we start on the clearing up?' he asked, glancing round at empty glasses and crisp packets littering the tables.

Ignoring his question, Katy climbed on to a bar stool. 'Come on, knock it back,' she called, holding out a vodka. 'Stop fussing and come and have a drink with me.'

Rafe approached cautiously. 'What if he finds out we've been having a go at the spirits? It's not like we're taking the odd beer while we're clearing the tables.'

'So what if he knows we had a drop of vodka? It's not a crime, is it? In any case, I had nothing but coke all night, and a few punters offered to buy me drinks. Their cash went in his till, so I'm owed a few, and anyway, we're allowed the occasional drink, now and again, aren't we? Tell you what, if you don't want it, I'll drink it for you. Don't mind if I do.'

She was as good as her word. Downing her own vodka, she drank his straight after.

'Down the hatch,' she called out cheerily, clambering down off her stool.

It wasn't like Katy to get drunk. Rafe wasn't sure whether to feel amused or irritated by her antics. She had been working there for longer than him, so she was in charge, but if she lost control he would effectively be responsible for the premises.

'Go easy,' he urged her, adding, 'I suppose you're all right to get home.'

'I don't want to go home. I like it here.' She waved her hand in a gesture that took in the whole of the bar. 'We can drink whatever we like here and it's all free.'

She giggled and staggered back to the optics where she poured herself another vodka. Rafe frowned. He could understand why she might need to let off steam. It had been a difficult couple of weeks. What with the shooting, and the young guy who had fallen on the railings, it had been harrowing. After that, police had been crawling all over the premises for days. No one had been able to step outside for a smoke, apart from tobacco, and the manager had been in a foul mood because the bar had been quiet once the initial fuss died down. They had begun to worry that someone might be laid off. Eventually the police left them alone and it seemed as though life would finally return to normal, only then Jack had been arrested for the shooting.

They were all shocked. They saw Jack at the bar every day. Rafe hadn't been working there for long so he was probably the least affected by Jack's arrest. All the same, Rafe knew him and liked him well enough. Remembering how Katy had been fond of Jack, he felt a wave of pity for her. She looked so vulnerable. He decided he would see to it that she got home safely. That was the least he could do for her.

'They got it all wrong,' she told him, as she came and sat down beside him. 'The police. Idiots. They got it all wrong. Here,' she handed him another vodka. 'The bottle was half-empty anyway. We might as well finish it off. Then we can put another one up and start all over again!' She burst into noisy laughter. 'Go on, drink up,' she added, sounding almost aggressive. 'It's good for you.'

She stared at him with glazed eyes as he sipped the drink slowly. He wasn't sure if she was able to focus on him at all.

'Are you all right?' He was afraid she might pass out. 'Do you think it's time you got off home? I'll help you. Where do you live?'

'They got it all wrong,' she repeated angrily. 'The fucking police. You know they got it wrong. You know Jack didn't do it. He couldn't have. Poor Jack. Why didn't you say something?'

Tears trickled from her bleary eyes as she reached out and took his shot glass from his hand. 'Not Jack. It wasn't Jack. You know it wasn't.'

'If he's innocent, the police will get to the bottom of it,' he faltered.

'Will they? You think?' She drained his glass. 'It wasn't Jack, but they still took him.'

'They have to investigate, and besides, they must have found some evidence. They can't just accuse someone of murder for no reason. What makes you think you know more than the police who are investigating it? I know you were friends with Jack, but you can't be sure it wasn't him.'

'I know it wasn't him because I was with him when that guy was shot. We heard it. We were in the other toilet together.'

'What were you doing in there?' he asked, realising too late how stupid his question was.

'We were screwing, you dickhead, what do you think we were doing?'

Her anger dissolved into laughter which turned to hysterical weeping. Rafe watched, appalled. He had no idea what to do with her.

'I'm calling you a taxi,' he said at last. 'Stop crying and try to act sober or they'll never take you home.'

'I can stay here,' she replied, her speech barely intelligible, 'plenty to drink here.'

'I'm getting you a coffee.'

By the time he came back with two cups of espresso from the machine, she had rolled a joint. She wasn't that far gone then, just upset. Watching her gulp the hot coffee, he wondered how on earth she could drink so much and still remain upright.

'You have to go to the police,' he said, when she had calmed down. 'You have to tell them what you know.'

'I can't. Jack made me promise never to tell anyone.'

'Don't be stupid. You have to. This is far more important than him worrying his girlfriend might find out he was screwing around.'

'Screwing around?'

'Well, OK, seeing you as well. You have to tell the police. If you don't, he'll be found guilty of murder, and the real murderer won't be caught.'

Katy began to cry again. 'I promised,' she sobbed, 'I promised Jack I wouldn't tell.'

66

GERALDINE RECOGNISED THE girl who worked with Jack although she had only met her once, briefly. Her pink hair helped make her memorable.

'Katy, isn't it? You work with Jack, don't you? Please, sit down. Now, how can I help you?'

Aware that she was going through the motions, Geraldine did her best to sound interested. She was almost sure this would be a waste of time. Katy would come up with some desperate plea, or she might try to persuade Geraldine that Jack couldn't possibly have shot anyone. 'I know him so well. There's no way he would ever do something like that. Jack wouldn't hurt a fly.' Geraldine had heard similar phrases so many times before. Katy's conviction that her colleague was innocent was touching, but worthless compared to the weight of evidence stacked against him: the gun, the location of the shootings, and the jacket found in Jack's wardrobe.

'I know Jack didn't shoot that guy at the bar,' she said, staring earnestly at Geraldine.

'I understand you're concerned about your friend, but we have compelling evidence against him.'

'It doesn't matter how much proof you say you've got, he didn't do it and I'm going to swear to that in court. Whatever evidence you've got against him is false. Someone's lying, and I don't know if it's you or if someone else is lying to you, but it's physically impossible for him to have shot that guy in the toilets.'

Geraldine asked her to explain why she was so convinced of Jack's innocence.

'I don't know anything about the first bloke he was supposed to have shot, but I know he didn't shoot the guy who fell out of the window at the bar.'

'What makes you say that?'

'Because Jack was with me when the guy was shot.'

Katy explained that she had been having sex with Jack in the toilet next door. He hadn't wanted his girlfriend to find out, so Jack occasionally went home with her after work, and sometimes they got together at work in the ladies toilet which was bigger than the men's cubicle. They were in there together when they heard a shot in the toilet next door.

'How did you know it was a gunshot?'

'I didn't, not at the time. I thought it was a car backfiring, only it sounded like it came from the other side of the wall. To be honest, I didn't really take much notice of it at the time only I noticed it because it was so loud. Anyway, we finished and I went out first to check the coast was clear, before Jack came out. We couldn't stay away long without anyone noticing. It was just a bit of fun, you know. Well, no one saw us – that was part of the fun, the risk we might be caught. Only when I got to the corridor I nearly had a heart attack because a woman ran past me.' She gave a mock shudder. 'She came out of nowhere and nearly knocked me over. Then Jack came out and we decided to pop into the men's, to see what the noise was all about, and there was a pool of blood on the floor and a gun in the sink! It was like we walked on to a movie set!'

This was a lot more interesting than Geraldine had expected.

'What happened to the gun?'

'I wrapped it in paper towels and gave it to Jack.'

'Why?'

She shook her head. 'I don't know. He told me to do it so I

did. I was so shocked, I didn't really know what I was doing, but Jack was cool.'

And Katy would have done anything he told her to do, Geraldine thought.

'Then we both went back to work. We couldn't stay away long without anyone noticing.' She shrugged. 'It was just a bit of fun, you know.'

'Didn't you mind that he had a girlfriend?'

'If it didn't stop him, why would it bother me?'

'But didn't you mind having to keep your relationship a secret?'

'No. It was part of the fun, really. I mean, it was only sex. It's not like either of us wanted to get exclusive or anything. It wasn't serious. We were just having fun. What's wrong with that?'

'What happened to the gun?'

'I don't know. Jack took it and we went back to work and then about five minutes later we heard shouting and sirens and it all kicked off.'

Geraldine asked the witness if she would make a formal statement. If her account was true, Jack was innocent of shooting Luke. While Katy was retelling her statement in greater detail to a constable, Geraldine studied her notes on the interview. As soon as Katy had finished making her statement, Geraldine spoke to her again.

'I've told you everything I know,' Katy protested. 'There's nothing more I can tell you. I just want to go home now. I've done what I could and I shouldn't even have told you anything.'

'Why not?'

'Jack made me promise not to.'

'Because of his girlfriend?'

Katy nodded. 'But this seemed like it was serious. I mean, a murder charge. He could go to prison.'

'For a long time,' Geraldine agreed. 'Thank you for coming

forward with your statement. Jack is going to be very grateful. There're just a couple of things I need to check with you. First of all, why didn't Jack tell us he was with you when Luke was shot?'

Katy shrugged. 'I don't know. You'll have to ask him that.'

'We will. There's one other thing. You mentioned a woman ran past you. Could she have come out of the other toilet?'

'Well, I didn't exactly see her come out, but there was nowhere else she could have come from, unless she was lost.'

'Who was she?'

'I don't know.'

'Can you describe her?'

Katy shook her head. 'She was just a woman. I can't remember what she looked like. It's quite dark along there.'

Gradually, Geraldine managed to wheedle a few details from Katy. She was sure it was a woman who had come out of the toilet. She had shoulder-length hair of indeterminate colour, and was wearing a coat. It could have been a duffel coat or an anorak, Katy wasn't sure.

'I'm sorry. That's all I can remember.'

'Would you recognise her if you saw her again?'

'I don't think so. I didn't see her face. Sorry. I'm not very good with faces.'

Geraldine wondered if Katy was making up the presence of a third person in the toilets at the time of the murder to lead the police astray.

'Were you the only one to see a woman in the corridor outside the toilets, or did Jack see her too?'

'He might've missed her, only she barged right into me so I knew she was there. As she was pushing past me he came out, and she ran off. I don't know if he saw her or not. You'll have to ask him.'

Geraldine thanked her again and stood up.

At the door Katy stopped. 'When you see Jack, tell him I

thought it was the best thing to do. I mean, I know I promised, but this is different. I mean, a murder charge. This is serious, isn't it?'

Geraldine didn't answer. Wondering if this new lead was genuine, she hurried away to follow it up.

67

ADAM NODDED AT a chair. Geraldine sat down. The detective chief inspector remained silent for a few minutes, reading something on his screen. Geraldine waited. He had summoned her, so she wasn't going to speak first.

'I wanted to discuss Katy's statement with you before we talk to everyone else,' he said at last. 'How reliable would you say her account is? Do you think she's telling us the truth or is this simply a fabrication in an attempt to get her boyfriend off?'

'I don't think we can discount it,' Geraldine replied slowly. 'It could be true, although she could just be making it up. It's impossible to tell really. He wasn't exactly her boyfriend, but she clearly had a thing going with him.'

'By "having a thing going", you mean they were fucking?'

'Yes.'

'Let's be clear what we're talking about. There's enough obfuscation and confusion in this case already without our adding to it with ambiguous comments. Basically, Katy's statement strikes me as a load of bollocks. Why didn't she mention it at the time?'

Geraldine had the impression the detective chief inspector was reluctant to take the new witness account seriously. As they talked it over, she struggled against being persuaded to dismiss Katy's account. It was very difficult to believe that Jack wasn't involved.

'Are we really to believe that David was shot immediately

after Jack stole his leather jacket, and then after shooting Luke the killer left his gun behind for Jack to find?' Adam asked her. 'It's just all a bit too much of a coincidence, isn't it? And I don't trust coincidences. One way or another, this new account doesn't make sense. She promised Jack she wouldn't tell anyone about their affair. Really? Someone's trying to pull the wool over our eyes and my money's on Katy. I still think Jack's our killer. He was there, for Christ's sake. And his brother had the gun. What more do we want? It had to be one or the other of them, and my hunch is that it's Jack. Otherwise, why didn't he tell us he was with Katy when Luke was shot? We have to get him to confess.'

They agreed they needed to check out what Katy had told them. To satisfy themselves that she was lying, they explored whether Jack could confirm her statement.

'Tell us about your relationship with Katy.'

'Katy? Katy what works at the bar?'

It took a while before Jack would admit that he had regular sex with Katy.

'Why you want to know? What's it to you?'

'Just answer the question.'

'Yeah, we was shagging. So? I get lots of pussy.' He glanced at Geraldine and made a hissing noise with his tongue. 'We done it at work mostly, in the ladies. There's more room there than the men's, and anyways it stinks in there. And the ladies got a lock on the door.'

'You also went to her flat for sex?'

'Sometimes we done it there. So what? The bitch is well up for it. Ain't no one's fucking business.'

'When did you last have sex with her?'

'What?'

'Just answer the question. And don't try pulling anything, because she's told us everything. Now talk.'

Jack's account of the evening matched what Katy had told

them, right down to the detail about her wrapping the gun in paper towels to avoid touching it. He took it from her and put it in his pocket.

'Why did you take it?'

'It's a gun, innit?'

'Why didn't you tell us all this before?'

Jack shrugged. 'I ain't gonna let you get my bro in no trouble. He ain't like me. He ain't like no one else I know. And I know he ain't done nothing because he was home that night. I don't never leave the front door unlocked. We take care of him, my ma and me. You ain't gonna fit him up for this.'

'So you were prepared to go to prison to protect your brother?'

Geraldine was surprised when Jack laughed at the question.

'I ain't going down for something I ain't done. No way. You got no proof. I knew I'd never go down for it. Something would turn up. It always does. I always been lucky. Anyways you don't scare me. Ain't no way you gonna get me.' He clicked his fingers.

Jack admitted he had given the gun to his brother to hide.

'I give the shooter to my bro, Theo, because his room's a mess – you seen it? He picks up stuff and hoards it, like a bleeding magpie, innit? So I think, if he hides the shooter in with all his gear, ain't no one gonna find it in there. Only the stupid asshole takes it out, and he gets picked up with it. He ought never to have got out. My ma and me, we keep the front door locked so he can't get out.'

Geraldine leaned forward. 'We need you to think very carefully now, Jack. Did you see anyone in the corridor outside the toilet when you came out?'

'Only some old tart.'

'A woman?' Geraldine and Adam exchanged a rapid glance. 'Who was she?'

'I dunno, do I? Just some old tart. I never seen her before.'

He looked up, his eyes alert with interest as he realised the significance of the woman's presence in the corridor that night. 'You think she done it?'

'Can you describe her? This is very important, Jack.'

'Yeah, I get you. You're just wetting yourself thinking you got a suspect. Well, you're in luck, because I'm good with faces. Yeah, I remember her. So what you gonna bung me for the info? You asking me to snitch. That's worth some dosh, innit?'

The lawyer leaned over and muttered to Jack.

'How about we substitute obstructing the police in a murder enquiry, withholding information, and accessory to murder, for starters, in place of a simple murder charge?' Adam exploded.

'Fucking hell, hush, man. All right then. This old tart, she was small with hair all over the place so I didn't get much of a look at her face, not that I was bothered. She was skinny, and her face was bad, what I could see of it, like she'd had acne real bad, innit? And she had this big warty thing on her chin.'

After speaking to Jack, Geraldine took a break. Seeing Sam in the canteen, she went over to her table. Although she would have preferred to have a quiet coffee by herself, remembering Sam's last words to her, she felt she ought to join her. Determined to avoid talking about anything other than the case, Geraldine launched into a theory that took account of Katy's statement.

'Basically, either Jack's guilty or he confessed to stealing the gun to protect his brother, in which case he must know Theo's guilty. Assuming that's the case, perhaps Theo followed Jack and saw him mug David for his jacket. Theo was watching and he shot David, maybe because David resisted Jack. It was probably just a lucky shot. Then after that Theo followed Jack to work. I'm not sure why he shot someone else.'

'Maybe he didn't do it deliberately. He's not all there, is he?'

'Possibly.'

'So let me get this straight,' Sam said. 'Now that we think it might not be Jack after all, we're going to try and pin it on Theo again. And he's an easy target, because we don't really need a motive with him, do we?'

Geraldine sighed. They seemed to be casting around in a fog.

'Katy was clear that she was with Jack when Luke was shot, but of course she could be lying to save his skin.'

'What about the woman they saw leaving?' Sam asked, dunking a biscuit in her tea.

Geraldine watched the chocolate on Sam's biscuit melt as she lifted it out of the tea. She craned her neck forward to eat it over the cup so it couldn't drip in her lap.

'Katy was pretty vague about her, but Jack gave us quite a detailed description. When I've finished my coffee I'm going to get an e-fit – hang on.'

'What is it?'

Geraldine stared at Sam, but the face she was thinking about didn't belong to her colleague. 'Jack said the woman they both saw had a wart on her chin.'

Sam stared back, oblivious of the drops of chocolate dripping from her biscuit on to the table. 'Hasn't Gina got a wart on her chin?'

'Let's go and find out.'

For once, Sam didn't complain about abandoning her tea as they hurried from the canteen.

68

'TAKE YOUR TIME, Jack. Look very closely at these pictures and tell us if you recognise the woman you saw in the corridor outside the toilets at the bar.'

Jack gave an anxious nod. He understood how much might hang on his identifying the right woman.

'I never got much of a look at her,' he mumbled, as he gazed at each of the images in turn. 'That's the one,' he cried out with sudden animation. 'That's the old tart what was there outside the toilets.'

Geraldine and Sam exchanged a glance. He had picked out the photograph of Gina.

'Are you sure?'

'She got that same fucking wart on her chin. How you gonna forget that? And her bad skin. If that ain't the one, she got a twin what looks just like her.'

Geraldine had heard enough. She nodded at Sam. 'Let's go and see what she has to say about this.'

On the way, they conjectured about the significance of this new development, wondering what might have motivated Gina to shoot David and Luke. There was some sense in her killing David, as they knew she had got her hands on the ring he had bought for Laura. Lenny's confession that he had stolen the ring from David could easily be a story he and his killer girlfriend had concocted to explain how his DNA came to be on the body, and how they came by the ring.

'So, Gina and Lenny are out together. They come across

David who's drunk and lost, and set about mugging him. But something goes wrong – perhaps he fought back when Lenny assaulted him – and Gina shoots him. That all fits,' Sam said. 'But what was she doing in the bar, shooting Luke, and how the hell did she get him out of the window?'

'He was quite slight,' Geraldine pointed out.

'Even so, it would have been awkward getting him over the window sill.'

'The window's above the toilet so he could have been trying to climb out, when he saw her aiming the gun. She shot him and he fell, or she gave him a final push, and he was out of the window and on the railings. She ran off, and slipped out of the place while the police were still on their way. Remember, everyone thought it was an accident to begin with. It wasn't until the post mortem that the pathologist discovered he'd been shot.'

Gina's heavy-lidded eyes glared up at Geraldine. 'He's out.'

'It's you we want to talk to,' Geraldine said, quickly putting her foot inside the front door to prevent Gina from closing it.

'I ain't got nothing to say to you.'

Gina's bony fingers tightened on the edge of the door.

'Gina James, I'm arresting you on suspicion of the murders of David Lester and Luke Thomas. You do not have to say anything –'

Geraldine continued with the prescribed words throughout Gina's shrill protests.

'Get your fucking hands off me! Get off me!'

Once they had Gina behind bars, Geraldine went to report the details of Gina's arrest. The problem facing them was that the CCTV in the bar hadn't been working that night. They had only Katy and Jack's word for it that anyone else had been in the toilet corridor when Luke was shot, and Jack was alone in claiming to recognise Gina. They didn't have to look far to find a motive for him to identify a fresh suspect. All the same, it seemed unlikely he had picked her out at random, given that she lived with Lenny who was involved in David's death.

A check of Gina's Oyster card showed no travel recorded on the night in question. She could have bought an individual train or bus ticket, or even taken a cab to cover her tracks, so the card didn't offer conclusive proof that she hadn't been in Central London that evening. The VIIDO team set to work looking through hours of CCTV from stations and nearby Oxford Street, to try and spot Gina in the area that evening. It was going to take days to complete the search, with no guarantee they would spot her on the busy streets and platforms, if she had been there at all.

'A confession would be helpful,' Adam said, as though it was in Geraldine's power to obtain one. 'See what you can do this time, Geraldine.'

With an anxious glance at the duty lawyer sitting at her side, Gina flatly denied having been in London on either of the two nights mentioned. As she spoke, her eyes darted nervously from Geraldine to Sam and back again. She was trembling, and her voice shook.

'I don't hardly never go out and I do know for a fact I was home the night Lenny was let out because I was at home waiting in for him only he never come home till the morning. No way was I going out when he might've walked in any time. Not in a million years. You gotta be joking. And the night the other geezer copped it, you told me that was when Lenny was banged up in custody again – for no bloody reason – so what the hell would I be doing out in London when he was inside? I don't never go out at night without him. Where would I go? I ain't got no dosh.'

'If you were there, we'll find out,' Geraldine said, in as menacing a tone as she could muster. 'If you were in London, near Oxford Street, on those two evenings, it would be better for you if you came clean straight away. You'll only make it worse for yourself if you lie to us.'

'Oh shut it, for fuck's sake. I told you I weren't there,' Gina snapped. Her words were feisty, but her shaking voice betrayed her terror.

'Just think about what you're saying –'

'My client has made her response to your allegations perfectly clear,' the brief cut in.

It was perfectly understandable for Gina to feel apprehensive. She had been arrested on a murder charge. But Geraldine wondered if there was another reason why she was so frightened.

69

'YOU'VE BEEN OUT and about a lot,' Neil commented when Geraldine returned to her desk to write up her log. 'You've hardly been here lately. I gather you're getting somewhere?'

She brought him up to speed. He must have known she was using the opportunity to review the case for herself, but he listened attentively all the same.

'So you've got a new suspect. That's good.'

'Yes, but we need to get something more definite than an identification by another suspect. He's obviously trying to get himself off the hook. And we've got no evidence to place her at the scene. CCTV cameras at the bar weren't working that evening –'

'Typical!'

'And the only other possible eye witness didn't get a look at the suspect's face. No one else working at the bar remembers seeing the suspect there that night, or any night come to that, and there's no sign of her so far on CCTV at or near local stations or bus stops. None of that means she wasn't there, but we've not got enough to place her there.'

'No telltale prints on the gun?'

'Nothing. That gun's been wiped clean so many times it's not true. Any prints that were there have been smeared and smudged into each other to make them all totally indistinguishable. It looks like it was handled with gloves, as were the bullets we found. It seems like a few people handled it without any direct contact. It's still being examined but if forensics haven't found

305

anything yet, it's unlikely they will. It's not that easy.'

Leaving the team studying video footage, Geraldine went home. It had been a long day, full of dramatic developments which had led nowhere. She opened a bottle of her favourite red wine, Montepulciano d'Abruzzo, poured herself a glass, and sipped it as she made herself a huge bowl of pasta, sprinkled with cheese. It was a simple meal, and quick to make. Ignoring a missed call from earlier on from Louise, she settled down and tried to relax. Sometimes inspiration could strike when she put an investigation out of her mind, but that wasn't easy to do. Finishing her pasta, she stacked the dishes in her small dishwasher, and returned to her sofa with the bottle of wine. She poured herself a second glass and leaned back, breathing deeply, doing her best to unwind.

In desperation, she reached for her phone and called Celia. If her sister's comforting chatter didn't succeed in distracting her completely, at least it would prevent her from opening her iPad and working. There was nothing really for her to do but be patient and wait for the visual images identifications and detection officers to do their work.

'Geraldine! It's so nice to hear from you. Tell you what, can I call you back? I've only just this minute got back from the hospital.'

Geraldine glanced at her watch. 'Hospital? It's a bit late, isn't it?'

'Oh, it wasn't a check-up. I had a bit of an accident, but it's fine.'

'Oh my God, what happened? Are you all right?'

'Yes, of course. But they wanted to make sure.'

'What happened?'

'Well, I was out shopping this afternoon and some idiot wasn't looking where he was going and he barged straight into me and I went flying. I had shopping bags in both hands – getting bits and pieces for the baby, you know. Anyway, I felt fine but Sebastian insisted on driving me straight to the hospital just to check and once you're there they keep you hanging around for hours, doing all sorts of tests, you know how it is. Anyway, everything was all fine but we've only just got in so I'll call you back, OK?'

'As long as you're all right.'

'I'm fine.'

'Well, let's speak later. And for goodness sake be careful.'

'I know my balance isn't the best, but this wasn't my fault, really. The idiot barged straight into me.'

Geraldine hung up and took another sip of wine. And another. She closed her eyes and pictured her sister being sent flying by some moron who wasn't looking where he was going. He had probably been in a hurry. The incident jogged something in her memory but she couldn't remember exactly what it was. She had drunk too much to drive to the station but the thought niggled her so much that she opened her iPad, reluctantly, and began scanning through Gina's statements. She found nothing there so she went right back to the beginning and read through everything Lenny had said, and then Jack. Again she found nothing that helped. On the point of giving up, she tried a search. It was the word 'barged' that had alerted her so she typed that in. At once the system called up a statement made by Katy. 'She barged right into me so I knew she was there.'

The contact between Katy and the woman in the corridor might provide the proof they needed. This couldn't wait until the morning. It was nearly ten o'clock. She grabbed her phone and called Sam.

'Sam? Are you sober?'

'Yes. Are you?'

'Are you sober enough to drive?'

'Yes. What's up?'

'Pick me up on the way. We've got work to do.'

'What?'

'We need to get forensics on to something. But first we need to collect the evidence. Just pick me up will you? I'll explain when you get here. I'd drive myself only I'm probably over the limit and in any case I want you to come along in case I miss anything.'

'I'm on my way.'

A few moments later, Geraldine's phone rang.

'I can't talk now. I've got work to do.'

'What are you talking about?' Celia replied. 'It's ten o'clock.'

'I'll call you tomorrow.'

'Are you pissed?'

Geraldine hung up and ran to the kitchen. She was gulping hot coffee when her doorbell rang.

'What's so urgent it can't wait until tomorrow?' Sam asked.

'She could go to the dry cleaner's! Come on!'

'Geraldine, what are you talking about? How much have you had to drink?'

'Enough to make me pissed, not so much that I can't still think clearly.'

'If you say so. Where are we going?'

70

KATY LOOKED TROUBLED at the sight of Geraldine and Sam standing on her doorstep at eleven o'clock at night. She opened the door with a tentative smile which faded at once.

'How come you're here so late?'

'May we come in?'

Katy looked nervously from Geraldine to Sam and back again. Detecting a strong scent of cannabis coming from the flat, Geraldine quickly assured her that they were there in pursuance of the murder enquiry.

'I figured. I mean, you investigate murders, don't you? To be honest, all right, I was just having a little smoke, but it's only a tiny bit, just for myself. Personal consumption's legal now, isn't it, so you can't bust me for the occasional spliff, can you? I mean, it's not a crime, is it?'

'Cannabis isn't legal, but if this is a first offence we'll just issue you with a warning,' Sam began.

Geraldine interrupted her colleague. 'But only if we catch you in possession of it.' She frowned at Sam who took the hint and stepped back, staring at her feet.

Katy's frown relaxed. 'I suppose you'd better come in then. I mean, I can't stop you, can I?' Geraldine didn't contradict her. 'Just give me a minute, will you?'

She closed the door and they waited impatiently for her to clear away her paraphernalia.

'Is this about Jack? Is he out yet?' Katy asked when they were all seated in her tiny living room.

A stick of incense on the table filled the room with its acrid scent.

'Would you mind extinguishing that?' Sam asked brusquely.

Katy shrugged. 'If you like.'

'We're still working on Jack's release,' Geraldine replied, quite truthfully, as she sat down. Her head was beginning to ache, but she pressed on. 'You're going to have to think very carefully, Katy, because we need to know what you were wearing on the night of the shooting where you work.'

'What do you mean?'

'Your clothes. What were you wearing that evening?'

'I'm not sure.'

Geraldine sighed. 'I'll try to explain. It's not very complicated.' She frowned, trying to gather her thoughts. 'You told us a woman barged into you outside the toilets just after you heard a gunshot. That was your word, wasn't it? You said she barged into you.'

'Yes.'

'So she must have touched you.'

'Well, her coat did, yes.'

'If we can find any fibres from her coat on your clothes, from when she brushed past you, then we may be able to establish her identity. We need to test the clothes you were wearing at the time. It's important they haven't been washed since the contact occurred. That's why we're here so late. We came as soon as we spotted this possibility. The longer we left it, the greater the chance was that you might wash your clothes. Please say you haven't washed them.'

Katy giggled.

'It's nearly two weeks,' Sam hissed.

Geraldine nodded. She knew it was a ridiculous question, but she had to know. 'Did you wash the clothes you were wearing that evening?'

'I must've washed my shirt and jeans, but possibly not my

jacket. I've got two, and one is dry clean only which is a pain but my mother bought it for me for Christmas –'

'Were you wearing the jacket your mother gave you indoors on that evening?'

'I can't remember. I don't even know for sure that I was wearing it at all that night. I might have been. I probably was. That one or the other jacket I use for work. But the other one might have been washed since then.'

'We need to borrow both of them.'

'Both of them? Oh all right.' She frowned. 'But how can you trace someone from a few fibres?'

'Leave that to us.'

There was no need to explain to Katy that they already had a suspect in mind, and would be able to get hold of her coat to see if they had a match. It just depended on the forensic team being able to find the matching fibres on Katy's clothes. They took both of Katy's work jackets away in a plastic bag. She had washed her jeans since the evening of the shooting but they took those as well. Ignoring her protests that she needed them for work, they took all of her shirts, as she didn't know which one she had been wearing on that particular evening.

'What am I supposed to wear for work now?'

Geraldine handed her a twenty quid note. 'Buy some clothes.'

It was past midnight by the time they reached Lenny's flat and knocked loudly on the door. He took a while to respond.

'What the fuck is this now?' he called through the letter box, without opening the door.

'Open up, Lenny. We don't want to have to break it down.'

Grumbling ferociously, he let them in. Dressed only in grey boxers and a grubby white vest he looked as though he had been in bed when they arrived.

Sam went straight to the bedroom to search the wardrobe while Geraldine checked the rest of the flat.

'What the hell do you want now? You got a search warrant?'

When Geraldine didn't answer, he asked her what they expected to find there. 'If you tell me what you're after, it could save us all a lot of time. Fucking hell, I want to get to bed tonight.'

Geraldine explained that they needed to examine any jacket or coat Gina owned. All they found in the flat was a grey cotton jacket. When she had been arrested, she had been wearing a duffel coat that was at the police station.

'Did she have any other coats at all?'

'I dunno what she had. I been away for a long time, or had you forgot?'

Back at the police station, Geraldine had all Katy's clothes bagged up and labelled, along with Gina's coat and jacket. Then she had the whole lot despatched to the forensic lab with specific instructions about what they were to look for. When she had finished, Sam offered to drop her home but she wanted to wait for the results.

'They'll be hours yet,' Sam said.

'You go home if you like. I'm staying here.'

In the end, Sam persuaded Geraldine there was no point in hanging around at the station. There was nothing to do there but wait, which they could do just as easily at home. It was nearly four o'clock by the time Geraldine climbed into bed. As she lay down and pulled the duvet up to her chin, she realised how worn out she was. Although she didn't think she would be able to sleep, she drifted off as soon as she had set her alarm.

71

GERALDINE'S PHONE RANG early next morning. Mistaking it for her alarm, she reached out to turn it off and realised just in time that it was a call. After a brief greeting, the forensic scientist informed her that they had established a match. Muzzy-headed with sleep, Geraldine responded to the speaker's excited tone before she registered who was speaking.

'Can you repeat that?'

'We've got a match. Item SH3 – that's the dry clean only jacket seized from Katy – had textile fibres from item SH7.'

'And SH7 was –'

'The duffel coat seized from Gina.'

'So Katy and Gina definitely had contact?'

'Yes. There was forceful contact between the right shoulder and sleeve of both items, and we can estimate approximately when the contact took place. In its own way, trace evidence from textile fibres is more useful than DNA in indicating a time frame.'

'When was it?'

There was a slight pause. 'Well, we can't pinpoint the time exactly but it was probably about a fortnight ago. I won't bore you with all the technical details but basically the potential redistribution of fibres due to the wearers' activity and the weather suggests a period of time of around a couple of weeks. It could be longer.'

'And all this is evidence that could be given in court?'

'With the provisos I've mentioned. We're interpreting the

evidence but yes, I'd say our conclusions are pretty accurate. Certainly, there's no doubt there was contact at some point within well – being conservative – within the three weeks. But I don't think it was that long ago.'

'Thank you. Please let us have your report as soon as you can.'

'Of course. I didn't work through the night to have my conclusions ignored.'

Geraldine smiled. 'Oh, this won't be ignored, believe me. Far from it. You may think you've just been sitting in a lab, but what you've actually done is nail a murderer.'

'Well, it's good to know that just sitting in a lab can be so useful.'

'You deserve a bloody medal. I hope they pay you well for working overtime.'

'Ha! Fat chance. Anyway, glad to be of help. It's all in a good cause.'

With a final word of thanks, Geraldine rang off. Adrenaline had cleared her head and she leaped out of bed and hurried into work.

Gina glared across the table at Geraldine. Her expression altered as Geraldine explained the evidence that had been gathered.

'All of which means that we have proof that you had physical contact with Katy exactly as she described it. Textual fibres can be transferred on the briefest of contact, and you barged right into her. We'll be scouring the toilets and the corpse for traces of your DNA, and we'll find it. You were there, Gina. You were seen by two people leaving the men's toilet just after Luke was shot, and we have forensic evidence that bears out their eye witness statements. You might as well start talking, because we have enough evidence to make a watertight case against you. No more wriggling, no room for manoeuvre. We can prove you shot Luke Thomas. All you can do now is cooperate with us in the hope the judge will be lenient when you're sentenced. But it's going to be difficult, with two murders –'

'I never done two!' Gina burst out in alarm.

'You admit you shot Luke Thomas in the toilet? Come on, Gina, there's no point in denying it now.'

'It's a fix. I been framed!' she shouted, turning to her lawyer in a panic.

'I'd like a word with my client,' the brief said.

After a break, Gina returned to the interview room white-faced.

'Look, I'll tell you all of it what happened, only you got to believe me I never shot that first bloke. That was Lenny and he's a bastard what I never should've listened to. He said he shot the bloke in the alleyway and then he come home and told me. He said it wasn't his fault, he was too drunk to know what he was about. And he told me he did it so as he could get the ring for me. He said he heard the bloke boasting about it in the pub so he thought he'd get it for me.' Her blemished features creased as she began to sob.

After a moment she sniffed, wiped her nose, and continued. 'I believed him. He said he done it because he loved me. But he's a lying bastard. He never got that rock for me, he got it for himself, only me, being a mug, believed him. He told me if he ever got nicked for shooting that bloke I was to take the gun and use it on someone near there, while he was in the nick, and then you'd think it couldn't be him what done it. So that's what I done. I put on gloves like he told me and I took that gun of his and I went to Oxford Street. I went in a bar round the corner from where Lenny shot that guy and followed a bloke into the toilets. Don't ask me why I done that. It just seemed like the best thing to do, because I thought no one would see me in there. So he sees me get out

315

the gun.' She shuddered. 'I don't know what I was thinking, only I done it for Lenny. I thought that way I'd get to keep Lenny and get my ring and I thought we was going to get married. He promised me.'

'I lifted up the gun and this bloke saw me and he jumped up on the toilet and opened the window like he was going to climb out. He never said a word. If he'd spoke to me, I would've bottled it, but he never said a word. He climbed up on the toilet and glared at me, like I was a rat. So I shot him. He fell backwards across the window sill and I run forward and give him a shove and he was gone. And then I legged it. Only I must've dropped the gun when I went to push him out the window, because when I got outside, I never had it. I wasn't going to go back in for it so I just went home. And Lenny got out. Only then the bastard tried to pull a fast one. He got the real diamond took out of my ring and a bit of shit glass put in, like I wasn't going to find out. Like I was some kind of idiot. After all I done for him, the lying bastard. He deserves all he gets. This is all his fault. I was only doing what he told me.'

She finished her account and began to cry again.

'Well, well, what people do for love,' Geraldine said.

'Love? He's a lying bastard and I hate him!' Gina shouted through her sobbing. 'I don't love him and I never did. But I thought he was going to look after me. I ain't never had nothing so nice as that ring. And he spoiled everything. I ought never to have listened to him.'

'You're right there.' Geraldine said, as Gina was led away.

Adam listened intently to the tape of Gina's confession.

'So it was the two of them all along,' he said, 'and because of Lenny's greed, two random innocent victims lost their lives. Don't you sometimes wish we didn't have to treat prisoners so well? I mean, when we *know* they're guilty of such vile crimes?'

'At least with the evidence we've got, and her confession, the case against them should be watertight.'

'Yes, and I don't suppose he'll like being locked up with seriously violent cons. He won't be mixing with petty villains banged up for larceny this time,' Adam added, with a grim smile.

Leaving Adam's office, Geraldine went to find Sam. 'Come on, Lenny's been brought in. Let's go and listen to what he has to say.'

'I can't believe it's over. It feels like this investigation's been going on for years.'

'I know. It's been a tricky case, but we got there in the end. Gina and Lenny. Who would have thought it? What a pair they make! And we make a good pair too,' she added, smiling.

Sam's broad grin reminded Geraldine how keen her sergeant was to earn her approval, and she felt a tremor of guilt at having been so dismissive towards her.

Sam's expression became thoughtful. 'I can't help feeling sorry for Gina, in a way. Rescued from a life on the streets by Lenny isn't much of a break, is it? Was he really the best thing that happened to her? Some people don't get much of a chance in life.'

For the first time, Geraldine felt she genuinely understood her mother's choice to give her up for adoption. Growing up with her birth mother, perhaps she would have spent her life avoiding the law, instead of serving it. She might even have ended up like Gina. In the end, it was her own happiness Milly had sacrificed, not her daughter's. Geraldine felt as though a dark cloud had lifted from the top of her head.

'Sam,' she said, stopping abruptly as they neared the interview room, 'when we've finished with Lenny, let's go out for that drink – no, for a meal. There's – things – been going on in my life that I want to talk about.'

'I'm always ready to listen.'

'I know that. I've needed to work through it on my own for a while, but I'm ready to talk now.'

'Any time. You know where I am.'

Geraldine smiled. 'Thanks, Sam. You're a real friend. Now let's go and watch Lenny try and wriggle his way out of this!'

A LETTER FROM LEIGH

Dear Reader,

I hope you enjoyed reading this book in my Geraldine Steel series. Readers are the key to the writing process, so I'm thrilled that you've joined me on my writing journey.

You might not want to meet some of my characters on a dark night – I know I wouldn't! – but hopefully you want to read about Geraldine's other investigations. Her work is always her priority because she cares deeply about justice, but she also has her own life. Many readers care about what happens to her. I hope you join them, and become a fan of Geraldine Steel, and her colleague Ian Peterson.

If you follow me on Facebook or Twitter, you'll know that I love to hear from readers. I always respond to comments from fans, and hope you will follow me on **@LeighRussell** and **fb.me/leigh.russell.50** or drop me an email via my website **leighrussell.co.uk**.

That way you can be sure to get news of the latest offers on my books. You might also like to sign up for my newsletter on **leighrussell.co.uk/news** to make sure you're one of the first to know when a new book is coming out. We'll be running competitions, and I'll also notify you of any events where I'll be appearing.

Finally, if you enjoyed this story, I'd be really grateful if you would post a brief review on Amazon or Goodreads. A few sentences to say you enjoyed the book would be wonderful. And of course it would be brilliant if you would consider recommending my books to anyone who is a fan of crime fiction.

I hope to meet you at a literary festival or a book signing soon!

Thank you again for choosing to read my book.

With very best wishes,

Leigh Russell

About Us

In addition to No Exit Press, Oldcastle Books has a number of other imprints, including Kamera Books, Creative Essentials, Pulp! The Classics, Pocket Essentials and High Stakes Publishing > oldcastlebooks.co.uk

For more information about Crime Books > crimetime.co.uk

Check out the kamera film salon for independent, arthouse and world cinema > kamera.co.uk

For more information, media enquiries and review copies please contact marketing > marketing@oldcastlebooks.com